The Group

by

Kevin R. Doyle

The Group

Cover Art by *Debbie Taylor*

The Wild Rose Press, Inc.
PO Box 708
Adams Basin, NY 14410-0708
Visit us at www.thewildrosepress.com

Publishing History
First Edition, 2021
Trade Paperback ISBN 978-1-5092-3935-1
Digital ISBN 978-1-5092-3936-8

Previously Published: MuseitUP Publications, 2017; Barbarian Books, 2014
Published in the United States of America

He clicked the mute button, at the same time placing the device on the coffee table.

"…official comment at this time. There have been some reports of a lone man seen entering the victim's apartment a few nights back, but those have yet to be confirmed. Glenn?"

In the background, Ron could hear Sarah resume eating her cereal.

"When's the last time you spoke to her?" Lynda asked him.

"You know when."

"Not really. I know when you told me was the last time. Now I want to know whether that was the truth."

He felt all the old pains coming back. The acid churning in his stomach, the tightening of his skin. Towards the end of last spring, when he and Diane had first met, he'd realized almost from the beginning that he wasn't cut out for intrigue, deception and sneaking around.

Now Diane was dead. Murdered, if the television reporter could be believed.

"I told you the truth," he said. "First week of October. That's the last time she and I spoke."

"So what do we do now?" Lynda asked. Behind them, little Sarah had again gone silent.

"Do?" he asked.

"Yes. For God's sakes, Ronald your—lover—was just killed. How long do you think before the cops come to talk to you?"

Other Books by Kevin R. Doyle

When You Have To Go There
And The Devil Walks Away

Dedication

For Sandy S.,
who told me that if I could do it once
I could do it again.
And darned if she wasn't right.

CHAPTER ONE

December 15

Even for the Midwest at the end of the year, it was far too frigid and blustery of a day to be standing outside looking down at a corpse.

Although December usually wasn't all that cold around here, despite what residents of Florida or California might think, the temps this year had been a bit lower than average since October, and today the cold had come slamming in from the north like a visiting mother-in-law.

On top of that, Detective Third Grade Jack Hollis had stayed up late the night before watching a boxing match on pay-per-view and hadn't bothered to catch the local weather. So had waltzed out of the house this morning wearing merely a mid-weight jacket, which he now cinched closer to his throat.

"You ought to dress warmer," said one of the patrolmen from the car that had first called in the incident. Hollis, at thirty five, nearly ten years the guy's senior, thought about retorting but figured it wasn't worth the effort.

Instead, he looked back down at the body.

The deceased, dressed appropriately for the weather, lay on the pavement behind a Chinese restaurant. With little blood and no obvious rigidity of the body, the death appeared relatively mild.

At first glance, it seemed as if the man had simply lain down face up on the asphalt and died.

Hollis knelt down for a closer look at the corpse.

"Where's your other half?" one of the patrolmen asked.

"Giving a deposition downtown," Hollis replied, not taking his eyes off the corpse on the ground.

Peering closer, he saw a thin tendril of blood seeping out from the back of the man's head. Hollis stood up and went over to one of the crime scene techs. He'd been jammed up interrogating a witness when the call came, accounting for his being among the last to arrive on the scene.

"Got any ID on him?" he asked the tech.

The young woman looked down at some notes she held in her hand.

"Yeah, we've already gone through his license and called in to records. Name's Randall Cummings, fifty-two years old. Records has him listed as the manager of a Save-Rite Furniture Store."

Hollis looked up and down both sides of the alley.

"A furniture salesman? Where's his store located?"

"We're not sure yet. There's three of the chain in town. One of them's only about twelve blocks away."

"Meaning that considering the time of day, he could have come down this way for lunch," Hollis said.

Before the tech could respond, one of the patrolmen called out.

"ME's here."

Hollis turned to see a blonde, around thirty or so, heading towards the scene of activity. As he went to meet her, she was pulling on a pair of thin latex gloves.

"Hey, Tracey."

"Jesus, Hollis," she said, "did you have to get me out on such a cold day?"

"Don't blame me, kid. Blame Randall there."

"Hmph." Just as Jack had done when he first arrived, she knelt down and performed an eyeball inspection of the late Mr. Cummings.

"Has he been photographed yet?" she asked.

Hollis glanced at the techs, received a nod in return.

"Yeah. He's all yours."

"Then let's see what we've got." As she spoke, the doctor cupped her hands under the dead man's shoulders and gently shifted him about a 45-degree turn.

"And there's your cause of death, at least nominally," she said, pointing to the small hole drilled into the back of his skull.

"Single bullet?" Hollis asked as he bent down for a closer look.

"Looks like," the ME said. "Which is actually a little odd."

"Why odd?" Hollis asked, though he already had a suspicion.

"Well, it looks small caliber. Probably .22 or so."

"Execution style."

She looked up at the detective. "You suggesting this guy was hit?" she asked.

"It wouldn't seem likely. A furniture salesman in his fifties? If he was hit, it's doubtful it was over something like drugs or women."

"Maybe gambling?"

"Maybe."

Hollis fell silent as the ME went about her business although even he could pretty much guess what had

3

happened. With no exit wound, the small caliber bullet had no doubt buried itself somewhere inside the skull, probably after ricocheting around for a while.

Still, cases weren't built on instinct or prior experience, so he stood back and let the lady do her job.

"So how many does this make?" she asked without looking up. "Have you all hit the triple digits yet?"

Hollis grimaced. Over the last few years, most of the force had become hypersensitive to the fact of their city ranking as the murder capital of the country. A while back, some web site or other had even listed it as one of the ten most dangerous cities in the entire world. The only consolation they all had was that, over the last few months, Chicago seemed to be gaining on them.

"Actually," he said, "we passed the hundred mark at the end of last month. I'm not sure what number this one makes."

"Well," the ME said as she stood up and stripped off her gloves, "I won't be able to put anything down officially till I get him on the table, but it's pretty obvious what happened here."

"One bullet back of the head," Hollis said.

"Right. Which gets back to the oddity."

"How did he end up lying face up?"

The young ME turned and faced Hollis straight on, flinching a bit as a sharp gust of wind knifed through the alley.

"Exactly. Even a .22, in the back of the skull, should have sent him tumbling forward. This looks almost apologetic. Could it have been some sort of a robbery?"

Hollis glanced over at a couple of the crime scene guys involved in categorizing the contents of the victim's pockets.

"What've you got?"

"Wallet," said one of the techs, a kid with curly red hair, "with a couple of hundred dollars and four credit cards in it. Look at his left wrist, and you'll see his watch still on him. Plus we picked up a cell phone and an I-pod."

"This old duffer with an I-pod?" the blonde ME asked.

Hollis shrugged.

"So we can guess it wasn't a robbery," he said.

"Unless your bad guy got interrupted before he could grab the goodies," the ME said.

"Maybe, but how to account for the corpse being laid out all nice and neat like this?"

Stripping off her gloves, the ME turned and motioned to a couple of ambulance attendants standing off to the side.

"That's the nice thing about it, Hollis. My part's easy. I just have to come up with the means. You guys get to do the whole motive and opportunity thing."

Hollis grimaced as she walked off.

"Oh by the way." She turned back to him. "I checked with the office before I left. This makes number one hundred twelve for the year. And only sixteen days to go."

INTERVIEW #4

February 26

He stopped just outside the office building to check himself out one last time. Despite the temperature hovering around freezing, there had been no precipitation for almost a week, and the sun shone almost as brightly as in August. The shiny steel front of the building reflected almost as well as a mirror.

He hoped no one noticed him stop to check the set of his tie, the hang of his coat or the part in his hair. Rather than when he first got up that morning, he had waited until one o'clock, half an hour before the scheduled interview, to shave. This assured him of as smooth and clean a face as possible.

Of course, it would have been embarrassing if he had cut himself while shaving. He couldn't imagine anything worse than going into a job interview with a swatch of tissue stuck to his face. Well, maybe tissue stuck to his shoe after leaving the bathroom stall, but that was about the only thing he could consider as worse.

But he hadn't nicked himself, had dressed as faultlessly as possible (not really all that hot considering how things had gone recently), and had spent almost the entire morning psyching himself up for 1:30 in the afternoon.

He had to get this one. Three strikes had been bad

enough. Lately Mary had made her thinning patience more than clear. While it tore at him when he kept losing out on these jobs, seeing his wife lose confidence in him as a provider, and more to the point a man, made his current circumstances even more unbearable.

When he'd first lost his job, Mary had been about as supportive as he could have hoped. But as the weeks wore on and the possibilities for new employment came few and far between, her attitude began to change.

It started when she went out to buy a birthday gift for her mother, only to find one of their Visa cards rejected. Although she used another card to make the purchase, the incident formed the first slight straw on her back. When she found herself having to budget for groceries and hesitating about buying a new dress for a New Year's party they'd been invited to, the strain began to show in her face and tone of voice.

Even more so, the strain manifested itself in their bedroom. By the middle of January, sex between the two of them became perfunctory and, judging by her reaction, not very good. He felt sure that another couple of weeks, or even worse, another lost opportunity, and she'd cut off relations altogether.

So yes, for more reasons than he could count, he simply had to nail this job.

Even so, he stood there for a long moment, the by now all-too-familiar doubt creeping in again. Watching Mary lose confidence in him had been bad enough. Even worse were the nights when he left their bed to go into the bathroom, turn on the light and stare at himself in the mirror.

During those interludes, in the middle of the night with no one except himself to witness, he began to seriously doubt if he would ever work in the field again. Of course a bathroom, with its array of razor blades and pills, didn't really rate as the best place to have such thoughts.

Each time, he managed to suppress the doubts and fears, but suppressing them only meant that they'd return, quite possibly when he could least afford it.

Today, facing the fourth interview since his life had begun to fall apart, counted as one of those times.

With a near physical effort, he shook himself out of his lethargy. Standing up as straight as he could, a confident smile plastered on his face, he entered the building.

He simply had to get this job.

****

He stepped out of the elevator and onto the tenth floor. Turning to the right, at the end of the hall he saw the company name he was looking for and headed in that direction.

He paused again, just before entering, and seriously considered turning back and walking away. From out of nowhere, the possibility of another rejection became almost more than he could stomach. A year ago, even with the economic turmoil swamping the country, he'd never have dreamed he would ever be one of the unemployed, much less that months after the event he still wouldn't be able to find work. For someone like him, it wasn't supposed to work this way.

He'd gotten through college on okay grades, not spectacular but good enough, then managed to snare a job, a real job, not an internship, in March of his senior year. The employment, of course, was contingent upon his graduating, which had actually been touch and go for a while. Like many students, he'd put off the introductory and required algebra course until his last semester and had, in fact, barely squeaked past it.

But clear sailing came after that. Decent entry-level job, adequate wage and, just as he was getting into the single, young executive lifestyle, along came Mary to complete the package.

And for the last fifteen years life had been great, outstanding in many ways, with a slow, steady rise up the ladder.

All of which had fallen to hell some months before.

True, he could turn tail and run, not risk the rejection he'd received three times before, but that course of action would provide only temporary relief. Mary would still be irritable and impatient, they would still need to put food on the table, and their savings would still be dwindling. While so far they'd managed to avoid touching their retirement accounts, if something didn't happen soon…

Seeing no good option before him, he once again straightened up, put the confident smile back on his face (though it didn't feel quite so confident as it had downstairs), and pushed the door open.

A blonde receptionist sitting behind a polished black desk looked up with a smile when he entered.

"Yes, sir?"

He gave her his name, and she glanced down at an appointment book lying open on the desk. With a brief nod, she picked up the phone, spoke briefly into it, then replaced the receiver and looked back up at him.

"Mrs. Grayson's office is the second door on the left. She's expecting you."

He blanched inwardly, hoping the reaction didn't show in his expression. At the same time, he hoped others would be present besides Paula Grayson, who he'd learned ahead of time was the head of Human Resources, in on the interview. He tended to do better with male interviewers than female, but at the same time he was honest enough with himself to realize that just maybe his experience with his last boss had soured him on the whole female superior thing.

However, judging by his success rate of those first three interviews, the idea of doing better with one gender over the other may have just been an awesome case of rationalization.

Although an urge to turn tail and run surged up again, he smiled at the receptionist, nodded and turned to go down the corridor. The receptionist was rather pretty, though somewhat too young for him, and he wondered if, simply by looking at him, she could tell the tale of his shrinking bank account.

Was she sharp enough to see the cracks and crevasses in his appearance signaling his status to anyone who could read the signs? Could she figure out that the suit he wore was at least three years old and had been worn nearly ten times without being dry cleaned? Did she bother to look down and see, through the fresh coat of polish put on last night, the definite scuff marks on his black tasseled loafers? Could she smell on his breath the generic lunchmeat from his sandwich earlier?

In another place and time, he would have made at least some effort to chat up such a pretty girl, even if she seemed a bit young for him. Especially considering Mary's recent attitude. He would have felt confident that, with enough time and patience, he could have taken her out to some nice restaurant, maybe some place a little way out of town, plied her with some top of the line wine, and put the entire evening on his Visa without thinking twice.

These days, the credit cards verged on being used for daily expense, and as meticulously as Mary pored over them, there was no way to cover up extraneous expenses.

God, how he wanted his old life back. But in order to get it, he'd have to get past Mrs. Grayson.

Taking a deep breath, he turned the knob and walked in to meet his future.

He hoped.

****

Although in retrospect, as he drove home, it wasn't the worst interview he'd had, it sure as hell didn't rank as the best. Grayson had been a surprise, a pleasant-voiced woman in her early forties, and she'd obviously done what she could to put him at ease. But no amount of smooth talk or relaxing furniture could hide the fact that, as his internal sensor had quickly picked up, he wasn't their top candidate.

Anyone in his position would, before too long, develop this instinctive radar. As he stared straight into her gaze and answered her questions directly, he picked up on the shiftiness of her own gaze, the constant looking down at papers on her desk, and the artificial smile that seemed pasted on her lips yet didn't quite reach the facial muscles themselves. He realized the odds of getting this job were long and possibly out of reach.

And gee, who could be responsible for that?

Still, the Grayson lady walked him through the procedure: explaining the work load that would be expected of him, the salary range they were thinking of offering (even though they really weren't) and the company policies on retention and promotion.

He knew he could handle the job with ease. It was more or less the same work he'd done for the last several years. And no one could argue his record in the business was exemplary. At least, up until last May.

As Mrs. Grayson glanced over his resume, though surely she'd already studied it thoroughly before he showed up, she made several approving noises. Even so, he could tell, again from experience at this old routine, when she got to the details of his last job. Her mouth pursed, just a fraction but noticeably, and an odd little look came into her eyes.

Oh crap.

Finally, she placed the paperwork down on her desk and looked up.

"Well, it all seems to be in order. Would you like a tour of our offices?"

And that was it. No offer to introduce him to any higher-ups, no specialized questions as to his experience and background, and no incidental talk about family life, hobbies or formative experiences growing up.

Would you like a tour of our offices?

No, he did not particularly want a tour of their offices. What he wanted, goddamnit, was employment, some work to put money in the bank and meat on the table. He wanted to be productive again, make use of the skills he'd acquired and honed over a decade and a half of solid effort.

That's what he wanted. Not a tour of their freakin' offices.

But on the off chance of candidate number one, or two or however many were ahead of him in their consideration, not making the cut, he let her take him around a short inspection of the offices.

Twenty minutes later, he was standing at the outer door, the blonde receptionist temporarily absent from her post, as Mrs. Grayson promised him they'd be in touch.

Yeah, sure.

Riding the elevator down to the ground floor, he wanted to spit and hiss and fume.

Instead, with other people riding the car with him, he just sat there and smoldered.

Scratch possibility number four.

CHAPTER TWO

March 4

Professor Ronald Green first heard the news about Diane on the television. It was early on a weekday morning, with all the usual bustle around their house that mornings brought with them. The baby was just beginning to wake up, in her raucous way, while little Sarah sat at the kitchen table slurping up, and spilling out of her bowl, equal quantities of milk and Froot Loops. Ron reached out to the sink for a dishcloth and discarded the first two he found as too dirty, at the same time contemplating going into the bedroom and asking his wife, Lynda, for help. Although he didn't really want to bother her, usually the time and effort spent wasn't worth the end result, it would have been nice to have an extra pair of hands.

As he rinsed and wrung out the third cloth, he looked up at the clock in the microwave, seeing he had at best twenty minutes before Ryan showed up. On Ryan's days to drive, he almost always arrived a quarter hour before the appointed time, usually anxious to get going.

"Lyn!" Ron shouted out. He wanted to ask if she had time to get Sarah cleaned and dressed, but before he could frame the question another slurp of milk whisked out of the bowl and onto the tablecloth.

"Dammit," he said, remembering to bring his tone

down to a whisper a shade too late. Always conscious of his language around Sarah, he'd recently been trying to refrain from even the mildest of curse words. He considered it the least he could do to preserve harmony in a household that had seen far too little of it lately.

Even so, his daughter's ears perked up a bit and she gave him a look.

"Sorry, sweetie," he said as he reached over to begin wiping up her mess. He heard footsteps finally coming down the hall.

"Ron," his wife said behind him, seemingly not even noticing the mess on the table, "did you remember to call…"

Her voice trailed off, in a manner to which he'd become all too accustomed over the last few months, and he paused in the middle of scrubbing Sarah's face to look up and see just what he'd done now. For once, Lynda wasn't looking at him in varying shades of disgust or disdain.

Instead, she was staring at the television in the living room. He hadn't had the chance to hear the news yet, but one quick glance from his wife to the television indicated he wouldn't be hearing much of anything else this day.

When he'd first turned the set on he'd muted the sound, and right now the silent newscast was showing a blown up face shot of a brunette woman in her early thirties.

The caption under the picture read "Local Graduate Student Murdered."

Ron's stomach did a slow roll, and goosebumps flashed across his body. For a moment, he wanted to blink or pinch himself in the hopes of waking up from a bad dream.

"That's her, isn't it," Lynda said. She stood only about fifteen feet away from him, as of this moment an even more nonnegotiable distance than ever. "That's her, right?"

Either she hadn't noticed, or didn't care, that Sarah still sat at the table, her spoon now laid down. She leaned forward tensely, no doubt picking up on the sudden tension between her parents.

"Yeah," Ron said, barely recognizing the croak issuing from his throat, "that's her."

He dropped the dishcloth onto the table, walked over and picked up the remote. As he did so, he naturally walked within a few feet of Lynda and was not at all surprised to note that she moved farther back, reflexively keeping a particular distance between them.

He paused, remote in hand, again vainly wishing it would all suddenly go away. But the photo and caption stayed on the screen while the normally perky, now exceptionally somber-looking blonde early morning anchor continued speaking silently, mouthing words Ron simply did not want to hear.

"Turn it up, goddammit," Lynda said. By now she had to be aware of their six-year-old daughter sitting just a few feet away.

She just didn't care.

She hadn't cared about a whole hell of a lot the last several months.

He clicked the mute button, at the same time placing the device on the coffee table.

"...official comment at this time. There have been some reports of a lone man seen entering the victim's apartment a few nights back, but those have yet to be confirmed. Glenn?"

Then the blonde anchor referred back to Glenn Robinson, the most popular morning newscaster in town, who proceeded to detail the latest trade dispute in Washington. Lynda picked up the remote from the coffee table and clicked the set all the way off.

In the background, Ron could hear Sarah resume eating her cereal.

"When's the last time you spoke to her?" Lynda asked him.

"You know when."

"Not really. I know when you told me was the last time. Now I want to know whether that was the truth."

He felt all the old pains coming back. The acid churning in his stomach, the tightening of his skin. Towards the end of last spring, when he and Diane had first met, he'd realized almost from the beginning that he wasn't cut out for intrigue, deception and sneaking around. He'd gone through nearly five solid months of alternating crests of excruciating pain and intense pleasure. Every time he'd come home after being with her, searching for a lie Lynda would believe, he'd felt these same physical torments.

When he'd finally broken the affair off, he'd been physically sick for days on end. However, the sensations had passed and, despite the friction and hostility Lynda kept throwing his way, he'd figured that at some point, with a lot of effort, he could put his life back on its normal track.

Now Diane was dead. Murdered, if the television reporter could be believed.

"I told you the truth," he said. "First week of October. That's the last time she and I spoke."

"So what do we do now?" Lynda asked. Behind

them, little Sarah had again gone silent.

"Do?" he asked.

"Yes. For God's sakes, Ronald your—lover—was just killed. How long do you think before the cops come to talk to you?"

He turned and stared at her. He'd proposed to this woman nearly ten years before. She'd borne his children, and at one time he'd considered her his best friend. Yet now he looked at her as if she was literally insane.

"Why would they come talk to me? I told you, I haven't seen her in months!"

"Oh, for God's sakes." Lynda turned on her heel and stomped away, back into the bedroom.

Her standard way of dealing with him for the last year or so—just walk away. Most of the time, in order to preserve the peace, he took the route of least resistance and let her go. However, this time was different, clearly more serious.

He started to follow her when Sarah called out from the kitchen table.

"Daddy, I'm done."

He halted, the desire to wring some kind of sense out of his wife warring with the need to take care of his child, another chore over the last few months falling more and more to him.

As if to make even the simplest decisions too excruciating to deal with, he'd only made it halfway to the kitchen when a knock sounded at the door.

Dammit, he thought again. *Ryan, as always, right on time and early as hell.*

****

"You want to talk about it?"

"About what?" Ron asked.

They were in Ryan's car, heading towards the university.

"I heard on the radio coming over. About Diane, I mean. Judging by the awkward vibes in your apartment, can I assume you and Lynda heard about it too?"

"It was on the morning news. But we had the set muted until the last few seconds, so I don't really know…"

"She was strangled. Sometime since last Friday. A neighbor saw her Friday afternoon, and her roommate came back from a trip last night and found her."

Ron grimaced at the thought of her roommate, a somewhat younger woman, late twenties at the most. Tall, red-haired and violently freckled, Beth had never much cared for him. He didn't know if it was his age; the unusual, slightly stalkerish way he and Diane had met; or the fact that Ron was a married man. He'd never mentioned his marriage to Beth, had only met her a few times and hardly talked to her at all, but with the way women talk to each other he assumed Diane had told her all about his home life.

How long before Beth told the cops all about her friend's older, married lover?

"Strangled?"

"That's what the radio said and something about her being beaten. But you know how this goes. The first one or two reports are almost always wrong. Especially on something as juicy as this."

"Strangled," Ron repeated before shifting to look out the side window.

Another few miles went by, and the outskirts of the university came into view.

"So?"

"So what?" Ron asked.

"So what do you think of it all? What are you going to tell the cops?"

First Lynda, now Ryan. Maybe it was time for Ron to face the fact. Sooner or later the police would no doubt get around to him. He'd done his best to keep his identity a secret around Beth, had even asked Diane to never mention his last name, and most of their "dates" had either been at some third location or when Beth wasn't around.

Yet at the moment, none of those precautions felt particularly effective.

"I don't know, guy. The truth, I guess. Christ, there's nothing I couldn't tell them that Lyn doesn't already know. We met, purely by happenstance, something clicked and I spent a short time pursuing her. Then we began seeing each other. For all of five months, then my wife found out and I had to break it off. Haven't talked to the lady since."

"Think they'll buy that?"

"It's the truth."

"Yeah, but will they buy it? If you step back a ways, you've got to admit that you're in the primo spot for being a suspect."

A murder suspect? He'd played many roles in his life: father, husband, student, teacher. And he'd once dreamed of playing numerous other roles, which he probably never would.

But considered a criminal? Much less a murderer? The very idea of his taking part in such a sordid scenario sounded so far beyond the pale that he could barely imagine it.

"Maybe," he finally said. "Then again, I've no clue

who else has been in or out of her life since then. Hell, for all l I know I was just another fling."

"Yeah, just another fling that lasted half a year and almost wrecked your marriage."

As they pulled into the north faculty parking lot, Ron lapsed into silence. He didn't want Ryan to know, as of yet didn't want anyone to know, but there was no "almost" about it. His and Lynda's marriage was in fact truly and completely wrecked. Since October, they'd been going through the motions until they figured out all the ramifications concerning their two kids. The scene this morning had merely been an aberration in terms of subject matter, not intensity.

They hadn't so much as touched each other, not just sexually but even in a casual manner, since the night Lynda had found out about Diane. Ron had made one or two attempts, as part of the "healing process," but that had proven to be just another joke. The fire wasn't just out, the embers had been thoroughly soaked and scattered to the four winds.

"Lunch today?" Ryan said as he coasted the car to a stop and turned off the ignition.

It took deliberate effort for Ron to pull himself back from the lonely place his mind had just gone to.

"Afraid I can't. Got some song and dance for the chair, and for some potential donors. One of the big agricultural companies upstate."

"Okay. Well, see you at the usual time."

After Ryan walked off, Ron stood on the sidewalk for a moment. He had only one class today, a morning one beginning shortly after ten. Then there was the lunch with the chair and the donors at noon, a backlog of e-mails he had to get to, and three articles that one of the journals had sent him to review. All in all, a fairly normal day.

He just hoped it would remain so.

CHAPTER THREE

His class that morning, an entry-level entrepreneurship course that everyone in the department dreaded doing, ended up nearly a complete disaster. A few years back, the chair had dictated all faculty in the department had to teach the course at least once every two years. As an untenured assistant professor, Ron received the luxury of teaching it every year.

The chair's dictate was understandable to anyone who happened to walk into one of the course sessions and see the nearly two hundred students filling up each section.

Still, it rankled some of the older hands, while Ron just looked forward to the day, in the not too distant future, when he became one of the old hands and could scale back to once every four semesters.

Still, this lecture, covering some of the basics of marketing, should have been a slam dunk, even with the luncheon with the donors breathing down his neck. Today, however, proved the exception.

Because of the scene with Lynda, and Ryan's arrival this morning, he hadn't had a chance to really process and deal with the news of Diane's death, so he stood in front of his class and began his lecture, going more or less on autopilot.

Ordinarily not a problem, seeing as how he'd delivered the same lecture numerous times. He managed to divide his attention in half, part of his mind going through the standard notes and lecture points while the other part tried, more or less futilely, to grasp the concept that a woman he'd known so intimately, with whom he'd shared bed and heart for nearly half a year and, at one point, had considered leaving his wife and children for, was now dead and cold. He tried, unsuccessfully, to wrap his mind around the idea she had been choked to death, strangled in her home by some unknown person. And, if Ryan had heard right, also beaten. But no matter how hard he tried, he just couldn't bring himself to picture it. At one point, a small, divided part of his attention briefly wondered if somehow the reporters had made a mistake.

In the second row, somewhat off to the right, sat a young student who, at a quick glance, looked much as Diane had looked as a teenager. One night, after an unusually intense bout of lovemaking, their pillow talk had turned kind of nostalgic, and over a second glass of Chardonnay, Diane got out some old pictures, from the days before everything became digital, to show Ron. Her hair had been longer then, of course, and her frame somewhat skinnier, but in the smiling, impish teen portrayed in the pictures he could clearly see the genesis of the adult woman lying beside him.

At the time, lying in placid contentment, Ron had no idea that within a month he'd be forced to break it off and some months later the warm, vibrant woman beside him would be no more.

The young student in the second row could have almost been Diane's twin. Her presence made him even more jittery than he would have been considering the morning's news.

He tried his best, so much so that it wasn't until he'd

answered two questions incorrectly (the students didn't catch his mistakes, but Ron did as soon as the words were out of his mouth) and repeated the same point three times in a row, that he realized he had to call it a day.

Looking at the young woman in the second row, he saw a combination of confusion, irritation and slight resentment on her face. Probably chafing at the idea of her, or somebody on her behalf, paying good money to have some doofus babble nonsense.

But the look almost stopped his heart. So similar to the look on Diane's face the night he broke it off with her. He'd tried to explain how his wife had thrown down an ultimatum that he wasn't ready to cross yet, but no matter what he said or how he tried to break it, her reaction came even worse than he'd expected.

Tears he could have taken. Yells, curses, even a few thrown objects he would have expected and understood. Instead, Diane had stood there, her frame seeming to draw into itself while a combination of silent emotions paraded across her face.

When he tried to explain further, she half-turned from him. When he reached out and touched her shoulder, she had actually flinched, a slight motion, though enough to get her point across.

Those had been his last moments with her.

And now here he had some student throwing that same look in his direction.

Too much.

Simply too goddamned much.

"Sorry, guys," he told the assembled class. "Think I had some bad Chinese last night. Thrown my system out of whack." He attempted a chuckle, which got no response from his students. "What say we shelve this for now and pick it up again next Monday. Any objections?"

It was a standard joke, one he'd picked up from an old Prof of his. Naturally, no one objected to leaving class early, and as Ron watched the students dashing out of the room, on top of everything else running through him, a pang of jealousy hit him hard.

No doubt most of them were looking forward to at least a little bit of downtime before the next item on their schedules. He, unfortunately, still had his business lunch to get through. And no clue as to how the hell he would pull it off while debating with himself as to whether to go to the cops.

As it turned out, he could have saved himself the worry of trying to make that decision.

****

They were waiting for him when he came back from lunch shortly after two. Heading down the hall towards his office, Ron noticed a man and woman hanging around his office door.

As he got closer, he realized they looked too old to be students, at least too old for the students normally around during the daytime, and they were dressed far too casually to be faculty, at least in this department. Most people didn't have to spend much time at all around the typical university campus before realizing the old cliché, which stated that most professors, no matter their rank or pay, dressed worse than the average student, approached absolute truth. In most other departments, one rarely saw a blazer of any kind, much less a tie. And some faculty, especially in the humanities, came to work wearing nothing but jeans and tee-shirts.

This was true almost uniformly, except for in the business department, where jacket and tie, if not full suit, still ruled. Almost every year, some new faculty member would commit the cardinal sin, usually early on, of showing up wearing something other than a solid-colored blazer, at which point his new colleagues would immediately set him straight.

So it didn't take much deduction at all to categorize this pair, both the man and woman dressed in jeans and casual blazers, as not connected in any normal way with the university, and from there it took Ron only a small leap to figure out who they were and more than likely what their business was.

As he came within ten feet of the pair, something in their posture, or maybe the set of their faces, served to validate his initial impression..

"Professor Green?" queried the female, a short, fairly pretty brunette in her early thirties.

"Yes?" Ron replied.

The next second or two unrolled almost like a movie or television drama. The woman held up a small leather carrying case, flipped it upwards to show an open compartment and reveal a shiny badge.

"Detectives Lipscomb and Hollis. Could we have a word?"

"Certainly." Ron hoped his tone sounded calmer than he felt. His underarms instantly soaked; his heart beat twice its normal speed; and the hallway seemed to swirl and dip around him.

Even so, he managed to unlock the door to his office and usher them inside. The woman came all the way in and took a seat at the single chair in front of his desk. The man, who still hadn't spoken, took up a standing position next to the doorway.

Ron hoped it was only his imagination making the

man appear to be blocking the only exit from the room.

"I guess I know why you're here," he said before either cop had a chance to speak.

"Oh?" This from the woman. The guy, standing about two inches taller than Ron's own five nine and looking like a prime athlete just starting to go soft, still kept silent.

"Diane Brewster, right?"

"So you know about her?" Ron glanced toward the male cop.

"Yes. My wife and I saw it on the news this morning. I wondered how long it would take for you to come around."

"So if you knew about it and was wondering," again from Detective—Hollis?–"why didn't you come to us?"

"Well," Ron paused, realizing how evasive anything he said would sound.

"Mr. Green." The woman again. "Did you know Diane Brewster?"

"Yes, I did."

Forthright. Look them in the eye, almost like negotiating a business deal. Supposedly, he knew all about business and deals and how to negotiate. He earned a decent salary teaching all that stuff, for chrissakes. But with the stakes so high, pray they don't see the sweating palms or twitching extremities.

"How did you know her?"

"Just by the fact that you found me, I'm assuming you already know the answer to that."

"Maybe so," said Hollis, still seemingly guarding the doorway. "But we'd still like to hear it from you."

Ron wondered, briefly, just how much they really knew. His dalliance with Diane had been mainly physical. Coming from the business environment, Ron knew all too well the damage excess documentation could do. So he'd kept his e-mails and phone calls to Diane to a minimum, and had made sure they never had their picture taken together.

"Professor Green?" The woman interrupted his thoughts.

But obviously they'd talked to Diane's roommate, would have done so early on, and here they were quizzing him about his relationship with Diane.

No doubt his fears of earlier in the morning, that Diane had, either knowingly or not, blabbed his identity to Beth, had borne true.

"Do I need a lawyer?" He directed his question towards the woman, Detective Lipscomb.

"Not as far as we're concerned. We're in the earliest stages of the investigation, naturally, and we just need some background information."

"How did you get my name?"

"Hey, buddy,"—this from the guy at the door—"We're the ones who're supposed to be asking the questions, and you're supposed to be—"

"Jack, he asked a legitimate question. Mr. Green," Lipscomb said, "what was your relationship with Miss Brewster?"

He noticed that, despite her seeming to want to get along, she'd sidestepped his question.

"None, lately," Ron said.

"But in the past?"

"In the past we–hell, you have to know all this anyway. We were lovers."

"Are you married, Mr. Green?"

"Yes," he responded, looking at the female

detective.

"How long?" The guy. Ron looked his way.

"Eight years."

"This your first affair?" The woman.

"I really don't see how that's any of—"

"It is our business," said Hollis. "You want to answer or you want to get a lawyer?"

A lawyer? Christ, what would Lynda think, what would his colleagues think, if he had to go out and retain a lawyer? He hadn't seen Diane in months, so how could he have possibly had anything to do with her death?

If they'd just broken up, he could see it. Yet after all this time?

"Do I need one?" Ron felt as though on some sort of eternal merry-go-round, always returning to the same starting point.

"You're not a suspect." The man.

An unspoken "yet" seemed to hang in the air between the three of them.

"How long did you and Miss Brewster have a relationship?"

Although this was all a new area for Ron, he fancied himself an intelligent enough man to adapt to any situation, even one this grim.

And the one thing he knew for an absolute certainty, the one thing obvious to any clear-thinking person, was to make sure you knew exactly what you were saying before you said it.

And even more important, make sure you knew exactly what they were asking.

"I think I want to speak to a lawyer," he said.

"Come on, guy," the male partner said, "how did you two meet?"

"Jack," the woman broke in, "he's asked for a lawyer. It's time for us to stop."

CHAPTER FOUR

"Well, whatcha think?" Hollis asked as they pulled out of the university parking lot and headed downtown.

"About our guy in there?" Helen said.

"Uh huh."

"Likely, very likely."

"Interesting how quickly he shut up," Hollis remarked.

"Yeah. As soon as we asked him about how long their affair lasted, he just stopped talking."

"Which could mean a few things."

"Such as?"

Hollis grinned. Although he and Lipscomb weren't officially permanent partners, they worked together more often than not, sometimes with himself as the primary and sometimes with her. In this case, Helen had caught the initial call, which automatically made her the lead detective on the case. Still, it was a fifty-fifty toss up with both of them having roughly the same amount of experience. It really only came down to a question of whose name came first on the reports.

"He could be merely a savvy citizen, innocent, who thinks it's better not to say anything to the cops without a lawyer present," Hollis said.

"Maybe." Lipscomb pulled up to a stop light and drummed her fingers on the wheel.

"Or he could be innocent but hiding something that

would make him look guilty."

"Such as?" she asked.

"Well, the most obvious would be if the affair didn't end like he said."

"Because if he was still seeing her, he'd be our number one looksee."

"Right."

The light turned green and Helen gunned the engine, causing a slight squeal of the tires.

"But he has to know," she said, "that we'll find out pretty quick whether or not they were still doing it, which if he lied to us will make him look worse."

"Doing it?" Hollis said.

"Huh?"

"You said whether or not they're still 'doing it.'"

"So?"

"Nothing. Just not very ladylike."

He grinned in anticipation of a comeback from her, a game they often played, but he didn't get it this day.

"You didn't see her, Jack. Not up close."

True. Hollis had been off duty the night before when the woman's body was discovered, and while he'd had time to skim Helen's initial report, which included the standard array of photos, obviously the actual scene had impacted his partner more than he'd realized.

"It wasn't just that the bastard, or bastards, strangled her," Lipscomb continued. "She was beaten first, or at least the ME thinks it was first. Won't know for sure until the autop. Nose broken, both eyes blackened. She even had a couple of teeth knocked out. The beating alone wasn't enough to kill her, but it sure softened her up for the final act."

Hollis, even with years of experience, shivered at

the thought.

"You saying there was some kind of passion behind it?" he asked.

"Either passion or rage. Lots and lots of one or the other."

"Which isn't too good for our buddy the professor, is it?"

"Not at all," Lipscomb said. "So we might as well look at the most likely possibility for why he's lawyering up so quick."

"Not only most likely," said Hollis, "but most common."

"Right." She jammed her foot on the brake for another red light. "Odds are, he's our guy."

CHAPTER FIVE

"A focus group?"

"That's right."

"You had an affair with a woman you met in a focus group?"

Walter Lowenstein was considered by most a decent lawyer, and even more, Ron counted him as a friend, not a great friend but a good one. Yet even as he heard the question repeated, Ron began to realize just how lame the story sounded.

"That's correct," Ron affirmed.

Walt sighed and reached over for a pen and legal pad. The two men were seated in Lowenstein's office, in a building just east of the city's downtown section, which he shared with four partners. Through the west windows Ron could see the sun beginning to descend. The highly-polished desk between them reflected glints of light from the window.

"Brewster, right?"

"Yes, Diane Brewster."

"I'm surprised the cops don't already have you downtown."

"Like I said, they came to see me, and when I stopped answering their questions they asked me to meet them tomorrow for a formal interview. Suggested I bring my lawyer."

"How do you propose to explain all this to them?

I'm assuming Lynda already knows."

"God does she." Ron wiped his hand across his forehead, even though the office's air conditioning kept the atmosphere comfortable. "Ever since she found out, life at home's been one unending series of torments."

"How?"

"How've I been tormented?"

"No, Ron. How did she find out?"

Ron took a deep breath, then laid his palms flat out on the chair arms.

"Same old story as always. Not one big revelatory moment. She didn't find any nude photos on my phone or anything like that. Didn't come home early and walk in on us making love. It was a matter of stories not meshing up, more than once. Maybe some odd little mannerisms on my part. I started taking better care of myself. Things like that. Then, when she had her suspicions, she went about checking up on me, and there you are."

"Such as?"

"Huh?"

"You said stories not meshing up. What stories?"

"What does it matter, Walt? The important thing is—"

"The important thing is that I need to know everything, guy. Every single little detail, if I'm going to decide whether to represent you. Because whatever little bits and fragments of information are out there, if the cops seriously like you for this you can damned well bet that they're going to dig it up. Quite possibly already have. So let's get with it, buddy. What kind of stories didn't mesh up?"

"If?"

"I'm sorry?"

"You said 'if' you decide to represent me. What's that mean?"

"It means that something this large is kind of out of my field. I usually deal with assaults and muggings, also the occasional drug dealer. But if we're talking murder here, whether first or second degree..."

"Still..."

"Plus, I'd have to run it by my partners. We usually give each other as much latitude as we can, but something like this could easily tie up a lot of our resources. Lots of downsides to murder trials."

"Any upsides?"

"Sure. If you win. If you lose, nothing but down. Among other things—and, Ron, please don't take this the wrong way—but if you're actually charged, let alone tried, with homicide, will you have enough to pay our bills?"

"I–I guess I really hadn't thought about that."

"Need to think about it, guy. And while you're thinking, don't kid yourself. If what you've told me is true, and can be confirmed as such, you're at the top of the cops' hit list for this one."

Ron felt his stomach sinking even more than it had in the afternoon when he'd returned to his office to find the two detectives standing outside his office. In all the chaos this day had brought on, he'd never once considered that Walter wouldn't help him out.

"So what can I do to help convince you?" he asked.

"Simple." Walter settled more firmly into his chair, placed the legal pad down on the table and poised his pen over it. "Tell me everything, everything you can think of. Don't leave a *damned* thing out, and we'll see what we can do."

"Okay." Ron suddenly felt more tired than he had in a long time. "But you may want to order out for some pizza. It's going to be a long night."

What the hell, he thought. It sure beat going back home.

CHAPTER SIX

Shortly after nine o'clock the next morning, Ron and his attorney walked into the central police station. They had to stop just inside, empty their pockets into a small plastic tray, and walk through a metal detector. Cleared by the machine, they consulted the uniformed officer manning the device, then made their way to the fifth floor, where the homicide division was located.

Detectives Lipscomb and Hollis were waiting for them just inside the door to the Homicide squad. After a brief greeting, Hollis held the door open for the two men as Lipscomb ushered them inside and directed them to a small room along the east side of the squad room. When they all got settled down in the small interview room, and coffee had been offered and declined, Lipscomb took a moment to look her visitors over.

Green actually looked like a little bit of hell had flown through the air and settled inside of him. He sat rigidly, hands down at his sides and jaw locked as tightly as it could possibly be. He wore a light tan, two-piece suit and light blue shirt, no tie, and the first two buttons of his shirt unbuttoned the only hints of casualness in his appearance. Even so, Helen thought, the man looked an absolute wreck.

****

The morning, so far, had been even more of a disaster than Ron had expected. When he'd gotten home from Walter's office the night before, he'd waited until Sarah and the baby were both asleep before trying to tell Lynda about his day. Originally intending to be as straightforward as possible, when the time came he found himself, for lack of a better term, chickening out.

He'd told her about his nervousness and distraction yet had neglected to tell her about the police visit. In the back of his mind he hoped, actually damned near prayed, that somehow or other the next day he and Lowenstein could make the whole thing go away.

Lying in bed , the invisible barrier that had existed between them for months felt even more ponderous than usual. Ron found himself staying so tightly to his side of the bed that at one point he felt he might fall off. Although he could tell, late into the night, that Lynda lay awake, her breathing too ragged for sleep, the few times he attempted to elicit some response or conversation he met only stone silence.

Even worse, he'd woken up in the morning to find his wife gone, a note on the kitchen table that she'd gone for a walk, whatever that meant. Even over the strain of the last few months, she'd never shirked her motherly duties. Now, she'd left her two kids alone with her husband asleep. Ron hurried to take care of both Sarah and the baby, getting the one ready for school and finding a sitter at the last minute for the other—thank God for grandparents—before notifying the university he would be out for the day and they needed to cancel all of his classes.

Then it was time to get ready to meet Walt at the central police station downtown and prepare for the grilling.

By the time he left the apartment around eight-thirty,

Lynda still hadn't shown up.

****

"Mr. Green, did you know Diane Brewster?"

Ron stared at the recorder, placed squarely between them on the table, and took a deep breath.

"Yes, I did."

"And what was the nature of your relationship with her?"

Ron glanced over at his attorney, got a nod of affirmation, and took a deep swallow.

"We were lovers."

"I see." Detective Lipscomb made a notation of some kind on her pad. Ron wondered why she was asking some of the same questions as the day before, but figured it had to do with some kind of formal procedure.

"Were you involved with her up till the time of her death?"

"No. We stopped seeing each other about five months ago."

"Was Miss Brewster a friend of your family or a friend of a friend?"

"No."

"Did you meet her in some kind of social setting? A bar or nightclub?"

"No. I didn't."

"Did she have anything to do with your workplace?"

"No."

The two cops looked up.

"No?" said Lipscomb.

"No. She wasn't associated with my work."

The detectives glanced at each other before Lipscomb continued.

"Dr. Green, you're employed at Tribune University.

41

Correct?"

"Yes, but..."

"And didn't Miss Brewster work at Tribune as well?"

"Not really, no."

Again, the glances between the two. At the same time, Walt looked like he wanted to kick Ron's shin under the table.

"Dr. Green, we've talked to the officials at Tribune University. They have her listed as an employee, so ..."

"They should have her listed as a graduate teaching assistant."

"That's not employment?" Hollis asked.

Ron sighed, suddenly realizing how far off into the weeds he'd managed to stray. This was supposed to be a simple in and out matter, and now he'd unnecessarily complicated it.

"Let me clarify what I just said," he said.

"Please do," said Lipscomb.

"When I said Diane wasn't connected with my job, I meant it from an academic viewpoint. Tribune's a big place, hell, you know that. And all told there's several hundred, possibly into the thousands, of people who work there."

"Okay."

He looked over at Walt, who seemed to have calmed down a bit. So he continued.

"I guess you could say it's a conceit on our part, but by and large the faculty out there, hell, probably most places, don't really consider teaching assistants as colleagues. To us, they're students who just happen to work part-time for their tuition."

"Pretty inflated opinion of yourselves, isn't it?"

Hollis asked, and now his partner looked like she wanted to kick his shin.

"Maybe," Ron said, "but that's just the way it is. On top of that, she worked in the sociology department."

"Problem with that, too?" Hollis said.

"No. But you've got to understand how big the university is. It's actually several schools in one. And it's almost unheard of for people in one school to know someone in another."

"Fascinating as this is," Lipscomb said with a slight, sarcastic twang in her voice, "how exactly did the two of you meet?"

This sounded, at least to Ron, like an actual question, not part of some pre-determined script. Was it possible the cops didn't know…

He looked over at Walter, who gave him a brief nod.

"We met," Ron said, "when she and I were both picked by the Amos Kettering PR firm."

The male half of the partnership, Hollis, had jumped in.

"Picked?"

"Yes," Ron said. "Picked."

"Picked for what?"

"We were selected to take part in a focus group for part of the advertising for Senator Rawlings's campaign."

The two cops looked at each other, and something Ron couldn't quite pin down passed between them.

"You mean for her re-election?" Detective Lipscomb asked.

"Yes. If you recall, she was neck and neck in the polls. So about six months before the election, her campaign team decided to scrap their advertising and promotions and start fresh."

"I heard about that," said Detective Hollis. "Neck and neck is a nice way of putting it. She was getting trounced. Didn't some of her people get fired during the shakeup?"

"I think so, but I was so busy at the time, spring semester and all, that I wasn't really following state politics all that much. I usually don't get interested until about September."

"Anyway," Lipscomb drawled out the word to get their attention," the two of you got picked for this group?"

"Right."

"And how exactly did that work?"

"I'm sorry?"

"How did you get picked? How did they go about selecting people for this group of yours?"

"Oh, well, in my case, I answered an e-mail that had been sent out campus wide. I don't know for sure, never asked, but I would guess they sent out a similar solicitation to all the schools in the area."

"So you saw this e-mail?"

"Yeah. At first, just glancing at the subject line, I assumed it was junk that hadn't been caught by the university's filter. But I knew of Amos Kettering as a legitimate firm. Heck, some of our students get internships there, so I figured what the heck and opened it up."

"And did Diane Brewster come into the group in the same manner? As a teaching assistant she would have gotten the same e-mail, right?"

"I would guess so. We actually never talked much about it, but it makes sense that that's how she came upon it."

So far, except for the initial whack on the shin, Walt Lowenstein had remained completely silent. Obviously, he hadn't considered anything his client had yet said as in any way harmful.

"So if I understand this right," Detective Hollis said, "everyone in this survey thing were associated with the university?"

"Actually, no. As far as I ever knew, just myself and Diane."

"Then how did the other people get picked? How many were there anyway?"

"There were twelve of us, all told. I'm sure the Kettering people contacted more, but you have to account for shrinkage on these things."

"Shrinkage?" Lipscomb said.

"Right. People who commit but don't show up, drop out at the last minute. That sort of thing."

"Okay. And the others got selected how?"

Ron leaned back somewhat. The tide had turned, at least temporarily, and swerved into the role of lecturing the two cops about an aspect of business work. He suddenly felt more like himself than he had in several days.

"I don't know for sure how the others got selected. None of us ever talked much about it. But there's two ways to go. Sometimes, these things require a really narrow audience. Like if you were doing a new brand of dishwasher soap or, in my field, a new textbook or teaching material. In those cases you want to get people as similar as possible, like from the same field or who share a similar activity."

"Not so for this one?" Hollis asked.

"No. For something like this, with a political bent, they'd probably want as wide a variety as possible. Adults of voting age, of course, but other than that they'd want a sample of people that mirrored the general population."

"That's all interesting, Mr. Green," Detective Lipscomb said, "but how were the various people picked?"

Ron suddenly felt something like an ass as he realized he'd been talking down to these people.

"Sorry," he said as he wiped his hands on his pants legs. "I guess I've been kind of running off at the mouth. Let's just say a lot of times companies forming general focus groups will put ads in the local media to solicit participants."

"But you don't know if that happened in this case?"

"Sorry, no. It's something we really didn't talk about."

"How long did this go on?" Hollis asked.

Ron glanced over at Walt, who still seemed content with the way things were going.

"It took about a day and a half."

"Doing what?"

"Basically, they had six different series of commercials. I think three or four in each series. We would watch a series, then one of the PR people came in and asked us several leading questions, and we answered them."

"What kind?" Detective Hollis again.

"What kind what?"

"What kind of questions? About politics?"

"Not so much about politics, at least not directly, more about the tone and vibes we'd get from the commercials. You know, did we agree with the idea? What was our gut reaction when we heard this phrase? Which way they had the senator posing was more appealing? That kind of stuff."

"You mean they even narrowed it down to different ways she was standing or walking?" Hollis asked.

"Believe me, they quizzed us over everything. Sometimes we'd see three different versions of the same commercial, with maybe the only difference being the outfit the senator was wearing."

"So you did this for a day and a half?" Lipscomb asked.

"Right."

"Seems like a long time to be watching campaign commercials over and over. Didn't it get old after a while?"

Ron merely shrugged.

"And somewhere during that day and a half, you and Miss Brewster got something going on?" Hollis asked.

Ron noticed Detective Lipscomb grimace at her partner's choice of phrase.

"It didn't exactly happen that way," he said.

"Then exactly what way did it happen?"

So far, Ron had been watching his attorney out of the corner of his eye. Now he turned and looked at Walt straight on. Walt nodded, like a calm and reassuring uncle, so Ron turned back to the detectives.

"Well, it was more like…"

****

The young office worker manning the reception desk had ushered him into the conference room. In tone and design, it looked a lot like the antechamber to the president's office at the university, the one reserved for board meetings and other weighty matters. Full of muted earth tones and dark polished woods, the room projected an air of business and luxury at the same time. As Ron thanked the young woman and turned to enter, he'd noticed her right off.

At no point would Ron have said he was struck with love at first sight or realized right away she was the woman he should have been with all his life.

It wasn't anything like that, but it was enough.

About fifteen people milled around the room. One or two stood out as employees of the firm, with the rest obviously participants like himself. In his suit and tie, Ron felt oddly out of place. He'd decided to go with his usual uniform during the work week, but the only other man dressed even close to what he wore was walking around with a clipboard in his hand, so Ron figured him for one of the PR people. And even he just had slacks and a blazer.

While a few of the women, Ron picked up on right away, wore skirts or dresses, most of his fellow participants, both genders, were wearing jeans or pants and a comfortable shirt or blouse. As he looked around, Ron saw a mixed group of ordinary people, most of them with a slightly-uncertain look on their faces, probably similar to his own expression, and Ron considered that this may not be the worst way to spend a couple of days off work. As he took a closer look at the crowd, one or two of them didn't quite seem to fit in, but overall they seemed a decent enough bunch.

Then he noticed her.

At one end of the table, nursing a Styrofoam cup of coffee and a plain cruller, sat a young woman who looked to be in her late twenties, though he would later find out she was over thirty. Average height and build, she wore jeans, a purple tee-shirt, and purple and white running shoes. She had her light brown hair done up in a ponytail and looked for all the world like a young woman on her way to the gym.

Ron looked away, then in another second glanced back at her.

As he stared closer, he felt an odd sensation growing, not just the obvious physical one but something else. A small vein began hammering in his temple, his breath literally quickened, and his palms began to sweat.

What the hell, he thought.

She wasn't even that attractive. Sure, she looked okay, and from what he could see her build while not scrawny, wasn't all that noteworthy either. Heck, on any given day of the week he passed dozens of university students hotter than her. Yet something, maybe the image of her sitting all alone in a roomful of people, or perhaps the fact Ron and Lynda had had another of their increasingly frequent arguments that morning, or maybe that he'd already well surpassed the seven-year mark where thoughts are supposed to wander, something about this young woman caught his attention.

He swung by the serving cart in the corner and got a cup of coffee, then began heading over towards her end of the table. Before he made it even halfway, the guy with the clipboard cleared his throat noisily.

"Good morning," he said. "I'm Jacob Vickers, and I'd like to welcome you here today on the part of the Amos Kettering firm. If you wouldn't mind taking your seats, we'll get started."

Before Ron could go another four steps, the chairs on both sides of the brown-haired woman were filled, one by a young black woman in a soft blue business suit and the other by an old geezer who looked to be at least seventy.

Oh well, Ron thought, *just as well*. Despite their constant bickering, both he and Lynda held out hope that somewhere down the line they could put things back together. (After all, their marriage wasn't seriously troubled, just running kind of stale, especially with the new kid.) So hooking up with some fresh young thing probably counted as the absolute worst move he could make at the moment.

Besides, he'd never considered himself a womanizer, so why the hell start now and with someone so clearly unsuited for him?

Sighing, he slumped into the nearest available chair and waited to see how the next two days would go.

****

"So when did you first talk to her?" Detective Lipscomb asked.

"Actually, it wasn't until the next day. They kept us pretty busy the first day, with only about a half hour or so for lunch and a few other breaks here and there, and by the time we wrapped up all I could think about was going home and crashing. You've no idea how boring it is to watch political commercials for nearly nine hours straight."

"Did you get paid?"

Ron shrugged.

"A little, kind of a token payment for something to be on the table."

"How much?"

"I don't really remember, probably around fifty dollars for the two days. I got the feeling most of us were doing it for the experience more than anything else."

"And so?" Hollis asked. "When did you two first talk?"

A few minutes before, the male detective had got up from his chair and moved to lean against the wall. He gave Ron the impression of a man who had too much energy to sit still very easily, which made Ron realize he never wanted to antagonize the man.

"The second day. At lunch."

****

By the next morning, the whole affair had begun to grow stale. Initially, considering his business background and work in academia, Ron had looked at participating in the focus group as an interesting experience. But after watching four of the six series of commercials, all about the same legislator who, to be frank, he'd never cared much for to begin with, Ron could clearly feel ennui setting in.

Besides, this was all for a state senator looking for a second term. And in the midst of a presidential election year, who the hell cared about state senators?

In truth, the only thing that kept him at all engaged the second morning was the young woman he'd noticed the day before. They all wore name tags, and there'd been a fair amount of back and forth discussion in each of the debriefing sessions, so he knew her name was Diane (though he still didn't know her last name) and that she also, surprise surprise, worked at the university as a teaching assistant, though in what field she hadn't revealed.

Interestingly enough, on the second day she had dressed up quite a bit, especially compared to the first day. She had on a charcoal-grey wool skirt, black turtleneck and modest black pumps. A simple gold chain looped around her neck hung about halfway down the turtleneck. This was particularly noticeable seeing as how most of the participants had, if anything, dressed down from the day before.

At one point in the morning, with one of the discussions ongoing, Ron took a few minutes to idly wonder about her change in appearance. He couldn't tell for sure, not being much of a player in these matters, but he couldn't help but wonder if maybe, just maybe, she was attempting to attract somebody's attention.

Then he wondered if, by chance, that person was him.

****

"So you actually first got together when?" Hollis asked, his annoyance now palpable, even though his partner still seemed unruffled. Ron wondered if this was some sort of variation of the clichéd good cop/bad cop routine.

"After it was all over, somewhere around two o'clock that afternoon. A few people had to leave right away, and one fellow even sulked out of there like he'd somehow been insulted by the whole thing. But most of us decided, what the hell, the day was already shot, we might as well all go out and have some drinks. We went to a little bar a few of us knew and sat around for a while BS'ing. Over the next couple of hours, one by one they all had somewhere to go or something to do, until finally there were only two of us left."

"You and Miss Brewster," from Lipscomb, a statement not a question.

"Yes. Me and Diane."

"And that's how it started?"

"Yeah," Ron said, looking down at the table because he suddenly didn't want to look any of these people, not even his own lawyer, in the eye, "that's how we started."

CHAPTER SEVEN

Last March

One by one the others had taken off, leaving just Ron and the dark-haired woman, Diane. He still had half a mug left on his latest beer (he'd only had three) with the lady in the process of polishing off her second martini. While both of them had had more than a little to drink, you could by no stretch consider either one of them drunk.

A little fact which became important to Ron later on when he tried to rationalize to himself what happened next.

"Well," she said, "I guess it's getting kind of late."

"Late for the afternoon," Ron said, "but still kind of early."

Now where the hell did that asinine comment come from?

"What time do you have to get home?" Diane asked.

"Who said I have to be home any special time?" Inwardly, he grimaced at how lame he must have sounded.

She grinned, though in a nice way, and pointed to his hand.

"That little band on your finger says so."

Laughing, Ron took a drink to cover his embarrassment.

Just what the hell, he wondered, was going on here?

"So," he said as he put his glass down, "where's your next stop after you leave here?"

"That depends," she said. "I've got a couple of different possibilities. On the practical side, I've got a paper to write on how the structural-functionalist concept will become irrelevant by the middle of the century."

"The what?"

She waved her hand in dismissal, managing in the same motion to brush back a lock of hair.

"Sociology stuff," she said. "After six years of studying it, I'm starting to think it's all just a bunch of blah, blah."

"What's the other option?"

"Well," she said as she cast her eyes partway down and twirled her glass between her fingers, "that's kind of open to discussion."

Even Ron, who'd been part of the staid married scene for nearly a decade, could read the signs here, and it kind of surprised him that he could so easily pick up on the signals again.

And it really surprised him that he hadn't bolted yet.

"I told my wife that I didn't know when we'd be done," he said.

"Hmm." Diane still hadn't looked up yet, and Ron wondered just how far she was willing to take this–whatever it was.

Wondering at the same time just how far he wanted it to go.

She looked up from her drink.

"Are you hungry? I know it's a bit early for dinner, but the lunch they served was pretty light today, and I'm feeling kind of…"

She looked at Ron expectantly as the words trailed off.

Ron himself was beginning to feel like twenty different kinds of an ass. Not only did he have Lynda waiting at home, but Sarah and the newborn as well. And yet, things at home had been so damned uncomfortable lately.

It wasn't just the second pregnancy, though it definitely hadn't helped things at all. He and Lyn had been having their issues for a while now, and it had taken a major effort on both their parts to keep it under wraps and away from Sarah's attention.

And while it would take an idiot not to see where this was headed, Ron figured himself at least ten years older than Diane. If it was just a matter of a casual dinner, maybe to talk over their experiences of the last two days, what could it hurt? As long as he kept it from going too far, and kept the drinking to a minimum, he could be in for a nice, casual interlude before going back to his real life.

"Yeah," he finally said, "I could eat."

"Here? Or …"

"No," he said, working to mask a sudden hoarseness. "Let's go somewhere else."

"I don't have a car," Diane said. "Poor grad student and all."

Ron understood this at the moment. He could still get up and walk away, say it was nice to meet her, and return to normalcy.

That's all it would take. Just sliding his seat back, getting up from the table, and walking away. A few quick flashes of synapses, and he'd be home free.

Yeah, right. Like he ever really had an option.

"It's okay," he said, "I've got a car."

****

And then, naturally, he had to take her home. They'd spent a quiet hour or so in a small Italian place just east of the downtown area, and while it was still fairly early when they left the eatery, evening was definitely coming on.

Ron had taken a minute, just before they left the bar, to call Lynda and let her know the focus group had just wrapped up and he'd decided to go over to the university and get some work done before heading home. As he'd ended the conversation and flipped his cell phone shut, a faint thread of queasiness wormed its way through his gut.

He had no way of avoiding the truth then. No way of brushing it off or throwing fate to the winds.

He knew exactly what he intended doing.

Twenty minutes later, they pulled up outside a small, two-story house in an older section of the city.

"You own your own home?" he asked.

"God, no. Not on what the university pays its TA's. Inside it's divided into apartments, two to each floor."

"Oh."

They sat there a moment, neither one speaking.

She finally broke the silence without looking at him, just staring straight out the window.

"Beth's out of town for a few days."

"Huh? Who?"

"Beth," she said, still avoiding eye contact. "My roommate. Works at a local cafe about twenty minutes away. She and her boyfriend went to a family reunion back east."

"Okay."

Ron suddenly realized he, too, had been admiring the view just outside the windshield, doing his best not to look at the young woman in the passenger seat beside him.

"Just me. Living the single girl's lifestyle. All on my own."

Ron didn't respond to that one, a few seconds later reaching over and stroking his hand across her knee.

He heard the slightest intake of her breath, felt her muscle tremble under his palm, then a second later her hand covered his.

Well hell, he thought.

CHAPTER EIGHT

"So how do you think we did?" Ron asked.

He and Walt were seated in a booth at a sports bar down the street from the university. They'd met at Ron's office that morning and driven over to the police station together. Now, at slightly past noon, they'd decided to stop first for lunch and a bit of beer before going back to their respective work days.

"Well, they didn't book you,'" Lowenstein said as a waitress approached to take their order, "so you may have made out okay."

"May?"

"Yeah."

Before he could explain further, the waitress arrived, and the next few minutes were taken up with the necessities of ordering their respective lunches. When the young blonde, who Ron vaguely recognized from seeing around campus, hustled off, he turned back to his lawyer.

"How do you mean 'may'?"

"Simple. If you were telling the truth about all of it, you'll have a chance."

Ron nodded but didn't say anything. He stared off to the side for a moment before Lowenstein prodded him.

"Hey, you were telling the truth, weren't you?"

"Sure, it's just–I haven't thought much about her for a while. Been doing my best not to think about her. I'd forgotten how hard that could be. It's been a lot of years since I've tried to force myself to forget about a woman."

"Trying to repair things with Lynda?"

"Tried. For the first few weeks, but it became pretty obvious pretty quick that the ship had sailed. Actually, we'd been having troubles for quite some time before Diane came along. So I've been trying to put things together, making plans to get on with my life, not to mention cushion the kids, then suddenly here's Diane back in my life."

"Don't think of it that way, guy. She's not actually back."

"Sure feels like it."

"Did these plans of yours have anything to do with her?"

"You mean get back with her after leaving Lynda?"

"Yeah."

"Well, I thought about it, sure. Never seriously. If I'm any judge, she was pretty hurt when I broke it off. Besides, let's face it, the best thing after leaving a marriage is probably taking some time for yourself."

"Maybe. You talk to anybody about this?"

"What do you mean?"

"Friends, co-workers, maybe a marriage counselor? Did you talk to anyone about potentially splitting from Lynda?"

"Probably."

"Probably?"

"Of course I did. Geez, Walt. Did you ever know anyone heading for divorce who didn't gripe about it?"

"No. But most people heading for divorce aren't possible suspects in a homicide."

"What's your point?"

"My point is that those two detectives we just dealt with are going to be going through your entire Rolodex talking to everyone you work with, socialize with or know. So any stray comments you made, anything that could be in any way misconstrued, they're going to find out and, being homicide cops, they're going to put the worst possible spin on it."

"Come on, Walt. You're not making sense. How does anything I may have said having to do with me and Lynda connect in any way to Diane?"

"Simple. Some could see her as the catalyst that broke up your neat little life. And some could see that as a reason to take her out."

Ron lowered his head for a moment and stared at the scarred wooden table.

"Okay, I guess I get that. But—do you know if they have any other suspects, any real suspects?"

"Not yet. Like I said, this is out of my line, but it's probably a bit too early yet. I tried sniffing around yesterday afternoon but didn't get anywhere. I'll try again in a few days. If they've developed any leads it should be obvious by then. Far as that goes, if there's anything to find out the media will probably get it before I do. In the meantime, and I know this sounds a little too pat and easier said than done, but you just have to go about your daily life."

"Go about my life?" Ron's hands shook, and he probably would have said more except that right then the waitress arrived with their lunch. He sat quiet, doing no more than giving his lawyer a baleful look, until the young woman went away.

"My life? Dammit, Walt. I've just been questioned in a murder case. You think I consider that as part of my life?"

"No. And you shouldn't." Lowenstein took a bite out of his cheeseburger, chewed for a moment, then continued.

"And that's the point I was just making. It's going to be almost impossible, but you've just got to go about things as you would have if you'd never heard about her death, and let me handle the legal end."

"Until?"

"Until we get it resolved one way or the other."

"Tell me one thing, though. Am I officially a suspect?"

"They didn't charge you and lock you up, which is good. But in all truth, like I keep telling you, it's early yet. As far as I could tell, yeah, they're looking at you. There's one tone with questioning witnesses and another with people they're actually focusing on. Whether they have any others or not, we'll just have to wait it out and see. But if it comes down to it …"

"Yes?" So far, Ron hadn't taken a single bite out of his chicken sandwich and had only idly toyed with the fries. He realized now that he'd screwed up by ordering a stein of beer because the damned thing seemed to beckon him to down it all in one gulp.

"More than likely, if you haven't done anything, you'll be okay."

"If?"

"Let me finish. You'll more than likely be okay. But if it gets bad, and I mean really bad, then we'll have to call someone else in."

"Why? You're a criminal lawyer, right?"

"I am. But dammit, you're not listening to me. Something like this is way out of my league. If it would, by any stretch, happen to get as far as a courtroom, we'll have to call in a bigger gun."

"Someone else from your firm?"

"Maybe, but I'd actually feel better with a few names I can think of on the outside."

Ron had thought, over the last twenty-four hours, his stomach couldn't lurch any more. Now, the thought of mounting, and major, legal bills facing him down, at the same time as dissension with his wife and children, made him want to go in a corner somewhere and curl up into a ball.

And the worst part was, he had absolutely no idea how long all this hell was going to last.

CHAPTER NINE

After saying goodbye to Walt, Ron had a little under half the day left, so although his classes had all been cancelled, he decided to head over to the university and try to get some work done, a task he found not as easy as it sounded.

After nearly two hours of staring blankly at his computer screen, his mind wandering all through the tangled labyrinth which his life had somehow managed to become in less than two days, he gave it up as a bad deal, shut down his equipment and locked up his office.

He got to the parking lot right around three in the afternoon. Approaching to within about a football field's distance from his car, he got his first inkling of the maze developing an entirely new twist.

Two men stood next to his light blue Focus. Assuming them to be another pair of cops, he slowed down and, teeth on edge, tried to figure out a way to handle this new obstruction. For chrissakes, they'd let him walk out of the central station house just hours before, what could they possibly want so soon?

A tiny worm of fear uncoiled in his gut at the idea the cops had stumbled upon some evidence, or what they considered as evidence, against him.

The most likely, of course, would be DNA. After all, when Beth hadn't been around he'd spent quite a lot of time in Diane's apartment. However, granted that he ranked as fairly ignorant in these matters, Ron had always heard it took a long time for DNA evidence to be processed by a lab. Surely more than just a couple of days.

Even more, how could the cops possibly have any of his DNA to use as a match? Rapidly, his mind went over the time spent down at the station today, searching for anything he might have done which would have allowed them to get sample of his cells. The only thing that came to mind was about half a cup of coffee he'd consumed while there, which may or may not have given them what they needed. Again, Ron was ignorant in this area. Yet, even if they'd somehow managed to swipe something off the cup, the time angle still didn't add up.

Even more, if they'd managed somehow to get a sample from him, was it legal to do so? Or did they need his permission? Dammit, he just didn't know.

Now about ten feet closer to his vehicle, walking almost by remote control, Ron got a slightly closer look at the two men. He also noticed the brightly-colored van with the logo of a local TV station on its side and the bulky item sitting on the ground next to them.

Oh Christ, he thought. *Please say it ain't so*. Even from this distance, the device on the ground looked an awful lot like a video recorder.

Shit.

The press. Ron would almost have welcomed another visit from the cops compared to this, and as the realization banged through his mind he slowed to a complete stop. He looked all around him, searching for some way to avoid simply walking up to his car.

Unfortunately, just then one of the two looked over and saw him. He nudged his companion, who bent down and picked up the video recorder. Then the two started walking Ron's way.

No way, he thought. They can't know who I am. Unlike some of his colleagues, Ron had never appeared in local media, never been asked his opinion about topics related to his field. So if he just kept walking as if he had nothing to do with anything, they'd go right by him. They couldn't possibly know what he looked like unless they'd managed to do some ungodly fast digging and research.

Or checked out the university's website, he realized ruefully.

Or happened to be on hand at the police station earlier.

Or had been given his description by somebody down at the station.

Or ....

By this point, they'd come in front of him, and Ron could tell the jig was up. The camera, in the hands of the shorter of the two wearing jeans and a cotton work shirt, was already rolling, while the taller one, in blazer and tie, who Ron now recognized from seeing on the evening news from time to time, had begun talking.

"Excuse me, Professor Green?"

Ron could see no point in trying to bluff it through. If he somehow managed to avoid them, they'd only track him down at home, or if not there ....

Christ, home. What if another handful of this bunch, either print or television, was already bothering Lynda and the kids? Ron would never hear the end of it. He desperately wanted Walt here to give him advice, which was obviously out of the question.

"Yes?" he finally said.

"John Andrews, Channel 6 News. I was wondering if I could ask you a few questions about the death of Diane Brewster?"

For some reason, only now did Ron notice Andrews holding a microphone.

"Excuse me?" he said, stalling for time.

"Diane Brewster, professor. The young woman found dead in her home yesterday. We'd like to ask you a few questions."

Ron found himself tempted to respond with "no comment." However, he realized it would only make him seem guilty, just what he'd always thought of people who fell back on that statement, and he struggled to maintain some decorum.

"Why are you asking me?"

"We understand you were questioned by the police, twice, in regard to her death."

How could they possibly know that? Ron struggled for an answer, hoping the camera pointed straight at him hadn't picked up the sudden sweat on his forehead.

But in the lull as he tried to find his answer, Andrews kept pounding in.

"Were you acquainted with the deceased lady, professor?"

Andrews, especially in his current pose, looked like the epitome of a television crusader. Standing somewhat over six feet tall with perfectly styled hair and capped teeth, he made Ron feel like some sort of inferior specimen.

Which was more than likely the whole idea.

"Look," Ron finally got in, "I really don't want to talk to you about this."

"But the police have questioned you, correct?"

Andrews persisted.

"Please," Ron said, "Miss Brewster is—was—an acquaintance of mine, and I'd rather not discuss her death."

Sensing Andrews prepping another question, Ron set his shoulders and, not seeing any option, bulled his way right past the two men and into his car.

It took him three tries to turn the key, and when the ignition finally did catch he nearly stripped a few gears with how quickly he thrust the tranny into drive. Calming down at the last nanosecond, he managed to avoid squealing out of the parking lot, which no doubt would have ended up at the top of the evening's newscast.

Even so, he kept his speed around ten miles over the limit on his way home. He needed to get home as quickly as he could to warn Lynda. He didn't need his family life getting even more complex than it already was.

****

As he entered their apartment, Lynda stood in the middle of the living room, a tumbler of Scotch in her right hand.

"Did you see them?" she asked.

Nodding, Ron walked past her and went into the third bedroom, long ago converted over into a work area for him, and deposited his briefcase on the floor.

He went from there to the kitchen and fixed a Scotch and soda, very light on the soda, for himself.

As he mixed the drink, he looked up to see Lynda standing in the doorway of the kitchen. He wondered if it was merely his own nervous condition making the apartment seem so silent, so tomblike.

"So you saw them?" she repeated.

"Yes," he said. "Had to go around the back way and

up the service entrance."

"They were waiting for me when I went to pick up Sarah at school," Lynda said, her voice in a near monotone. "I had Kimberly in my arms when they came up to me with their damned cameras. You forgot to tell me a few things yesterday, didn't you, Ron?"

Ron suddenly understood why the apartment seemed so still and quiet.

"Where are the kids?" he asked.

"They're at Mom's for now. You forgot to tell me something, right? Yesterday, when I asked you if anything happened?"

He drained about half of his drink in one swallow while staring at the white kitchen wall. After a while, he might possibly shift to looking at the ceiling. Anywhere except at his wife.

"I didn't forget," he finally said. "I just didn't know how to tell you yet."

"Tell me what? That my husband was questioned by the police, had to call in a lawyer?"

"That didn't happen until this morning," he said, still hedging the truth a bit.

"Oh wonderful."

Lynda threw up her hands in the air, for the first time since he'd entered the room some animation coming into her voice.

He wasn't sure if that was a good or bad thing.

"What else haven't you told me?"

He finished the rest of his drink, rinsed the glass out, and placed it in the sink.

"What else?" Lynda repeated.

"Like what?"

"Oh, I don't know. Like how hard did they question

you, maybe do they have any evidence against you? Hey, here's an interesting one. Tell me, Ron, did you actually kill the bitch?"

"Of course I didn't. Damn, Lyn. How could you even ask ...?"

Without waiting for him to finish, she turned and stomped into the living room. A second later, she reappeared with a copy of the day's paper.

"You know how many people get murdered in this city each year, Ron?"

"Not offhand but—"

"Enough that one, more or less, isn't that big of a deal. At least that's what they say. Half the time, the story ends up somewhere in the back pages of the local section. But when the victim's a pretty young manstealer killed in her own home. Well, hell."

She threw the paper onto the floor between them, the front page facing up. Diane's picture stared up at him, giving him shivers even in black and white newsprint.

"Nearly four days later," Lynda said, her voice somehow more controlled now, "and she's still front page news, and guess whose name is prominently mentioned? So tell me, my husband, just how long are our lives going to be fucked up over this?"

Ron felt what amount of self control he'd managed to hold onto over the last two days starting to slip away.

"How?" he said. "How could they have—"

"Are you serious? Don't you think it's possible, just possible, that somebody leaked your name so they could feel important? Don't you get it, Ron? They think you killed that girl. And now our lives, not just yours but mine and the kids as well, are in the dumper, all because you couldn't keep it in your pants."

Ron realized now he'd been feeling somehow detached and apart from all of this. Suddenly, though, it all came together inside of him, and a surge of nausea nearly overwhelmed him. Without answering, he shouldered past Lynda and headed towards the bathroom, praying he would get there in time.

INTERVIEW #5

March 24

Five will get you ten, the old saying went. Five will get you ten that X will happen. Or five will get you ten such and such was the reason. He had no clue where the cliché came from or what it actually meant.

He just hoped it wasn't true.

These days, he could barely afford the luxury of hanging out in a bar and sloshing himself blind drunk. If Mary found out about it, there'd be a lot more than hell to pay.

But at the moment, he simply didn't care.

He just hoped the old saying wasn't true.

Because if five will get you ten, he didn't think he could take it. He'd just had number five, earlier this day, and if he'd screwed it up as badly as he thought he had, he couldn't take the thought of five more of these, for a total of ten.

At some point in the last month or so, he'd managed to move past the point of moaning and bewailing his fate. Once, he'd seen himself as the boy wonder, the man on a straight trajectory to the top who'd never be out of work.

Now, as he sat in this darkened bar just a few blocks away from the building he'd left an hour or so ago, he didn't know how much more he could take.

It wasn't any single part of the process; it was the whole damned thing put together. First, the applications, which had come a long way, baby, since the days of "send us your resume and we'll look it over." He'd had to accustom himself to the process of applying online, not a big thing in itself, until they listed all the ancillary material they wanted, and most of it you just knew the people on the other end were never going to look at.

Then, of course, came the whole references thing, which seemed the most futile waste of time because by now surely everyone in the business, at least within this part of the state, knew what had happened at his last gig and how his standing in the industry had taken a fall. And as the months went by with nary a nibble, the universe of people willing to vouch for him continued to dwindle.

But hey, at least five times he'd made it through all of that and actually gotten in the door. Only to crash and burn each and every goddamned time.

Including, he had no doubt, today as well.

A large mirror covered the wall behind the bar. Silently, he raised his glass in a mock salute to his reflection. The bartender looked at him for a moment, no doubt noticed his glass still around half full, and walked the other way.

Even the freakin' bartenders didn't want anything to do with him.

Draining his glass in one gulp, he swivelled around and looked out over the premises, wondering just what kind of people inhabited bars in the middle of a work day.

As he roamed his gaze over three or four old men playing checkers in a corner booth, a handful of out and out losers gulping down the cheapest whiskey available (and no, it didn't escape his notice that he had himself just now gulped his drink) and one obvious prostitute sitting in a corner looking bored and lonely, he realized just what kind of people sat around drinking in bars in the middle of the afternoon.

People with no jobs, prospects or hopes.

Just like himself.

"Another one?" The bartender had reappeared in front of him, holding the bottle canted at half mast.

For a moment, he thought of refusing, saying he had to get home to his wife. Then he pictured Mary waiting for him, waiting to hear word, her stomach probably twisted in knots in the hope that this time, finally, their luck had turned.

And he knew he couldn't possibly face her without more artificial courage than he possessed at the moment.

"Sure," he told the bartender. "What the hell. Fill 'er up."

CHAPTER TEN

March 26

As one of the youngest detectives on the force, Janey Turner had little direct experience with homicide. Despite her city's annual triple digit murder rate, Janey's first several months as a detective had been concerned mainly with robberies. However, a shift in manpower had found her at the first of the month transferred over to the Homicide division, which led to her standing here in the bedroom of a midtown apartment on a windy March morning.

Her first corpse that, as the initial detective answering the call, was all hers. *Yay me*, Janey thought.

"Photos been taken yet?" she asked one of the uniforms standing off to the side.

"Not yet. Guy called just before you got here. He's tied up on the east side, some sort of gang banging over there, and he'll be here as quick as he can."

"What," Janey said, half to herself and half to the uniform, "there's only one photographer in the whole metro area?"

The kid grinned, probably less intimidated by Janey, considering her youth, than he would be by a more experienced detective.

"No, we've got more than one. But you know. It's been a busy winter."

Janey grimaced, well aware of just how bad the winter had been. Already, just in the last week, they'd eclipsed last year's rate for the first three months. If it kept up like this, the department would celebrate another banner year.

"Looks pretty rough, doesn't it?" the young uniform said, causing Janey to realize that since entering the room she'd been looking everywhere except at the corpse splayed out on the bed. Now, she turned in that direction.

The woman, lying on her back and staring sightlessly up at the spackled ceiling above her, looked to be no more than 30 years old, quite possibly closer to mid twenties. A fairly slender African American, she was clothed, partially, in a powder blue nightie, now ripped practically in two and torn aside, revealing both breasts and most of one hip. Rigor didn't seem to have set in yet, at least by sight the limbs still looked fairly supple.

"Rough way to go," the uniform said. "Personally, I think I'd rather take a bullet in the head than go like that."

It did look rough, and had probably felt even rougher. Although no one from the ME's office had arrived yet, it didn't take someone with thirty years experience to determine just exactly how this young lady had gone to her reward.

Whoever the brutal bastard was, he must have been one powerful dude to do so much damage. Powerful, or maybe just enraged. Janey could guess that the blows to the face alone must have numbered at least ten, while the woman's entire midsection resembled one giant bruise.

"Look down there on the floor, to her right," said the patrolman.

Bending down, Janey lowered her head below the

top of the bed to look at three small objects laid out in a semi-circle.

"Good Lord," she said, recognizing the items as three of the victim's teeth.

"Yeah, ain't it something."

Before Janey could reply, another patrolman, red-haired and violently freckled, entered the apartment.

"Detective?"

"Yeah?"

"Just got done talking to the landlady. The victim's name is Lisa Willard, she thinks twenty-eight or so, but she's not sure."

"What'd she have to say about her?"

He glanced down at a small notebook he held. "Said she works as an accountant, though she's not sure what firm. Said she was a fairly quiet girl …"

He froze as he noticed the soft glare Janey sent his way.

"Sorry, fairly quiet woman. Anyway, said she didn't have any problem with her. Paid the rent on time, never much commotion except…"

"Yeah?" Janey stood up from her crouched position. "Except what?"

"Said there was some trouble a few months back with a boyfriend. Loud, yelling type. The neighbors in the next apartment over complained a few times, said they thought there was something bad going on in here."

"Anything more?"

"Not from the landlady. But before I came in here I called downtown, had them run a quick check. Turns out Miss Willard took out a restraining order about a month ago."

Janey felt her heart leap. Could her first homicide

wrap itself up so easily?

"Restraining order against whom?" she asked.

"Guy named Damian Pendleton. Guess he's an old boyfriend or something. The order made a specific reference towards her tires being slashed not long before."

Janey turned to the officer who'd been in the room when she first arrived.

"Stay here. When the techs get here, if they ever do, keep the place secured so they can do their thing. Tell them I'll check in later for their results."

The young man nodded as Janey turned towards the red-haired cop.

"You got an address for this guy?"

He glanced again at his notebook. It must be a nervous tick, seeing as how she'd asked such a simple question.

"Yeah. The computer had one. Current as of last week."

"Then why don't you come along with me. We'll go in your car and pay Mr. Pendleton a visit."

CHAPTER ELEVEN

As lunchtime rolled around, Ron Green discovered he had absolutely no appetite, a condition that had come upon him more than once in the last few weeks. He supposed having your marriage fall apart and being suspected of murder would do that to a guy. And while he hadn't seen any physical effects yet, he tried to take some consolation in the idea that, if nothing else, this ordeal might eventually result in losing those twenty extra pounds he'd managed to accumulate over the last few years.

But while he didn't feel at all hungry, and his schedule for the day didn't hold time for any sort of leisurely meal, he also knew, what with all the stress he'd been under lately, he had to keep some sort of regular nutrition entering his system, even in the loosest possible sense of the term "nutrition."

So with about forty minutes between the end of his late morning class and a meeting with his department chair (with another round of budget cuts looming they had to decide on at least eight courses to cut in the department) he locked up his office and headed over to the Student Union.

He decided to leave his suit jacket behind, it being a rather warm day for late March. Typical Midwestern weather. Just yesterday it had been damned near freezing, today everyone was running around in shirt sleeves. The university rec center, which held the Student Union, stood only about a block away from the Business Building, which on this day Ron found rather comforting.

He wouldn't go so far as to say that in the three weeks since Diane's death his department had ostracized him, but the writing was on the wall. In the intervening time, the cops had searched his apartment once and his car twice, questioned all of his neighbors and several of his colleagues at the college and eventually hauled him downtown for a second round of questioning. After that incident, Lowenstein had told Ron if it happened again he'd demand they either charge him with something or by God leave him the hell alone.

But while ostracize would be too harsh a word, Ron had noticed a decided cooling in his colleagues and acquaintances' attitudes. The two assistant professors with offices on either side of him still treated him, for the most part, like a normal person, though he couldn't be sure if their attitude stemmed from common consideration or the desire not to alienate a soon to be higher-ranking member of the department. Ron himself could well remember those first several years of employment when he would have done anything rather than tick off any of the entrenched faculty, and while he wasn't entrenched yet, that particular rung in the ladder loomed right around the corner.

But other than those two, there'd been a definite cooling on the part of practically everyone else. Ryan was coming up with more and more excuses not to carpool, and even the department chair, a friend of going on seven years now, seemed to be going out of his way to avoid spending time with Ron, their meeting today being their first get together in over two weeks. And as for the other members of the department....

As intelligent as he was, his instincts debated whether this might be merely a matter of perception, the ordinary reaction of a man watching major chunks of his life falling apart around him and naturally assuming that all the other chunks were disintegrating as well.

But while he still retained some uncertainty in terms of his co-workers, he had absolutely no doubt concerning his students. For the last few weeks, his classes had been moribund, to put it best. He'd gone through his lectures by rote, with nary a question or comment from any of the participants. The number of students coming by during office hours with questions or concerns had dropped to practically none. And weekend or late-night e-mails concerning an upcoming project in two of his courses, once a common occurrence, had ceased entirely.

Even worse, though, much more damning than anything else, was seeing young people, whether coming down a hall or out on the campus grounds, half turning away, pretending not to have seen him waving, gesturing a hello. Such flagrant avoidance stabbed at him every time he encountered it, and each time he did so Ron's irritation at the unjustness of his situation compounded.

It would be better, he sometimes told himself, a whole lot better if he'd actually been guilty of killing Diane. Then, at least, he could see some justification for everyone's actions. Forget trial and conviction. He hadn't even been charged, and yet here he stood, in the eyes of almost everyone he knew already a condemned man.

Ron remembered the time shortly after 9/11 when the anthrax attacks began. A series of envelopes, addressed to various people, most of them in the public eye, filled with suspicious white powder. The government had, quite naturally, gone on a tear, leaving no clue unfollowed in terms of who was sending those deadly missives. Before too long the media and authorities had singled out one man, a scientist and bio-weapons expert, as something called a "person of interest," a completely made up term.

Ron remembered that, at the time, he'd caught a whiff of unfairness in it all. If a person was a suspect, dammit, then call him such and charge him. Or her. But to apply this new label, which could mean anything from a suspect, to someone who had seen something, to someone who had known the victim ten years ago who might have some random information, seemed beyond unfair.

The public, of course, when they heard the term "person of interest," always imagined the worst.

Early on, in fact on the same day as his confrontation with the television crew in the parking lot, the authorities had named, and the media had reported, Professor Ronald Green as a person of interest in the death of Diane Brewster.

So it was that, as he made his way the short block from the Business Building to the rec center, no one he passed, even though he knew several of them, greeted, waved or even nodded to him. Maybe he had to pay some penance for his adulterous dalliance. Still, he couldn't help wondering just how long he'd have to live under this cloud.

Surely it will end sooner or later, he thought. *Eventually they'll need to realize I'm innocent.*

He entered the rec center, passed by the university

book store and went up the single flight of stairs to the second floor which held, among other facilities, the student union. Any lunch he'd obtain there would come from one of several kiosks leased out by fast-food franchises, but at least it would be quick, hot and some sort of nourishment.

He finally decided on two slices of pizza and a large Coke, paid for his purchase, took his food and went over to one of several empty tables. In fact, of the ten booths and twenty tables occupying the common area of the union, only two booths and one other table were occupied. Sitting down, Ron felt a faint stirring of resentful nostalgia.

In his own student days, any time the union was open you could find throngs of people studying, eating, or just hanging out. These days, what with everyone having a laptop and all the various social network sites, the damned place was practically a wasteland.

He sat down at a table fairly close to one of the large screen TV's hanging from the west wall. Coming in, he'd noticed this particular set tuned to one of the local channels, and figured if nothing else he'd catch a few minutes of the noon news, provided some soap opera wasn't running instead. Immediately after Diane's death, and in the initial flurry of attention he'd received, Ron had more or less avoided local news, both print and electronic, though in the weeks since, with no real developments, the news media had more or less gone on to other things. In fact, considering the amount of time gone by, the city had probably easily seen another dozen or so murders.

Regardless, it had been nearly ten days since Ron had noticed any reporters lurking around his home or office.

On the screen in front of him, an anchor was recapping the national and international stories, closed captioning scrolling across the bottom, which seemed safe enough to watch. Barely through three bites of pizza, Ron noticed the anchor switched to a local crime story, and the photo of a young black woman appeared on the screen.

Ron dropped the food as if it had scorched him and stood to get a closer look at the screen. A second later, he realized he'd been focusing so much on the picture that he'd neglected to hear or read what the anchor was saying. So he got only the last line or so of the prepared script, but even that was enough to give him the gist of the story.

He dug his cell phone out of his pocket and hit the speed dial for Walt Lowenstein's number. Unfortunately, he only got his attorney's voice mail.

"Walt, it's Ron," he began, the phone literally shaking in his hand, "I just saw something on the news. Call me back, please. As soon as you get this, call me back. I think I'm in a lot worse trouble than we thought."

He snapped the phone shut, dropped it back in his pocket and, unable to stop his trembling, slumped back into his seat. He saw a couple sitting in one of the booths staring at him but at the moment had no time to deal with incidentals like that.

It was her, he knew that for a fact. He didn't know her full name, had only known her first name once upon a time and couldn't remember it at the moment, but the picture was clear as could be.

It was her.

Dear God, he prayed, what the hell is happening?

CHAPTER TWELVE

"Here it is," Walt said from in front of his office computer. "They posted the first story around 10:30 this morning, which made the noon newscast."

"What was her name?" Ron asked.

"Lisa Willard. It says she worked for an accounting firm. Found this morning by her landlady."

"Lisa. That's it."

Ron remembered now. The tall, slender black woman. Dressed both days in conservative suits, one dark grey and one navy blue. Trim, business-like haircut. She was one of the more animated ones, but during the discussions she focused more on the actual political messages rather than the splash and dash of the commercials.

"And you're saying she was a member of the same focus group as you and Diane?" Walt asked.

"Yes. Does the story say anything about how she died?"

"No, they're withholding details at the moment."

Lowenstein turned away from the computer screen to face Ron.

"I don't quite get this. What's your point here?"

"Two women dead."

"Yeah. In a city this size, that's not exactly earth-shattering news."

"Probably true. But in this case, they were both

connected with me."

Ron's hands began trembling again.

Lowenstein raised an eyebrow.

"Wait a minute. Hold on here. Were you and this Willard woman …?"

"No, hell no. Nothing like that. I'm just worried that, what with me already a suspect in Diane's murder …"

"You're not officially a…"

"Is there anyone else they're even looking at?"

"No," Walt said, looking somewhat crestfallen, "at least, not as far as I've been able to dig up."

"So let's cut the bullshit, okay? And if they're after me for Diane's death, then how long before they start looking my way for this one?"

"Now wait a minute." Lowenstein stood up, moved away from his desk and began pacing between desk and the windows. "Why would they look at you for this woman?"

"Because of the obvious connection, Walt. All three of us were in that damned focus group. Good old Senator Rawlings. I'm just saying that they may see a link between the three of us and take the line of least resistance."

"Did you know Lisa Willard before you met her in the group?"

"No."

"Ever see her afterwards?"

"No."

"Was she part of the little coffee clatch afterwards?"

"I don't know for sure."

"Try to think."

"God, Walt. It was a year ago. Like I told the cops, most of us went out afterwards to kind of unwind, but other than Diane and myself I'm not sure who did or didn't stay."

"Most of you." Suddenly Lowenstein's voice had taken on a speculative tone.

"Huh?"

"You said most of you got together after. That's what you told the cops the other day. But not all, right?"

"Right. A couple of them said they had things to do. And one or two others just drifted off. Look, Walt, what the hell's the point of all this? Shouldn't we be worried about keeping me out of this latest killing?"

"I really don't think we need to worry about that."

"You serious? Two women connected with me are murdered, and you don't see it as a problem? Especially when I'm the number one guy tagged for one of them?"

"Look, Ron. Despite how you may currently feel about them personally, the cops aren't dumb. Or ignorant. By your own admission, there's absolutely no connection between you and the Willard woman, and they're not going to want to waste their time chasing phantoms, even if they somehow got a whiff of it. As far as that goes, if you're really concerned, there's an easy way to put the whole thing to rest, at least in terms of the Willard case."

"What?" Ron asked.

"We'll go downtown and confront them with it ourselves."

CHAPTER THIRTEEN

"Come again?"

When they'd arrived at the central station downtown, Det. Hollis had been unavailable, which suited Ron just fine, but Lipscomb had been up in the homicide unit's squad room. A call from a uniformed officer downstairs had brought her right down, and in no time at all the three of them were tucked away in one of the cramped interrogation rooms.

Ron didn't like the setting at all. It reminded him too much of when he'd been here before, and the only saving grace, at least in his mind, was that this time his conscience was about as clear as could be.

"Lisa Willard," Lowenstein repeated, "the woman found dead this morning."

"What about her?' Lipscomb asked.

"How was she killed?"

"Come on, counselor. You know how this works. If we didn't release it to the press, we had a reason. So why would I tell it to you, even if it was my case? And what difference does it make to you guys anyway?"

"Maybe nothing," Ron interjected, ignoring the glare that Walt sent his way, "but maybe everything."

Lipscomb had barely looked at him since they sat down, reserving most of her attention for his lawyer. But at his interruption she turned his way, giving him a quizzical look.

"Excuse me," she said, "but I've got a lot of work to do. If you've got something to tell me, just come out with it. Just remember that I can use whatever you say. Now just what is it you've come down her for, and whatever you say, please don't waste any of my time."

"It's simple," Ron said as Lowenstein figuratively threw up his hands, "Lisa Willard, the woman who was murdered yesterday, was also in the group with me and Diane."

Lipscomb leaned back in her chair and gave him the hardest look, quite possibly, that he'd ever gotten from anyone. True, she was a woman, and smaller and lighter than him, though no doubt more physically capable, but he felt that if he'd walked in there with any guilt at all the balefulness of her glare would have shriveled him in no time, if not broken him.

But he didn't have any guilt, not this time around, for anything, and in fact he felt as if he could glimpse, however dimly, a possible faint gleam at the end of the tunnel.

"In the group?"

"Yes."

"The focus group?"

"Yes."

"With you and the Brewster woman?"

"Yes."

"Over at, where was it, Amos Kettering PR. For the political thing?"

"Right."

"You recognized her name on the news?"

"No. When we took part in the group, we didn't know each other by more than first names. Even had to wear those dorky stick-on name tags so we'd know what to call each other. But I saw it the story on TV today at lunch, and I recognized her picture."

"Excuse me," Lipscomb said as she pulled out her cell phone and rose to step out of the room.

As she shut the door behind her, Lowenstein turned and glared at Ron.

"You ever consider letting your attorney talk for you?"

"Sure. And I would have on something important. But this seems pretty straightforward."

"Oh? Just how do you figure?"

"Well, if someone else from the focus group's been killed, it means ..." Ron trailed off, a befuddled look on his face.

"No," Lowenstein said. "Don't stop now. This Willard gal being killed means exactly what? In terms of Diane Brewster?"

"Well, it means–uh–I mean—"

"It means exactly nothing, other than that two women who barely knew each other, met for a day and a half something like a year ago, ended up dead. You even know anything about how this Lisa Willard got it?"

"I didn't take time to–oh hell."

"Exactly. You come tearing into my office and, with me as your counsel, head down here. I had a plan, a tactic in mind to help you out. You, on the other hand, charge in here thinking you've got some great big secret to share with them. And your great revelation is?"

"Walt…

"I'll tell you what it is. It's that two women got killed. Big whoop. What's even worse is that there's no connection between the deaths at all."

"No connection? But…"

"But what? Sure, they're both women. How many women in this city? They're both under forty. Same question. Even if we go with women under forty, you're still talking a hell of a lot of people. Both single? Add that in and you trim it down somewhat. If it turns out they were killed the same way, then maybe we have a possibility of throwing out a serial killer hypothesis. They didn't live in the same part of town, didn't work in the same profession, and most likely didn't share any of the same hobbies. When you consider that, female or no, they weren't even of the same race, things become even vaguer. So the only link we have is this panel thing of yours, which doesn't amount to a whole hell of a lot."

Ron felt as if his last cord had been cut.

"So why are we here?"

Walt sighed, as if dealing with a recalcitrant student.

"I'm not sure about you. What I'm trying to do is sow the seeds of doubt, to make them think there's some linkage, even when there isn't. We're engaged in a legal tactic here, Ron, and the best way to successfully execute a legal tactic is to let your lawyer do it. Got me?"

Before Ron could think of an answer, the door opened and detective Lipscomb walked back in, stuffing her cell phone into her pocket.

"We appreciate you taking the time to come down here, Professor Green." Her expression, though, looked anything but appreciative. "But I don't think we'll take any more of your time. Have you ever heard of a man named Damian Pendleton?"

"No. Who—"

"I probably shouldn't be telling you this, but they'll have it on the five o'clock news tonight, so what the hell. He's the main suspect in Mrs. Willard's death. They had a relationship for quite a while, and when it went sour a while back she had to file a restraining order to get him to leave her alone. And right now we've got him down the hall."

"But, wait a minute…"

Before Ron could continue, Lowenstein began dragging on his arm, pulling him up out of his chair.

"Come on, Ronald. We've got places to be."

"But what about—"

"I said come on!"

His attorney nearly yanked Ron out of the interrogation room. When they made it into the hallway, Walt released his grip.

"You've got to realize something, my man. You're still a suspect in Diane's death. They're not calling you one officially, but you and I, and that detective in there, know damned well that that's what you are. So I'm telling you right now to, dammit, steer clear of these people and let me do my job."

Ron stood silent, his faint hope of getting out from under his personal nightmare now gone.

Silently, his attorney took him by the arm again and walked him out of the station.

CHAPTER FOURTEEN

After Green and his lawyer left, Helen turned and headed down to the other end of the hallway. Entering the last door on the left, she made sure not to turn on the lights. Another detective, seated at a table and taking notes on a legal pad, looked up and gave her the slightest of frowns.

"May have something to do with a case I'm working," she said.

The other cop nodded and motioned her towards the other seat at the table.

The room's arrangement was one easily familiar to anyone who watched even a modicum of TV cop shows. A large pane of glass dominated one of the walls, allowing anyone in the room, currently Helen and the other detective, to view events in an adjacent room without themselves being seen.

But at the moment, nothing much seemed to be happening.

The room she looked into was a carbon copy of both the one she currently occupied and the one where she'd recently been conversing with Green and his lawyer. It held a plain wooden, black-topped table and three chairs, two of them currently occupied.

Detective Janey Turner, who Helen knew on a casual basis, sat in one of the chairs, facing the man sitting in the other. He was a tall, lean black man with a shaven head and trim goatee. For an instant, when Helen first looked at him, she thought of the actor who'd played Hawk on the old *Spenser* TV show her dad had watched when she was a kid. On closer inspection, he didn't quite have the muscle to fill that role. The third person in the room, a middle-aged uniformed officer, stood off to the side, tense and wary.

"Any progress?" Helen asked the cop next to her.

"Not so far. A lot of denial, and he's come close to asking for a lawyer a couple of times but hasn't quite gone there."

Helen turned back to the window. An intercom device allowed them to hear what was going on in the other room without being heard themselves.

"…last time?" asked Turner.

"I told you. About five weeks back. I went by her place and wanted to talk."

"Five weeks, that would be …" She consulted a sheaf of notes on a clipboard, though she no doubt knew all the information on it by heart, "just about a week before she got the restraining order against you, right?"

The prisoner shifted uncomfortably and looked down at his hands for a minute.

"Yeah," he said, looking up again, "five days before I got served with the notice, to be exact."

"So I'm guessing when you went over there, she didn't want to see you?"

"Didn't want to see? Hell, she didn't want anything to do with me."

"And this was after you slashed her tires, right?"

"I didn't slash the damned tires. That was just some street kid bein' thuggish. But with all the other stuff, she wouldn't listen to me. Dammit, how many times should

I have had to tell her I was sorry?"

"Sorry for what? What'd you do to piss her off so bad?"

****

Back in the adjacent room, the detective taking notes glanced up at Helen.

"What'd you say your interest in this is?"

"Maybe nothing," she said. "Scratch that. Almost assuredly nothing. You heard about the Brewster killing a while back?"

"That the young gal got strangled?"

"Right. Well, it was suggested to me–not by a very reliable source–that there may be some connection between Diane Brewster's death and your case."

He dropped his notepad and turned all his attention to Helen.

"Were the two women friends?"

"No."

"Coworkers?"

"Nope."

"Clearly not relatives."

"Not even remotely."

"So how'd they—"

"Supposedly, and I haven't had a chance to check it out yet to see if it's true or not, they met each other, briefly, about a year ago."

"And from that you think their murders are linked? Seriously?"

"Of course not." Helen had to fight to keep a snappish tone out of her reply. "Like I said, the person who gave me this isn't to be trusted at all. But since you've already got your suspect and he's right here in the building, I figured I might as well step in for a minute."

"Suit yourself, but it sure sounds like a waste of time."

"Probably," she said, "but it doesn't hurt to be thorough."

The two of them turned away from each other and back to the conversation in the other room, which had become, to put it mildly, heated.

****

"...For the last damned time, I'm telling you I haven't seen her. Haven't seen, haven't talked to her and for damned sure didn't beat her to death."

"But you did slash her tires, right? That was the final straw that sent her to the judge, right?"

"Alright, yes goddammit. I slashed her goddamned tires. So what's that say?"

"It says that you were around her place at least once with violence in your head."

The suspect had half risen out of his chair, and from behind the mirror Helen could see Janey Turner still seated, seemingly unruffled. The uniformed cop tensed himself, but before things could get out of control, the suspect puffed exasperatedly and plopped back down in his chair.

"Don't know what to tell you," he said, "because no matter what I say you won't believe me. Can sit here and tell you all night that I didn't kill her, but that's about all I can do–talk."

"So what are you saying, Damian?"

"Saying it's about time you all get me a lawyer. If talking won't do me any good, then I'm done talking."

****

Back in the observation room, the detective with the note pad capped his pen and placed it in his pocket.

"Guess that's it," he said. "Guy wants a lawyer."

He looked at Helen, who had stood up and was headed towards the door.

"What about it?" he asked her. "Think this has anything to do with your case?"

"No," she said as she swung the door open, "I'm pretty sure my 'tip' was just a desperate man trying to divert attention from himself. Funny thing is, it's going to backfire on him big time."

"Meaning?"

"Meaning," she said as she stepped out into the hallway, "that I'm more convinced than ever. If he tried something this lame to make us look the other way, he's definitely got something to hide."

CHAPTER FIFTEEN

After leaving the station with Lowenstein, Ron headed back to the university, his workload piling up the last few weeks. When he entered his office, neat and almost clinically organized as most business professors' offices were, two large piles on his desk confronted him. One was a stack of papers, memos and journal articles he needed to review, all connected in some way with his normal duties. However, as much work as the first stack represented, he found the second pile, only slightly smaller, more intimidating.

Taking off his jacket, he dropped into his chair and stared at that second pile, a regular Gordian knot he had no clue how he was going to cut through.

His bid for tenure was scheduled for the next academic year, in just a little over seven months, and the pressing deadline formed the reason for the second pile.

It contained a collection of letters from colleagues around the country, his curriculum vitae, photocopies of the last three articles he'd had published, three different review of a book he'd written on entrepreneurship profiles a couple of years ago, selected student evaluations, progress reports from the administrators of his department, a proposal for a grant he was trying to acquire from a private charity, and the outline and initial notes for another book currently only in the planning stage.

And while the current computer age provided such things as flash drives, personal web sites and assorted other gimcracks for the transmission of information, Ron still needed to keep hard copies of all that stuff, and sometime before the beginning of the next academic year have it collated, bound and distributed to the various members of the university, only one from his own department and only two from the actual business college itself, who would eventually meet to decide the state of his employment for the rest of his life.

And all with a potential murder charge hanging over his head. He could only hope the entire mess was cleared up sometime before the next year began.

Sighing, he got up and, changing his plans on the fly, shrugged back into his jacket. Hell with it. It would all keep till tomorrow (although it really wouldn't), and right now he desired of life nothing more than to spend some time with his two kids. He locked up his office and headed out.

Towards home sweet home.

****

He found the note waiting for him when he got there. Not in plain sight, but in a place where he'd be sure to see it.

Unlocking the door and stepping into the apartment, a complete absence of any normal sound took Ron by surprise. A small apartment with two kids, one almost six and the other just a baby, shouldn't be this quiet even if both were sound asleep.

When he noticed, a fraction of a second later, that all the lights were off, a nervous qualm began clawing at his gut. Dropping his briefcase, Ron raced through the apartment.

He found the note in the bedroom.

Now his nameless fear had a name, yet he could think of nothing to do other than to walk calmly over, pick the paper up off the pillow, and sit down on the bed to read it.

****

The phone was ringing. Had been, off and on, for some time in fact. Both his home phone and his cell, resting in the pocket of his jacket that he'd flung down on the bedroom floor.

Ron rubbed his eyes, trying to keep the room from swaying on him. He had the blurred sensation that either the home phone or his cell had been ringing on a somewhat regular half hour basis.

He grimaced, and his stomach clenched, when he saw, out of the corner of his eye, the empty Wild Turkey bottle resting on the floor. A few moments of silence passed, then the phone in his jacket began chirping again. He rolled off the couch, made his way to his feet, and staggered over to his jacket.

Fumbling the phone out of the inner pocket, he punched at the green button twice—missing it the first time—and muttered a hushed hello into the mouthpiece as he stumbled back into the living room.

"Ron? That you?"

"Huh?"

"Ron?"

"Ryan," he mumbled. His old carpool buddy Ryan, who hadn't wanted to be seen around him much the last few weeks. "Whatcha want?"

"Are you home? Where are you?"

"Home," Ron muttered. "Home sweet home."

"Jesus, man. How drunk are you?"

Ron shook his head back and forth, decided he didn't want to do that again, and sat up straighter on the couch. He blinked a few times, and a bit of lucidity seemed to come back to him.

"Say what, Ryan?"

"I asked how much you've had to drink."

"Not nearly enough. I'm home, buddy. And they're gone."

"Huh? Who's gone?"

"Lyn and the kids. She even left me a note, propped up on the pillow. How romantic can you get?"

"Ron, man, let me—"

"Says that the last few weeks had been the last straw. Says she's been working hard for months to get accustomed to living with a cheater, and that it's been pretty much a losing battle."

"But why now does she ...?"

"Note says that a cheater is bad enough, but a possible murderer is too much."

"Oh shit, man."

"Goes on to say, this is the longest damned note you've ever seen, that she doesn't feel safe in the house with me. For either her or the kids. Can you beat that? She actually thinks I might do something to my own kids."

"You think she really thinks so? Or just that it will look good in divorce proceedings?"

Ron blinked, a little more of the inebriation leaving him, and sat up even straighter.

"Damn. I hadn't thought of that. Hell, if the cops don't get off their asses and find Diane's killer, I may end up having to fight two legal battles at once."

"Or maybe three," Ryan said

"Huh?"

"It's the reason I've been trying to call you forever and a day, man. I picked up some scuttlebutt at a meeting today, over in the main admin building."

"What about?"

"I don't want to come out and say it, just in case I'm wrong, but you may want to check your e-mail as soon as you can."

"What?"

"Dammit, Ron. Sober up and check your freakin' e-mail. Then decide what you want to do from there, if anything."

A faint click sounded in his ear, signaling to Ron that his good friend and colleague had abruptly hung up. On the one hand, he had at least another six pack of beer somewhere in the fridge, and he really didn't want any more bad news tonight.

On the other hand, if things were about to get as bad as he feared, he really needed to have a clear head.

And really, how much worse could things get?

He walked into the spare room he used as an office and snapped open his laptop. A moment to boot it up and he was accessing his departmental e-mail. The first message in the roster was from Dean Hastings himself.

Oh crap, he thought. *This can't be good.*

CHAPTER SIXTEEN

It was routine in the homicide division that every Monday morning the ranking detectives would all meet in their lieutenant's office for an informal roundabout. They would update their supervisor on all current cases, bounce ideas off each other, and usually manage to throw in a dirty joke or two.

As one of the few female detectives in the department, and at second grade the highest ranking one, Helen never really cared much for these meetings. Not only trying to cram nearly thirty bodies into the lieut's office formed something of a logistical nightmare, but more from the fact these meetings always felt like a huge waste of time.

On this last Monday in March, however, she was looking forward to the confab with something almost approaching eagerness. Their fair city usually had more than its share of violent crimes, including homicides, but in the last year things had really began to pop. Aside from her own main priority, the Brewster case, and the death of Lisa Willard a few weeks back, the department currently boasted a total of twenty-five unsolved homicides on its hands. Several of these were clearly gang related, which as of a month or so back put them in the province of a special task force. But even though the task force had taken over those investigations, the ordinary homicide division still had its quota pretty well full.

Among the others was an assortment of domestic disputes gone horribly wrong, common street muggings, and a handful that had no easily-discernible cause or explanation. The division detectives usually referred to these as "stranger killings," the term an extreme bit of inside jargon because in ordinary law enforcement circles stranger killing referred to any murder where the perpetrator was unknown to the victim. But in this department, they used the term to refer specifically to those crimes for which no obvious rationale existed.

As Helen opened the door and squeezed herself into the office, now almost two-thirds filled, her first look at Lieutenant Jarvis seemed to prove the joke.

Pushing sixty and slated for retirement next year, his full thirty intact Jarvis still had his full head of hair and stern eye that he'd had on Helen's first day in his command nearly three years before. The stoop of his shoulders and the scrawniness of his neck, somewhat out of place on a man of his girth, gave evidence to the pressure the man had recently experienced.

As she managed to snag a personal spot in one corner, Helen reflected that, if anything, she was somewhat ahead of the game compared to most of her colleagues. In her main case of the moment, the Brewster killing, she at least had a viable suspect. And so far, Green's story had held up. True, the Brewster apartment had been lousy with his DNA, but the fact that he'd admitted a months-long affair with the victim kind of nullified the forensics.

But Helen hadn't yet given up hope, and while she'd been looking at a few other people, Green still ranked as the most likely possibility. On the other hand, there was the whole Lisa Willard angle….

As their boss began going over a series of routine reports, Helen felt an elbow nudge her side. Standing to her left was Janey Turner, who she'd observed interrogating Lisa Willard's ex the other day.

"So what do you think?" the other woman asked, "see any connection between our two victims?"

"Other than the fact that my guy knew both of them?"

"Yeah. I wondered about that too. Thing is, if he had anything to do with one or both of them, why would he give us a heads up?"

Helen frowned, sifting that thought through her mind for a moment.

"You thinking he may be on the level?"

"Maybe. Or it could be that he did the number on your vic and is trying to muddy the waters a bit. Get you off on a new tangent."

"Possible," Helen mused, "but if you go with that reasoning, it was awful fortunate for him that…"

She trailed off, as a new thought made her heart skip a beat. Her companion blanched, and Helen assumed she'd had the same thought as herself.

Without another word, they turned their attention back to the official goings on. One by one, the various detectives in the room gave Lieutenant Jarvis a rundown on the progress of their cases, and when it came time to review Helen's case, she gave the most perfunctory report she could.

When Helen had concluded her report, the lieutenant frowned.

"And you've been at this how long?"

"The investigation's been ongoing for about four

weeks," Helen replied.

"Any other suspects than that professor?"

"A couple. She's had a few other boyfriends over the year, and there's a few of her students she'd reported as acting kind of hinky. But nothing that really seems as strong as Green himself."

"What about the wife?"

"Sir?"

"Green's wife. The woman scorned? Could she have played a role in it?"

"We thought of that, naturally, but so far nothing's really come to light in terms of that connection. Almost from the jump, Green's been the main focus. However, Janey and I were talking a few minutes ago, and we think there may be a new angle to look at."

"A new suspect?" the lieutenant asked.

"No, sir. The same guy. But we think–there's a possibility–that Ron Green may have killed Lisa Willard as well."

Everyone in the room turned to look at the two women.

"Come again?" Jarvis, known as a nuts and bolts guy who liked simple, easy to follow solutions to cases, didn't look very happy.

"Green, the Brewster woman and Lisa Willard all took part about a year ago in some kind of survey deal for a PR firm. That's how Green and Brewster first met."

"And now Brewster is dead and Green is a suspect," the lieutenant said.

"Yes, sir."

"And the Willard woman comes in how?"

"As I said, all three were in this survey thing. It had something to do with Lucy Rawling's re-election bid."

"In which she got creamed."

"Yes, sir. But that's beside the point."

Helen was becoming a little breathless realizing she'd been holding a running dialogue with one of the city's top cops for several minutes, with a goodly number of her co-workers as spectators, but she wasn't through yet.

"And how did you uncover this connection between the three? How long did you say this survey thing lasted?"

"From what we gather, about a day and a half."

"Okay. So two murder victims and a prime suspect were briefly together about a year ago. Again, you discovered this how?"

"Actually, Green told us about it."

"Told you?"

"Yes, sir. He came to us the other day and informed us of the connection."

Helen's palms were sweating, and she really wished Janey would jump in at some point. A small crease between the lieutenant's eyes clearly indicated his dislike for the current conversation.

"Green divulged the connection to you?"

"Yes."

"And he came in to do this? It wasn't part of any questioning instigated on your end?"

"No, sir. Obviously, for the last few weeks he's been under investigation. We've had two interviews instigated by us and performed some searches. But for this one he came in on his own."

"Ms. Turner." Helen exhaled slightly as the lieutenant's attention turned to the woman at her side.

"Yes, sir?"

"From what I understand, you have a strong suspect in the Willard case."

"Yes, sir. Damian Pendleton. He and Willard dated for a while some time back. They broke up, and not long after she had to get a restraining order."

"Any physical evidence to tie him to the crime?"

"The scene, yes. Obviously, since they dated, her apartment's lousy with his traces. But for the actual crime itself, not yet. However, he does have a history of violent acts concerning her. But the lab's still working on it."

"Do you think he's your guy?"

"It's early yet, but if I had to stake money on it, yes. I'd say he's the guy."

"So why," the lieutenant's stare turned back to Helen, "do you see a connection between this Green fellow and the Willard case?"

Helen took a deep breath. She was about to go out on a limb here, and if she ended up proven wrong she'd fall a notch or two in her boss's estimation. But the thought rambling in her head was nutty enough, flat out insane enough, that it could possibly be true.

"This is just an idea, sir," she disclaimed, "but the fact that Green knew both victims, however briefly he knew the one, and that he brought their connection to our attention—"

"Yes?"

With every eye in the room locked on her, Helen went for broke.

"I think there's a chance he killed the Brewster woman, for the reasons we think, and then followed it up by killing Lisa Willard as well."

Helen's ears literally hurt from the absence of sound

in the room as everyone waited for the lieutenant's response.

"Why?" he finally said.

"In order to divert attention from himself. To get us to think that there's some kind of serial killer out there, which he may be, and that in the Brewster case he's just the innocent victim of circumstances."

"That's a rather wild theory, Helen."

"Yes, sir. I know."

Another long silence followed before the lieutenant nodded.

"But it wouldn't hurt to follow it up."

CHAPTER SEVENTEEN

Monday afternoon

Ron tapped his feet on the carpet, the only outward sign of how nervous he felt. The e-mail he'd read a few nights before had been guardedly worded, and even reading between the lines it had been difficult to parse the exact meaning. But Ron's gut had gotten the message loud and clear, and he felt almost as nervous now as on that day weeks ago when he'd first been hauled into the police station for questioning.

But with his lawyer along he'd at least had some control, no matter how slight, over that situation. If this meeting with his dean went as Ron expected, he'd have almost no control left over his life.

As it was, considering Lynda had skipped out and taken the kids with her, he'd spent most of the weekend in a semi-drunken state. If he didn't watch it, this whole ordeal would end up turning him into an alcoholic.

Actually, he considered himself lucky to have tied his shoes this morning without breaking down.

The phone on the secretary's desk buzzed. She picked it up, murmured something into the mouthpiece, and hung up.

"Dr. Hastings will see you now."

Ron stood up, smoothed the crease in his pant legs and walked about fifty feet down the hall to the office of

Dr. Franklin Hastings, the dean of the business school.

He rapped his knuckles on the door, then went in without waiting for an affirmation.

Dean Hastings stood behind his desk, his hand outstretched.

For a moment, Ron considered spurning the shake, but realized the action would appear petty and self defeating. A slim chance still existed things wouldn't go as badly as he feared.

"Good afternoon, Ron," Hastings said as they shook, then broke the clasp as they both sat down.

"How have you been?"

A new bolt of acid shot through Ron's stomach.

"I think you know how I've been, Franklin. It's probably the number one topic all around the campus."

Hastings leaned back slightly, stared up at the ceiling for a moment, then brought his gaze level with Ron's.

"You're right. And I'm sorry for the useless platitude. We both know the situation you're currently facing, though you feel it much more directly."

"They haven't charged me yet. And my lawyer says there's a better than even chance that they never will."

"Maybe, but surely you know they've been all around the campus, questioning everyone who works with you and, if we hadn't put a firm stop to it, talking to your students as well."

"Yeah, I've heard."

"Heard" was a mild way to put it. Ron would have had to be flat out deaf, if not blind as well, not to have been aware of the activity swirling around him. How many times had he walked down the halls and seen strange people talking to his colleagues in their offices?

How often had he carried a tray into his college's cafeteria at lunchtime, only to have everyone he knew suddenly turn their backs and hunch over their plates while he looked for a place to sit?

How often had students come to his office door, started to come in, then seemed to change their minds and walk away?

Yeah, Ron knew all too well. Just as he knew that his gut had been right about this meeting.

"Of course," Dr. Hastings broke into his reverie, "it doesn't help any that the woman in question was a student here."

"Grad student," Ron muttered, looking for any straw at all to stave off the inevitable. "Even more, a teaching assistant."

"But a student nonetheless."

"For God's sake, Franklin, she was thirty-one years old," Ron muttered. "And she didn't even work in the same college, let alone our department."

Hastings stood up and walked around his desk to perch on the front edge.

"And while you and I and a lot of other people around here can see that distinction, the general public can't. All they see or hear is professor/student/affair/murder."

The public, of course. The almighty public opinion against which everything must bow.

"I didn't kill her." Ron's mutter was lower this time, almost inaudible even to his ears. Dammit, he wanted to sit up straight and confront his fate head on, but he just couldn't find the strength to do so. He could only slouch and mumble.

"I'm sure you didn't. But, hard as this is, that's not

really the point here. The point is…"

"I know what the goddamned point is, Franklin." Now Ron had managed to find some fire, now when it was probably too late. "So why don't you save us both some time and hassle and get to it."

He almost regretted the words, but only almost. Every word, motion, and exhalation since he'd entered the office told him they had preordained his fate and, as the old time Puritans had believed, nothing he could do would change it.

So to hell with it.

Get it over with.

Rip off the goddamned scab.

"Fine."

Hastings stood up, walked back behind his desk and sat down again.

"Ron, I want you to drop your bid for tenure at this institution. I want it in writing by the end of the week."

And there it was.

The kiss of doom itself.

"And if I don't? I've worked damned hard for the last six years. Considering all the new standards and requirements, I've done easily three times the work those with tenure had to do back in the old days. So what if I don't withdraw it?"

The dean placed his hands flat on the desk and fixed Ron with a stare unlike any he'd ever seen before. Even when the cops had interrogated him, that lady detective hadn't drilled into him so mercilessly.

"I'd advise you to go ahead and withdraw, Dr. Green. Because if you don't, I can guarantee that not only will you not keep your job here, but with even more publicity piled onto what you've already got, you'll be lucky to find a job anywhere within the next five years."

Ron stood up, somehow finding the fortitude to look Hastings in the eye.

"Can I assume I'll at least have the standard year's grace period to find another job?"

"No. I'm sorry if that sounds harsh, but the truth is, we just can't afford to have you around here. You need to be gone by the end of the summer. And I want that withdrawal in writing."

"End of the week?"

"Yes. Make it official by then. That's as far as I can stretch it. You think you're under pressure. Try having the university president and the board bearing down on you like I do. If they had their way, you'd be out on your ear today, contract or no contract."

"Yeah," Ron said, "I'm sure you know all about pressure."

Not the most graceful of exits, but at least he managed to get out of there without breaking anything.

CHAPTER EIGHTEEN

The house was a pale blue two-story number. Situated on the very outskirts of the city, in one of the quieter residential areas, it literally had a white picket fence bordering the front yard. As Helen pulled up on the street and shut the engine off, she grimaced in distaste at the task ahead of her.

She knew, from a quick records search, that Lynda Green née Marshall had grown up in this house. Furthermore, Helen knew that this home was more than just an ordinary home; it was a throwback to an almost-forgotten time.

Lynda Marshall's parents had lived here for nearly forty years, until about a year ago when John Marshall had died of a massive coronary. Karen Marshall, pushing eighty-years old, still lived here and, since it hadn't taken much checking to uncover that Lynda Green had separated from her husband, it stood to reason that this was the obvious place to start looking for her.

Even so, no matter how logical, the idea of the questions Helen had for the woman made her more uncomfortable than she could remember being for a long time.

The picket gate creaked slightly as she opened and closed it, and Helen automatically glanced down to see just the slightest traces of rust.

Still, all in all, the place looked remarkably well kept

up.

Her initial knock on the door elicited no response, but a second, more insistent knocking brought her face to face with a slender, almost petite woman in her late seventies.

"Mrs. Marshall?"

"Yes," acknowledged the woman.

Helen flipped open her badge.

"Detective Lipscomb, I wonder if you could tell me …"

Before she could finish, a slight twist of distaste floated across the old woman's face, and she stepped through the screen door and out onto the porch facing Helen, letting both front and screen door snap shut behind her.

"Didn't take long, did it?" the old woman asked.

"Excuse me?"

"Lynnie said that it wouldn't be hard for you all to find her, but she was hoping for at least a day or two of peace."

"I'm sorry, but I don't follow."

Mrs. Marshall rolled her eyes heavenward.

"You think it's easy for her to up and take her kids away from their dad, even with what everyone's saying about him? You may think it was a snap decision, but it wasn't. In the end, she just had to get away from all that, even if only for a while. And now you come out here and…"

"Momma?" The voice that came from around the corner of the house sounded more like a little girl's than an adult woman's, but the owner of the voice clearly fell into the grown up category.

As Helen saw Lynda Green for the first time, she

116

wondered again, as she often did, just why some men felt they had to cheat. Mrs. Green wasn't a raving beauty by any standards, and she could possibly have shed a couple of pounds that seemed to have hung around from her last pregnancy. But even so, she definitely ranked as a pretty woman, and she sure looked better than any number of stick figures you saw on the cover of magazines. At first glance, practically any man in the world should consider himself lucky to have her in his bed.

But then Helen realized just how short sighted she was being. She knew from bitter experience that a person's appearance held no indication of how they were to live with, and there could have been any number of problems, on either side, in that marriage. So, odd as it sounded, she was being grossly unfair to judge Ron Green's actions based solely on his wife's appearance.

Then again, the guy could just be a horndog.

Quite possibly a murdering horndog.

The older woman turned at her daughter's approach, and the curl of distaste she'd held for Helen grew, if anything, even more pronounced.

"Lynnie, you can go back in the house if you want to," she said.

"That's okay." She swivelled to face Helen directly. "I guess you want to talk to me, don't you?"

"Yes I do, Mrs. Green. Just a few questions, if you don't mind."

"Let's go on in the living room. I've got about half an hour before I have to pick Sarah up from school, and I just put the baby down for the afternoon."

"Fine." Helen followed the woman into the house, feeling the disdain of the mother trailing behind her.

****

"First, I want you to tell me something. Is my husband your main suspect?"

Helen hesitated. On the one hand, standard policy dictated that you not let the interviewee chart the course of the discussion. On the other, Lynda Green could possibly provide valuable information to help cinch the case, but for her to do so Helen had to get the woman on her side.

She mulled it over for a few moments, as Mrs. Green shot questioning looks her way, before deciding to shade the truth just a little.

"No," she finally said, "not the only one. But I have to tell you that at the moment, and barring the introduction of further evidence, he's the one we're primarily looking at."

For a moment there, Helen felt as if the woman sitting across from her was looking, not specifically at her or anything physically in the room, but at some point in the far distant past, a time when everything had looked rosy and life held nothing but fun and games.

Then the look faded, and Mrs. Green came back completely into the present.

"Okay," she said, "what do you want to know?"

****

"She says that she didn't have a clue, pun intended," Helen said.

"And do you believe her?"

Janey Turner sat across from Helen, the two of them occupying a corner booth in one of the little coffee shops downtown. Helen had wanted Jack Hollis to come along with her to question the Green woman, but he'd been hauled into a deposition scheduled to take up most of the afternoon, leaving Helen to deal with Mrs. Green alone.

"Believe her? Not entirely. Of course, it's possible she did like a lot of women and deliberately ignored the signs."

"Especially with a baby on the way at the time."

"Exactly. So when she says she didn't know, she could be telling the truth as she knows it."

"But when the evidence became overwhelming, she finally had to break down and admit the truth."

"Right."

"Which, according to your guy, is when he had to break it off."

"Uh huh." Helen stopped talking as their waiter came by with their drinks: a plain coffee for her and some sort of overcompensated caramel and whipped cream laden concoction for Janey.

Helen sighed at the thought that she'd probably never be able to ingest something like that on a regular basis, at least not without bloating up like a diseased whale.

"Do you think he really did?" Janey asked in between sips of whatever the hell she was drinking.

"Did what?"

"Do you think he really did break it up with Diane when he says he did? Or was that just a show for the little wifey?"

Helen drummed her fingers on the table for a minute.

"Well, Hollis and I have gone through Diane's phone records, her e-mail accounts, both personal and professional, and her social pages, and we can't find any trace of him after the first part of October. Even more, according to the roommate she didn't see him around from early fall on, though she can't remember the exact date."

"Does that really mean anything? Didn't you say that, according to Green, she kept their affair low profile anyway?"

"Yeah."

"So did you find any trace of anything?"

"What do you mean?"

"Well, like her social media pages. Was there any sudden appearance of ranting or raving? Any communications with anyone where she showed any hurt or rage? Anything like that?"

"Not to speak of."

"So she was either a real expert at concealing her feelings . . ."

"Or she didn't really have that strong of feelings to begin with."

"Right."

"Green was just an uncomplicated lay, and when he said arrivederci, she figured she'd just go on to the next prospect."

"Or?"

Helen frowned and sipped her coffee as she organized her thoughts. "Or he told her that the wife had found out, and they would have to be even more circumspect than before," she finally said.

"Which does your gut tell you is true?"

"It's not sure yet. But while I sort it out, let's see how things link up with your case."

"Well, for one, we're pretty sure that Damian Pendleton is our guy."

"Pretty sure?"

"Right."

"But not positive?"

"Fairly close to positive, but I've got to tell you, Helen, your guy showing up and bringing us this wild story about a focus group is actually making us take a second look at Pendleton."

"Why?"

"Well, for one thing, like in your case we've got nothing tangible on the guy at all."

"Beyond the restraining order that Lisa Willard took out."

"Right. No neighbors had seen him around her place for the last several weeks, even though they were definitely aware of his presence before then, and according to his employer, a trucking outfit out on the west side, he's been putting in some heavy duty overtime."

"Trying to reform and become a model citizen?"

"Not likely. Especially considering the time he took a blade to her tires. But from what we've gathered by interviewing friends and co-workers, he's been talking a lot lately about saving up what money he can and heading down to Florida. His home town is Sarasota."

"Giving you the impression that if he's leaving town, he'd probably decided that Lisa Willard was a no go, and he's wanting to start fresh back home."

"Yes," Janey said.

Helen looked down at her empty coffee cup, then stared enviously over at her colleague, who still had almost half of her drink to go.

"But there's another possibility," she continued.

"Right," said Janey, "that maybe he wanted us to think he'd given up on the Willard woman, deflect attention from himself for when he did get his final licks in."

Helen sighed and pushed the empty Styrofoam container to the center of the table.

"So in both of our cases we have a guy who maybe is or maybe isn't our killer, and in both cases there may or may not be some deflecting going on."

"Right," said Janey. "However, if I had to pick, and I'm not saying this just because it would make it easier on me, I'd say that the more likely scenario concerns the common fact in the two."

"Green." Helen spat the name out almost venomously.

"Yeah. The fact he knew, even if briefly, both the vics tells me he's somehow connected to the two killings."

"And his cockamamie story about meeting them both in that focus group thing…"

"Is probably true."

"So we're both thinking along the same lines here."

"Probably."

"That my guy Green killed both women."

"Right. Diane Brewster in some fit of passion or rage because, while he may have made it appear differently, their affair was still going on."

"But he's not a professional criminal or anything," Helen said.

"Not at all. At least, not yet."

"And as smart as he is, a professor and all that, he may have been completely blindsided by how fast we got on to him."

"Which left him grasping for straws on how to get out from under suspicion," said Janey.

"Which led him to kill Lisa Willard, hoping we'd think there was some kook running around knocking off the members of that PR group."

The two detectives paused to fully digest what they'd just sorted out.

"But if that's true," Janey said after a minute or two, "how did he manage to track her down? From what I understand, in those kinds of situations most people just know each other's first names. How did he find her?"

"Here's an idea," Helen said as she stood and drew on her jacket, "why don't we go ask him?"

CHAPTER NINETEEN

With more people than usual crowded in, the interrogation room felt even more cramped and confined than Ron's previous experience, and not even the presence of his lawyer could keep his stomach from doing a slow burn. He kept his hands under the table, fearful someone in this bunch would notice them trembling and assume the wrong thing.

Barely an hour before, Ron had been sitting at his own desk in his office at the university, gazing at the accumulated pile of material that constituted his now never-to-be-completed tenure bid, when he'd looked up to see two detectives standing in his doorway. Lipscomb, of course, he knew, and he'd been wondering when she would show up again. The other cop, also a woman, was a stranger to him, but he'd figured her presence didn't signal anything good.

Turned out he was right.

Despite the man's distant attitude during their first encounter, Ron almost wished Detective Hollis had come to take him in. Maybe it was the idea they were looking at him for a woman's death, but the idea of two female detectives approaching set Ron's teeth on edge.

They made it clear he still wasn't under arrest, but when they'd asked him to come down to the station to answer some more questions, he'd done so only after calling Lowenstein.

So now here Ron sat in, as far as he could tell, the same interrogation room as the last two times, only with more people.

There was Lipscomb; Hollis; the other female detective, who he guessed had something to do with the Willard murder; an older man introduced as their lieutenant; and, the one who really made Ron's stomach queasy, an assistant district attorney. Combined with both himself and Walt Lowenstein, it made for quite a congested room.

Before the ADA, who'd introduced himself as Larry Moren, or any of the detectives could get the ball rolling, Lowenstein kicked the whole thing off.

"Up front, can you please spell out exactly what my client is being charged with?"

Attaboy, Ron thought. *Get confrontational as hell. Piss them off, especially considering that I haven't done anything wrong.* Something in his face must have shown his concern because Walt almost immediately laid a placating hand on Ron's arm.

"He's not being charged with anything, yet." This from ADA Moren. He looked to be in his mid thirties and, adding to Ron's discomfort even more, seemed competent as hell. Although they'd just been introduced, he carried himself in such a way as to make it clear to everyone that he was in charge of the show.

"No charges?" Lowenstein continued. "Okay, that helps clear that up. Now, just what exactly is he being suspected of?"

Moren and the women detectives sat at the table and their lieutenant leaned against the wall, all looking back and forth at each other.

"Actually, I wouldn't even go so far as to use the

word 'suspected' at this point," Moren said.

"But he is a suspect, right? In the Brewster murder?"

"At the moment, he's more of a person of interest."

"Goddammit!" Lowenstein slammed his palm on the table, making even the detectives jump. "Enough with this 'person of interest' crap. You guys have been throwing that at the press for the last month. Is Ron a suspect in the death of Diane Brewster or not?"

Again, the looks all around, but this time it was Helen Lipscomb who answered, while receiving a glare from ADA Moren.

"Yes," she said, "he's our main suspect in the Brewster murder."

"Meaning that you think somewhere around the first of March, my client entered Miss Brewster's home and strangled and beat her."

"Yes." Again from Lipscomb, and another glare from Moren, though not quite as sharp as the first.

"And?" Lowenstein asked.

"Excuse me?"

"Well, since you've already questioned him concerning Diane Brewster's death, not to mention having searched both his home and vehicle, and since you've brought him down here again, I'm assuming there's something else you want to talk about."

"Walt—"

"Quiet, Ron. Let's get it all out on the table right now."

The five members of officialdom acquired harder, more determined looks than they'd worn previously, and at this point Moren resumed the talking.

"We also have reason to believe he may be connected with the death of Miss Lisa Willard."

"Say what?" Before Lowenstein could restrain him, Ron had risen half out of his chair.

"You heard me," Moren said. "Lisa Willard, who I understand from the detectives, you knew. We're looking at you for that one, too."

"Ron, goddammit. Sit down!"

Lowenstein reached over and forcibly yanked his client back into his chair. For an instant, all three of the police officers in the room tensed themselves, as Green appeared about to physically jump someone.

After an instant, though, the tension seemed to leave him and he sank down into his chair.

"I don't get this at all. I came to you about her. I explained all that."

He'd directed the words towards Helen, as if seeking her support.

"Yes," Moren said, pulling Ron's attention back to him, "you came in, voluntarily, and provided some information about knowing the Willard woman last year."

"Meeting her. Not knowing her. The entire two days I doubt we spoke more than half a dozen words to each other."

"But you spoke considerably more than that to the Brewster babe, right?"

"Larry," Lowenstein cautioned, at the same time shooting a glare in his client's direction to keep him quiet.

"Sorry." Moren didn't look very sorry at all. "Didn't mean to be flippant. My point is, exactly why did you come in here to talk about Lisa Willard? You knew you were a suspect in one murder. Why get mixed up in another?"

Before answering, Ron looked again at Detective Lipscomb. He'd come to her in good faith before, but if he expected to see anything there, she disappointed him. She gave him merely a blank stare.

Ron looked at Lowenstein, who gave him a brief nod.

"I just thought it odd," he said, "when I saw the news about Lisa's death. Two women who just happened to appear in a random grouping together. I thought maybe …"

He trailed off as the inanity of his original idea finally sunk in.

"Yes?" Moren prodded. "You thought what?"

"My client's under no obligation to reveal his—"

"I thought the two were connected," Ron blurted out, cutting off Lowenstein. "I figured that whoever killed Diane might, just might, have also killed the other one. For some reason or other. So I came to you guys to notify you of their connection, even if it was kind of slight."

"All of which," Moren said with a noticeable sneer, "is based on the presumption that you didn't murder Diane Brewster yourself."

"Lawrence." Lowenstein's admonition was louder this time.

"Sorry. I'll take that back, for now. So let me get this straight, Mr. Green. You wanted to give the police a heads up that the same person who killed Miss Brewster may also have done in Mrs. Willard?"

"Yes."

"That maybe some serial killer was offing the women who'd been in this focus group for the senator?"

"Well, I wouldn't go that far. In fact didn't think it

all the way through. But yes, essentially you're right."

"And that they should stop wasting their time on you and go after the 'real killer,' eh?"

"All right," Lowenstein interjected. "I've had just about enough of this. Either straighten up your attitude or we're walking out."

ADA Moren's eyes flashed with irritation, but in a moment he'd taken on a more neutral tone.

"Mr. Green..."

"Professor," Ron interrupted, deciding the time had come to play some hardball of his own. As soon as the words left his mouth, though, he inwardly grimaced at the thought that, barring some miracle, he wouldn't hold claim to that title for much longer.

"Fine. Professor Green, surely you understand that the detectives, on both cases, found your–*input*–flimsy to say the least."

"What are you saying, Mr. Moren?"

Everyone in the room, even a legal neophyte like Ron, caught the sudden shift to formality with Lowenstein's question.

Ron noticed the detectives, both standing and sitting, shift backwards a little, as if sensing the song and dance coming to an end.

"What I'm saying, Walter, is that a much more logical rationale is that your client here is attempting to develop a connection between the two deaths. One that will get him off the hook."

Without another word, Lowenstein stood, grabbing Ron by the arm and yanking him to a standing position as well.

"Come on, Ron. We're out of here."

"Wait a minute …"

"No. No waiting. We're leaving now. Unless–" Ron's lawyer turned to the ADA, "you're ready to charge my client. Otherwise, we're gone."

"I still don't see…"

"It's simple, Professor Green. I'm sure your attorney will explain it to you in full, but the basic gist of it is—"

"Now, Ron." Lowenstein tugged even more ferociously on his arm. "Let's go."

"Not yet." Ron managed to jerk his arm free. "I want to hear this. Right from him."

Moren, who still hadn't moved from his chair, looked up at Ron and smiled.

A smile that made Ron's insides turn to mush.

"What we suspect, Mr. Green, and what we damned well intend to prove, is that you killed Lisa Willard in an attempt to deflect our attention from you in the Brewster case."

This time, Ron didn't resist as his attorney dragged him out of the room and, almost in the same motion, nearly out of the station itself.

Quite simply, he felt as if his final cord had been cut.

CHAPTER TWENTY

Ron hesitated before knocking on the door. It felt unreal to be an intruder, an encroacher, on a property you'd been invited to numerous times in the past. Merely another in the long line of adjustments he was having to make to his way of thinking.

Clearly, she was here, at least if her vehicle in the driveway indicated anything. But whether she would open the door to him was yet to be seen.

Still, he'd gain nothing by merely standing around out here in the evening air, so he raised his hand and knocked.

It took only the one rap to have the curtain over the living room window part, although so slightly that Ron couldn't make out the person on the other side.

A second later, the door opened.

"Hello, Karen."

Lynda's mother looked him over through the screen door.

"You didn't get the message when she didn't return your calls?" she asked.

He took a deep breath in order to keep his composure. He'd never had what you'd call a bad relationship with his mother-in-law, but he'd hadn't had a very good one either.

And he could only imagine what she must think of him now.

"Actually," he said, "the message did come through loud and clear. But I thought if I came by…"

The old woman turned her head and glanced over her shoulder, then looked back at him, opened the screen door and slid out, shutting both doors behind her.

"The cops were here the other day," she said. "Some woman detective. Questioned Lynda right in my living room."

"I'm sorry about that."

"I'll just bet you are."

She sighed, rubbed her hands across her face, then looked up at him.

"What happened to you?" she asked. "We, Lynda's father and I, always thought you were decent enough. Help me understand, okay? When did it all go wrong?"

The nervous tension that had kept him moving forward since he and Walt left the police station suddenly deserted him, and Ron's knees began to quiver. He walked over and sat down on the old-fashioned, wooden porch swing.

"I really wish I knew. I know it sounds lame to say I never meant to hurt anyone, and if I were to say that things just happened it'd make me sound like the weakest sort of wuss. It probably doesn't make any difference, but I've spent a whole lot of sleepless nights lately trying to figure out the answer to your question."

"And have you gotten anywhere?"

"Not far enough for it to matter."

She came over and sat down next to Ron, placing her hand on his knee.

"I know you and Lynnie have had your problems, and this latest thing is probably the worst of them all."

"It is."

"Like I said. But I know you pretty well, Ron. And I know at heart that you're a good man. But even good men make mistakes."

"I've made a couple of doozies."

"That you have. And unfortunately you've probably got some more payback ahead of you before your accounts are balanced out."

"I kind of figure on that."

"But mistakes and accounts set aside, I don't for a moment think you're guilty of what you're being accused of."

Ron sat rigid, his facial muscles locked absolutely tight. At that moment, he wanted nothing more than to break down and cry on this old woman's shoulder. But he also knew that if he broke down now, he'd probably never recover his composure.

"You know," he told her, "you're the first person since this started who's shown any confidence in me."

"I figured. The problem is, I've been trying to get that through to Lynnie for the last few days."

He turned and looked at his mother-in-law, feeling a fresh round of horrified expressions crossing his face.

"She doesn't actually think I did it, does she? I know she's asked me about it but—"

"Ron, you've got to get it through your head. Right about now, she doesn't know what to think. So if you want to talk to her, and if she's willing, go ahead and try. I'm just saying don't expect too much."

"Could you tell her I'm here?"

"Don't have to. She already knows." Mrs. Marshall stood up, her face grimacing as her knees creaked slightly. "Wait just a minute and I'll see."

It actually took closer to five minutes before the

front door opened and Lynda stepped out. Again, Ron almost thought he would faint when he saw that she had the baby in her arms and little Sarah trailed right behind her mother. He took this as a good sign, that she'd felt confident and secure enough to bring the kids out as well.

But when he got a good look at her face, he realized he'd been a bit presumptuous, and that things were probably about as good as they'd get.

****

Some two hours later, Ron felt composed enough to call his lawyer. He didn't really have any legal questions or concerns, besides the obvious. He frankly just needed someone to talk to.

"Hello?" Lowenstein's voice sounded a trifle weary.

"Hey, Walt. It's me."

"Yeah. What's up?" Suddenly the man sounded tense, energized, as if he feared some other shoe had just dropped.

"I'm sorry to bother you at home. I just…"

"That's okay, guy. What's going on?"

"I–I just came from talking to Lynda."

"Yeah?"

"She let me see and talk to the kids. Well, talk to Sarah, at least. Got to hold the baby for a while, too."

"Give me the big picture, Ron. How did it go?"

"I asked her to move back home. Told her that I needed her and the kids. Needed some stability so I could get through this."

"Sounds right. How did she take it?"

"Better than I thought she would. But not good enough. She wouldn't come home."

"Well, you told me that things were pretty much shot even before…"

"Before Diane's death, yeah. Thing is, before that happened I was just another guy wanting to split with his wife and go on to something new and different. Not very admirable, but at least kind of normal."

"Okay."

"But then this all happened. And it wasn't just her dying. It was being the one they're looking at, and now with the Willard thing."

"Need to keep perspective here, Ron. Despite what we tried to convince the cops of, that could just be a really isolated coincidence."

Ron leaned back in his chair and stared at the ceiling. Its blankness seemed to reflect the state of his thoughts. Ever since leaving Lynda a few hours back, he'd felt simply drained. So exhausted that it had taken practically everything he had to even pick up the phone and dial Walt's number.

"Maybe you're right," he finally said, "but at the moment I can't think that way."

"Why not?"

"Don't you see? If it's just a coincidence they were both killed, then that still leaves the cloud hanging over my head for Diane. But if it's something bigger, something wider, then that lets me off. Right? Except that's not how the cops may see it."

Ron waited for an affirmation from his lawyer. When it didn't come, he felt like his heart should sink all over again, but it didn't. That blank weariness still gripped him.

"So how did you leave it with Lynda?" Walt finally asked.

Ron sighed. "She gave me two months."

"Two months? For what?"

"To get out of the apartment. Turns out I was already too late by half. She saw a lawyer yesterday and is initiating proceedings. Said she wants to keep it amicable, but I guess you know more about the odds of that than I do. Anyway, she asked me to be out of the apartment within two months so she and the kids could move back there."

"You don't have to do that, you know. I can talk to Jerry Robinson, one of our associates, tomorrow and get started on counter proceedings."

Ron thought about it for a while, looking up at the ceiling for some kind of guidance.

He didn't find it.

"I don't know," he said after a few minutes. "I'm not thinking too clearly right now. Let me get some sleep and I'll get back to you."

"Okay. Anything else?"

"Yeah, something I just thought of. Can we sue the city?"

"Excuse me?"

"The city. Can we sue them? For defamation or whatever?"

Over the phone, Ron could hear Walt's breathing quicken.

"Ron, is there something you haven't told me?"

"Why? Isn't what they've done to me enough?"

"It's part of the department's charter to investigate crimes, buddy. As long as they do so in good faith, regardless of how wrong they may be."

"I've lost my job."

"Come again?"

"The dean called me in yesterday. Said to withdraw my tenure bid for next year."

"Aw shit, guy, I…"

"Won't even give me the standard year's grace period. Got to be out by the end of July."

"Ron, I—"

"So that makes reputation, marriage, and job that they killed. Well, maybe they didn't kill the marriage, I've got to take some fault for that. But they sure didn't help it any. So can we sue them?"

"Ron, go to bed. Get some sleep and we'll talk in the morning."

"Just answer my question, Walt. Hell, you're probably going to put this talk on my bill anyway, so let me know. Can we?"

"If, Ron. If we can get you cleared, it's possible that we may have a case. But we can't focus on that just yet. We've got to get you cleared first. That's job number one."

All through the conversation, Ron's gaze hadn't left the spackled white ceiling above him. With it shrouded in shadows, he'd strained his eyes looking for something tangible to hang his future on.

And had found nothing.

"I didn't kill her, Walt. I didn't."

"I know."

"Or the other one. I'm a lot of things, buddy. But I'm not a killer."

"I know."

"But I'm afraid."

"Afraid?"

"Yeah. I feel almost certain that I'm going down for this."

"We'll try to avoid that," Walt said.

'Yeah. Let's do that. Let's *try*."

JOB INTERVIEW #6

State Capitol (80 Miles from home)
March 30

Gas prices had shot up, again, and as he pulled into the Conoco station he tried to do the math as to how much it would cost to fill his tank.

As he unscrewed the gas cap and stuck the nozzle into the slot, he punched the little square on the faceplate of the pump that said "Pay Inside."

A few seconds later, he punched it again.

And again.

The line of digital numbers on the pump silently read eight.

"Excuse me, sir," a scratchy, electronic voice squawked at him, "but you have to prepay for that pump."

He peered at the entire surface of the pump, nowhere seeing any sign or warning to prepay. Grumbling, he rehooked the nozzle and trudged through the rain to the interior of the store.

Two people stood in line ahead of him—a young kid buying a Slim Jim and some sort of soft drink, and a middle-aged man nervously holding a Visa card.

As he waited for the kid to pay for his junk, he examined the man standing right in front of him. To the inexperienced observer, the man might have simply been any ordinary guy engaging in a minor bit of commerce. There were so many similarities between himself and the man in front of him: the hunched shoulders, slouched posture, slightly run-down clothing that had once been nice, and sweaty grasp of the credit card. He could easily recognize a brother in suffering.

Without even striking up a conversation, without asking a single question, he knew that the man in front of him was also out of work, had more than likely been unemployed for some time, and was beginning to fear he'd never find work again.

The kid took his Slim Jim and soda and went off, and stepping up to the counter, the man with the Visa card began to examine the array of lottery tickets beneath the glass-topped counter.

Seriously? Lottery tickets with a Visa?

He stood there, shifting from one foot to the other, as the man seemed to take forever to make his decision. In the end, he purchased nearly twenty different cards, paying for them all on the credit card, before turning away from the register. As he did so, the gazes of the two men locked, and they both recognized kindred souls.

After the lottery buyer left, he stepped up to the counter to prepay for his gas. He pulled his own Visa out of his wallet before remembering Mary had mentioned they had less than a hundred dollars left on it. He placed it back in its slot, nearly fumbling it out of his grasp, then pulled out his Discover.

They'd managed, thank God, to get by this long without touching the MasterCard, though no doubt its time was coming.

And soon. If he didn't get some work.

"Forty dollars, please. On pump thirteen."

The cashier took his card, did her thing with her machines and handed it back.

"Need a receipt?"

Yes, he most definitely needed a receipt. For nearly a year now, he'd been keeping track of every conceivable expense in some way related to his job search. He hadn't initially, mainly because when he'd first left his last firm he hadn't dreamed that it would take him so long to find employment.

He'd figured it would be a cinch to find a new job.

Even in this economy, and even considering his profession.

So while the first few weeks of expenses had been lost to oblivious naiveté, he wasn't about to ever make that mistake again.

He contemplated getting a medium-sized soda, but decided against it. Taking his receipt, he thanked the woman and headed back out to pump his gas.

Forty bucks didn't quite get him ten gallons.

Ten gallons wasn't quite half his tank.

But it would be enough to get him home, which at the moment was all he could hope for.

In desperation, he'd applied for, and received an interview, at a firm here in the state capital. Eighty miles from home but, if one were frugal, and more importantly if it involved a paycheck coming in, within commuting range.

Now, he was returning home empty-handed.

He'd lost this opportunity as well.

And he simply did not know what he would do next.

CHAPTER TWENTY-ONE

April 1

Johnny had dozed off during the ten o'clock news, something he found himself doing more and more these days, so he had no clue how long someone had been knocking at his door before the noise finally roused him. Struggling to an upright position on his old, cracked leather couch he blinked a few times at the clock over the fireplace before realizing his glasses had slipped off during his slumber.

Another knock came, this time sounding kind of frantic. He snagged his glasses from the floor in front of the couch and focused on the clock face.

Eleven thirty? Who the heck would be calling on him this late at night?

Another rap on the door, a three-beat tattoo, and Johnny began to get a bit worried.

Anyone who needed to see him this late should have called ahead first, and the fact they hadn't made him wonder just what was up.

Still, he wasn't some silly old duffer who would leave himself wide open. Forty years in the service had left him with his share of toughness, and although he lived in a decent neighborhood, he wasn't naive enough to blindly open the door in the middle of the night. Had Lisa still been alive, he would have sent her into their bedroom and shut the door behind her.

But she wasn't here anymore.

And someone was knocking on the door at nearly midnight.

Johnny sidled up to the door, turned himself partially sideways and looked with the edge of his eye through the peephole. It wouldn't completely fool someone, but it seemed a hell of a lot more subtle than looking straight through and casting a full shadow.

A lot less subtle was the aluminum Louisville Slugger leaning against the wall just a few inches away.

As far as Johnny could tell, only one person stood on his porch. A man of average height and probably weight (although the distortion of the peephole made it difficult to tell) and wearing what looked like slacks and a windbreaker.

"Yes?" Johnny said through the door.

"Mr. Caldwell?"

"Yes? What do you want?"

"Mr. Caldwell, we need to talk."

"Who are you?"

"We met last year. Don't you remember?"

The younger man didn't look familiar at all, and as the seconds went by and the fog of sleep lifted, Johnny cudgeled his brain, trying to remember the fellow's face. But, try as he might, he just couldn't place it.

"Who are you?"

"Come on, Mr. Caldwell. We met last year. Down at Amos Kettering?"

Johnny gave up on recognizing the man, but even so he felt reassured. It was late to be calling, but somebody trying a home invasion, or any kind of troublemaker, couldn't possibly know about his time spent at the Amos place last year.

Obviously, the younger man must be one of the bunch Johnny had spent time with, and it was just his old fart's brain that couldn't pin down the memory.

He threw the dead bolt and safety chain, the Slugger now entirely forgotten.

"Hell, son," he said as he swung the door open, "you've got to pardon me not recognizing you. Why just this morning I lost track of…"

The sudden swing of a ball peen hammer, the rounded portion connecting directly between his eyes, cut off Johnny Caldwell's greeting. With a soft grunt, he fell backwards, his head narrowly missing the arm of an old green La-Z-Boy as he landed on his back on the floor.

His visitor, moving as swiftly as he could, flashed inside the house and used the heel of his left foot to swing the door shut. Then he looked down at the old man lying in front of him.

The eyes were glazing over. He'd swung as hard as he possibly could, but they still held some awareness. Not much and not for long, but enough.

"You have any idea who I am?"

"Uhh." A drab of bloody spittle flowed out with the syllable. No doubt in his fall the old man had bitten into his tongue.

"Know why I'm doing this?"

Another subdued grunt, and it almost looked as if the geezer tried to shake his head, but that was probably just imagination.

"No matter," his attacker said from his crouched position, "the others have probably figured it out by now. Why don't you ask them when you see them."

And with that salutation, he raised his arm and, face

beginning to mottle in his fury, brought the hammer down again.

Several times.

CHAPTER TWENTY-TWO

April 2 (Early A.M.)

"Hey, Hollis, how'd you get stuck doing graveyard?"

As Jack stepped over the threshold onto the crime scene, he grinned at Stan Blunter, the fiftyish patrolman who'd greeted him.

"Everyone's having to pitch their weight lately, Stan. In case you hadn't noticed, our fair city's in the midst of a short-term crime wave."

"Yeah," Blunter snickered, "short term for the last half decade or so. And this one here isn't going to help our stats any."

"I can see that."

Hollis walked a few steps closer to the corpse that lay on the dull brown carpet. He couldn't get too close because the area around the body held such a God-awful mess.

For this one, two different people from the coroner's office had been called out.

"Anything for me yet?" he asked the two ME's.

"Not yet," said the older of the two, a black man pushing retirement age whom Hollis had worked with on several occasions. "Only been able to eyeball it. Your tech people have been working all this time."

And indeed the crime scene guys, four of them,

roamed all over the house, mainly in the living room and around the body, but also moving back and forth throughout the place, doing their thing.

"Pictures been taken?" Hollis asked no one in particular.

"A while back," someone replied behind him. "Photog left about ten minutes 'fore you got here."

Hollis grunted, then edged a little closer to the mess on the floor.

The guy looked old, for sure, which led Hollis to initially think this could just possibly be a random home invasion. But while home invaders often killed their targets, they usually did so in the quickest way possible.

What Hollis saw in front of him could in no way be called quick.

"Who called it in?" he asked as he attempted to mentally count the number of impact points he could see on the face and body. He gave up at eight, even then none too sure that he'd figured right. There was such a mess there, the face literally beaten to a pulp, making it too damned hard to tell.

"Neighbor," said Blunter from behind him. "Believe it or not, an old lady out walking her dog. Kind of late for that, but what the heck? She saw his light on, got concerned at how late it was. Guess the guy's been a widower for a few years and is in the habit of going to bed by ten or so."

"So when she saw his light on this late?"

"Said that she came up to the porch just to make sure everything was all right. When she saw the door open and living room lit up, she got scared and scampered on home. But at least had the gumption to call us."

"Forced entry?" Hollis asked.

"Doesn't seem to be. Door was just half open, and no damage on either the jamb or knob."

Hollis grunted and looked around the living room. It took up, at a guess, about half the space of the house, one of those old-type home constructions almost extinct these days. Most of the furniture, though obviously kept in decent shape, looked between ten and twenty years old. The leather couch cushions had a lot of cracks, but other than that, things didn't look too bad.

Except for the fine layer of dust coating practically everything.

"You said he's a widower," Hollis asked.

"Yeah, according to the neighbor lady a couple of years now."

A long, flat glass case suspended over the fireplace caught Hollis' eye. Circling around the scene on the floor, he walked over and peered up at it.

"Anybody here been in the service?" he asked the room in general.

"I was, sir." One of the crime scene techs had just come out from the rear portion of the house. "Five years in the Marines. Whatcha need?"

Hollis motioned towards the case.

"Can you tell me what branch these medals come from?"

The case contained a varied assortment of nearly twenty medals and ribbons. Hollis, a civilian his entire life, saw nothing but a mass of color.

The tech came up closer, peered just a second, then stepped back.

"Looks like navy, sir. And judging by some of them, I'd say he was in over several years."

"Hey, Bluntner."

The uniform stepped up.

"Yeah, Jack?"

"What's the name the neighbor lady gave you?"

"Said his name was Caldwell. John Caldwell."

"Buzz the central house and have them run it through records. Not just the usual search, go through the Defense Department as well. See what we can get about this guy."

"Sure thing."

As Bluntner walked off, Hollis bent down again for a closer look at the body.

"How many does this make?" one of the techs, a middle-aged Asian woman, asked.

"Huh?"

"On your plate? How many homicides you currently got open?"

"Why? You keeping score or something?"

"Not really." She shrugged and continued wiping some sort of chemical onto a portion of the carpet. "I just wonder if you all ever get burned out on all this stuff."

"Actually..." Before Hollis could finish, another uniformed officer came from the back part of the house.

"Found a wallet, sir. Has a driver's license in it."

"Made out for John Caldwell?"

"Yes, sir. Gives his age as seventy-three."

Hollis glanced back down at the corpse before turning back to the Asian crime scene person.

"And there's your answer," he said.

"Huh?"

"To whether it ever gets to me."

"Yeah?"

"It never has," he said, "until just now."

CHAPTER TWENTY-THREE

April 4

Helen stood on the other side of the mirror and observed the interrogation room. At the moment it held only one occupant, and even though an officer had offered that person the chance to consult a lawyer, the offer had been turned down. Now the occupant of the room, clearly nervous, sat and waited for someone to come in and tell her what the hell was going on.

The door behind Helen opened, and Jack Hollis came into the room. He walked up to her side and took a good look into the other room.

"Looks pretty normal," he said, "your typical suburban housewife."

"That's what she looks like," Helen replied, "except she doesn't live in the suburbs and, at the moment, her life is anything but typical."

"Think she knows why she's here?"

Before Helen could answer, the woman in the other room stood up and began pacing back and forth, agitatedly swinging her arms.

"You've talked to her just the once?" Hollis asked.

"Yep."

"So she thinks she's answered everything?"

"At least she probably did until you called her," Helen said. "You said it was just for some follow up, right?"

"Right. Although she sounded, at least over the phone, a bit put out to be talking to a man detective."

"But you didn't give any indication . . ."

"Come on, Helen. Give me a little credit."

"Sorry."

"Don't worry. When I asked her in I phrased it in such a way that she should still think we want her to help us get the goods on dear old hubby."

"Okay. Even so, she looks nervous to me, but not really guilty."

Hollis glanced at his colleague. "You having second thoughts?"

"Not at all. We have to consider her. At least until we can rule her out. She had almost as much motive as Green to want Diane Brewster dead."

"Maybe." Now Hollis's tone sounded uncertain, and it was Helen's turn to glance over.

"What do you mean 'maybe'?"

"Well, have you had the chance, or any way, to determine whether or not the Brewster woman was the first?"

"The first? You mean his first affair?"

"Right. After all, most guys don't do that kind of thing only once."

Helen tapped her fingers on the sill of the two-way mirror. The woman in the other room had stopped pacing now and sat back down, her legs crossed and her left foot gyrating.

"I hadn't thought of that," Helen finally said.

"Don't take it personal. Cavemannish as this may sound, you're not a guy. Trust me, of those guys who're inclined to that sort of thing, it's rarely a one-shot event."

"And would she have known?" Helen asked, pointing through the glass at the woman in the other room.

"What do you think?"

Helen pondered for a moment, her gaze fixed on Lynda Green's wobbling foot and ankle.

"If it was fairly common," she finally said, "she either knew or strongly suspected."

"Yeah," Hollis said, "but the question is, does that give her a motive or take one away?"

Helen looked at her partner as he stepped back from the mirror and smoothed his suit jacket down.

"Start the recorder," he said, "while I take my crack at her."

He walked out of the room, made it the three steps to the interrogation room and, without knocking, opened the door and went in.

****

Up close, Lynda Green looked even more nervous and irritable than she had through the mirror. Still sitting down, she looked up and frowned as Hollis walked in.

Hollis guessed that standing she'd be fairly tall, around five nine or so, and she had her dull reddish hair pulled back into a tight bun. Her clothes, skirt, blouse and cardigan sweater, looked fairly expensive, but the colors, all muted shades of grey, didn't flatter her at all.

"Detective Hollis?" she inquired.

"Right."

Without offering his hand, he walked over to the head of the table and pulled out a chair.

"So what do you want?" Mrs. Green asked. "I thought I answered all the questions the other day with that lady detective."

"Sorry about that. We've had a busy couple of months around here. But there are a few items I need to go over with you. Just a few things to double check."

Lynda's stiffened posture indicated she was about to bolt. Either that or she really didn't want to be questioned by a man. After a second, she relaxed a bit.

Hollis sat across from her and placed a legal pad and pen on the table in front of her.

"I'm really sorry to do this to you, Mrs. Green. But we need to acquire as much information as possible in order to…"

"Just get to it." She sighed. "I don't know what I can tell you more than I said the other day, but if you want to waste your time, feel free."

Hollis wondered if her tone came from exasperation or fear, but either emotion would potentially give him a lead, so he let it go.

"How long have you and your husband been married?"

Mrs. Green glared at him without saying anything.

"Mrs. Green?"

"I already told you people. I thought you had some new questions for me."

"As I said,"—Hollis worked to keep his own tone as placating as possible—"we need to go back over some stuff."

"Why?"

"Routine questioning." That usually worked to quell any objections.

He could see her debating it, a virtual panoply of emotions racing across her face.

Then eventually her shoulders slumped and she looked down at the floor.

"Eight years."

"Has the marriage been, at least in your opinion, a happy one?"

"Where's that other detective, the woman?" Again, the agitation. "I'd rather talk to her."

"Detective Lipscomb isn't available right now." As he spoke he made sure he didn't even momentarily glance at the mirror that filled the back wall. "And I don't want to sound harsh, but the sooner you answer my questions the sooner you can leave. So again. Was your marriage a happy one?"

Another sigh, louder and more obviously forced this time.

"You mean as far as I knew?"

"Yes. As far as you knew, up until recent events."

"Sure." She shrugged. "I mean, we had our ups and downs of course. But I never suspected him of being anything other than a normal husband. At least, not until…"

"Yes," Hollis said. "When did you learn about your husband's involvement with Diane Brewster?"

"You're just determined to keep retreading the same ground, aren't you?"

"Afraid so."

"Fine, but please keep it as brief as possible. I found out somewhere around the first of October. I don't—I don't remember the exact date, but Ron had been back at work about a month or so."

"You mean back at the university?"

"Yes. And they always start up again right around Labor Day."

"So how did you find out? What tipped you off?"

"I really don't want to—"

"Mrs. Green, please. How did you discover about your husband's affair?"

"Little things. Little things that kept adding up. Him having trouble some days looking me in the eye, coming home from work and jumping right into the shower, odd little things like that got me wondering."

"So you started checking?"

"Well, not at first. Dammit, I wanted to trust my husband. But all those little details kept piling up."

"How did you confirm your suspicions?" Hollis asked. "Did you check his e-mail or computer?"

"First thing I thought of, even though Ronald isn't exactly the most up to date person when it comes to technical stuff. It wasn't too difficult to check his phone or e-mail without him knowing. But that netted me exactly zero. So I had to get more basic."

"More basic?"

For the first time since Hollis had stepped into the room, the Green woman actually smiled. Only for a moment, true. But it was there for a second, long enough for Hollis to realize that, without all the angst confronting her, Lynda Green could be halfway pretty.

"I followed the bastard," she finally bit out.

"How long did it take you to confirm—"

"About half a day. Either I got unbelievably lucky or he was a lot busier than I'd imagined."

"So how did you handle it?"

"Handle it?"

"Yeah. Did you confront her? Confront your husband? How did you go about it?"

The hesitation again, somehow deeper this time.

"I'm sorry, detective, but I really don't see how that matters."

Hollis knew this could go either way. The idea of sending in a strange male to question her was rooted in the principle of trying to agitate her, to see which way she would jump. However, one of those possible directions was to completely clam up and refuse to give any more answers.

He couldn't even come close to letting her realize she was a possible suspect, but at the same time he knew that he wasn't facing a stupid woman. So he had to be cautious here.

"We're trying to reconstruct the timeline of Miss Brewster's life," he said. "And to do so, we need as much precise information as possible. So when you confirmed your suspicions, how did you proceed?"

"Well for one, I never even met Diane Brewster, if that's what you're asking. As soon as I had the proof I needed, I confronted Ron as soon as he got home. Said I had something important to talk about, took him out in the hall so we wouldn't bother the kids, and had it out."

"How did he respond?"

"Respond?"

"Yes," Hollis said. "Did he act angry, hurt, confused or what? Did he try to deny it?"

"You could tell he wanted to, but I had all the stuff I needed right in my hand. Actually, if anything I guess you'd say he seemed—deflated. In a flash, he went from being a solid, imposing guy to someone who looked like everything had been sucked out of him."

"And did he agree to break up with her right then?"

Lynda Green shrugged.

"Like most men,"—a bit of a glare in her response—"he tried to weasel out of it a little. But as soon as I hit him with taking the kids away, he folded. Turned right around and headed off to call it off with her."

"And did he?"

"Huh?"

"Did he really break it off, or was he possibly just acting to fool you?"

A sharper look, one of almost disdain this time.

"I doubt he was acting," she said, her voice almost glacial. "He came back an hour or so later and didn't say two words for the next several days. Whenever he thought I wasn't watching, he looked like a little boy who'd lost his puppy."

"So as far as you know, he did, in fact, break it off with Miss Brewster?"

"As far as I could tell, yes. And believe me, I kept tabs on him for the next several weeks."

Throughout all of this, Hollis had been scrutinizing the woman as closely as possible, knowing full well that on the other side of the glass Helen was doing the same.

"Is that all you needed?" Lynda Green asked, half standing up. "Can I go now?"

"I'm sorry, no," Hollis said, "there are a few more questions I need to ask."

She heaved a disgusted sigh and sank back into her seat.

"What questions?" she asked.

****

"So what do you think?" Helen asked. She and Hollis sat at opposite desks, both with their feet kicked up. It was late, going on eleven at night, and considering it was a weeknight the detectives' squad room was empty except for the two of them.

"You mean do I think she could have done it?"

"Yes," Helen said. "You saw and talked to her up

close and personal, same as me. Think she has it in her?"

"Hard to read that one. She's glacial as hell, that's for sure. Frankly, I could easily see her capping another woman."

"Glacial? That's what you saw?"

"Sure. How did you read her?"

"I saw a woman uptight, trying her best to keep her emotions from spilling out all over the place."

Hollis gave her a questioning look.

"But maybe I'm putting myself in her place too much," Helen said.

"Meaning what?"

"Meaning that my ex, at least as far as I know, never cheated on me. But if he had, it would have been tough, damned near impossible, for me to just smilingly accept it. So maybe I empathize with her too much to be objective."

Hollis shrugged.

"Maybe. Or maybe we're just seeing two sides of the same thing, which was kind of the idea. But let me ask you this. If your ex had cheated and you found out, would it have made any difference whether or not you had kids?"

Helen didn't even have to think about that one.

"Sure. If Thomas had pulled any such stunt, I probably would have left him flat out. But if we'd had kids—"

"Right. So that's where the Green lady's at. She wants to keep her family together, which is understandable. But my reading of the interview with her is that she'd do damned near anything within her power to do so."

"Including murder?"

Hollis shrugged again.

"I could see it," he said.

"I still like the husband for my primary, though."

"Yeah, I would too. But probably shouldn't rule the wife out yet. Anybody else on your list?"

"Not a one. I've managed to rule out the few other possibles, and outside of the affair she had, I can't find any other feasible motive for her murder. The Green guy is it, I'm almost positive. But dammit, I don't have any evidence to back me up."

"It's a bitch," Hollis said, "but sometimes it works that way."

"Speaking of which, I hear you caught a particularly nasty one the other night."

"You mean the old Navy guy?"

"That the one got bludgeoned in his home?"

Hollis grimaced, and for a second Helen thought she saw a kind of sickened look cross her partner's face.

"Yeah," he said, "that's the one. John Caldwell. Just be glad you weren't catching that night, Helen. We've both seen bad stuff, hell, everyone in the division has, but this was about the most brutal thing you can imagine."

"Any ideas on it yet?"

"No, that's the hell of it. Just an old, retired widower, as far as we can find not an enemy his whole life. On top of that…"

"Yeah?" Helen prompted.

"Well, it's just that it's been quite some time since I've seen such–rage, I guess–in a crime scene. I mean, look at your victim. Whoever took her out obviously had to be ticked at her, but once the job was done it was just done."

"So?"

"I just got the preliminary coroner's report on Caldwell before I came over here. They won't know for sure before they do a full autopsy, but they said it sure looks like the poor guy was dead with the first blow. Even so, whoever did him in kept pounding and pounding on him over and over."

"Which is probably your key."

"You think?"

"Sure," Helen said. "Sounds to me like your kindly old septuagenarian had something he'd done that engendered that kind of anger. Once you find out what it was, you've got your guy."

"Maybe," Hollis said. "I can only hope it goes that easily."

CHAPTER TWENTY-FOUR

"You're thinking the wife now?" the lieutenant asked.

"Maybe," Helen said. "My feeling's not as strong on her as it is on the husband, but there's quite a lot of coiled tension there."

"Understandable, considering the turn her family life has taken."

"Yeah, and maybe that's all it is. On the other hand, she definitely had motive."

"But what about all the other stuff? Means? Opportunity?"

"She's a stay-at-home mom."

"How many?"

"'Scuse me?"

"Kids. How many and what ages?"

"Two, including one under a year old."

"So we're probably talking about as much as she can handle," the lieutenant said.

"Probably."

"So how does that give her opportunity?"

"Well, for one thing she does have time during the day It wouldn't take much to have a friend or relative sit the kids for a while and—"

"Maybe." Her boss's expression showed just how thin he considered her theory. "But weren't you working off the assumption that the Green fellow had killed the other woman too? The Willard woman?"

"Never hurts to run down two possibles at the same time, sir."

"Okay, what the hell, run with it if you think there's a chance. See if you can get a warrant, for both the apartment and her car, if she has her own."

"We've already searched their place, and she's not currently living there," Helen reminded him.

"Where's she staying?"

"At her mother's. Literally a white picket fence house."

"Okay, but when you searched the apartment you were looking for evidence against Green, not against his wife. If you go in with a different orientation, you may find something you missed before."

"What if we can't get a warrant?"

"Cross that bridge when you come to it, Lipscomb. Don't borrow trouble. Take it one step at a time."

Helen stood up and headed out of the office. She had a lot to do and not much time to do it. If in fact, Lynda Green had any connection to the Brewster killing, she would probably sooner or later start to get nervous.

"'Nother way to look at it," the lieutenant called right before she stepped out.

"How's that, sir?"

"What if she did the deed, wanting to make it look like her husband was the killer?"

Helen couldn't help but grin.

"Wasn't there a movie, or book, or something like that some years back?" she asked.

"Of course, Lipscomb. Where do you think I got the idea?"

CHAPTER TWENTY-FIVE

Helen wasn't sure what she expected when she knocked on the door to the Green apartment, but it sure wasn't what she got.

Lynda Green answered the knock with a baby in her arms and a little girl clinging to her leg. Helen blinked, as if suddenly blindsided.

"Yes?" the woman standing in the door said, obviously not even bothering to hide the sarcasm in her tone.

"Mrs. Green, I'm sorry. I didn't expect you to—"

"The kids and I just came by to pick up a few extra items. I called Ronald to make sure he wouldn't be around, but what are you people doing here?"

Silently, Helen held up the new, updated search warrant. As she did so, she mentally scrambled to get ahead of the game. The lady being on site had not been part of the plan.

"You've got to be kidding me," Lynda Green said as Helen attempted to hand the warrant over. She didn't accept the proffered papers, instead merely glaring at the collection of cops standing in the apartment hallway.

"We have a warrant to search this apartment," Helen said.

"So search it. But unless you want me to drop my baby I'm not taking that paper from you."

Helen decided not to push the matter, instead

motioning the assortment of crime scene people into the apartment. Mrs. Green grudgingly stepped back for them to enter, at the same time looking down. Little Sarah's face was screwing up and turning red.

"It's okay, baby," she soothed before turning back to Helen. "Didn't you people already do this a few weeks back?"

Again, Helen did her best to ignore the sarcasm.

"That's why you need to read the warrant, Mrs. Green. When we were here before, we were looking for evidence concerning your husband's involvement in the death of Diane Brewster."

Something got through to the woman. She knelt down and handed over her baby to the five-year old, still working to fight back tears.

"Honey, why don't you take the baby and go into your bedroom and shut the door, okay? Do it for mommy?"

As she watched the little darling sniffle, then nod her head and take the toddler by the hand, Helen wanted nothing more to just turn around and walk away. Unfortunately, she had her job to do and she didn't see any way to do it that wouldn't end up causing these kids any more harm.

After the two had wandered off, Mrs. Green turned back to face Helen.

"Explain yourself please."

"Mrs. Green, we're looking for any evidence in your home that would serve as proof of your involvement in the Brewster killing."

"You have got to be kidding," she said, just as a technician moved past them and accidentally bumped into her, causing her to cant off balance.

"What the…"

"Watch it, Tim," Helen said.

The technician shrugged, muttered an apology, then moved on.

"Me?" Mrs. Green almost snarled.

"Yes, ma'am."

The two women watched as three of the techs, loaded down with equipment, headed into the master bedroom. Lynda Green cursed and headed off in their direction, causing Helen to whirl in front of her.

"Mrs. Green, if you interfere in any way with those men, who are executing a lawful warrant, I'll have to arrest you. And I don't want to do that, don't want your children to see that."

"You really think I had something to do with that little slut's death?"

"I'm not sure. But my boss and I have determined that you're a valid suspect, and so…"

The sound of a vacuum hose, coming from the bedroom, partially drowned Helen out. She took Lynda by the arm gently, and herded her out into the hallway, shutting the door behind them so they could talk.

"So I get it," Lynda said, "when that other cop, the man, called me in with some more questions about my husband, that was an interrogation, wasn't it? Ron wasn't the one he wanted information on. Hell, you must already know all there is to know about him. It was me you were interested in, wasn't it?"

"'Fraid so."

"And that one man questioned me without even allowing me a lawyer?"

"You weren't under arrest, Mrs. Green, so he didn't have to read you your rights. Even so, if you'd asked for a lawyer he would have stopped talking to you."

"That's a fancy way of saying you people tricked me."

"Maybe, but regardless, we played by the rules."

"So now you think I killed her, don't you?"

"We have to explore all of the—"

"To hell with this," Lynda muttered as she turned and opened the door.

Helen followed her in, unsure of her intentions. However, the woman looked neither right nor left as she went down the hallway to the room into which her kids had vanished.

So far, the crime scene techs were still in the master bedroom, and Helen hurried after the Green woman.

As she got to the bedroom, Lynda left the door open when she swept in and gathered up her children. She hoisted the toddler into her left arm and took the little girl by her hand, then headed back out into the living room, catching Helen flat footed.

Barely looking at the policewoman, she kept going forward, deviating at the last minute to grab her purse off the couch. Pausing only long enough to sling the purse over one shoulder, she linked hands with her daughter again, while tears of confusion ran down the kid's face, and went to the front door.

She stopped there and turned back to a confused Helen.

"If you happen to see my husband, tell him that I've had enough."

She slammed the door behind her, leaving a roomful of cops looking at each other.

CHAPTER TWENTY-SIX

April 14

One thing about this town, it held plenty of coffee shops, with most of them relatively empty during the daytime. Over the last few weeks, since that disastrous second meeting down at the police station, when he'd come to understand they now considered him a suspect in two murders instead of one, Ron had taken to spending more and more of his days hanging around coffee shops, mindlessly roaming the Internet on his laptop and chugging down far too many various foamed, sweetened and caffeinated drinks. Already, he'd noticed a distinct tightness in the waistband of his slacks and unusually restless nights.

So much for his earlier hope that stress would cause him to lose weight.

Still, considering all of it, it was amazing he could get any sleep at all. The stray hour or two he managed to catch sometime around dawn ranked as a veritable snooze fest considering his current life.

Actually, he thought as he reached the halfway point on his latest unpronounceable beverage, he really shouldn't be hanging around these hideaways, swigging coffee. At least nominally he still had a job, even though the majority of his current students had stopped attending his lectures altogether. And a normal academic, faced with the certainty of losing out on tenure, at least had the option of staying on another year at his institution and planting seeds for his future.

In Ron's case, Dean Haskins had made it totally clear he had no future beyond the next few months.

So what the hell did he have to lose? Coffee shops it was.

He hadn't heard from Lyn and the kids for nearly two weeks and, considering the way she took off the second time without any notice, he figured he wouldn't hear much of anything from her. For a while there, he'd at least expected her to ask for money to help her get along, but nada.

As far as he knew she was still at her mother's house, and past midnight on more than one night, half drunk and feeling like crying his heart out, Ron had picked up the phone and started to dial their number. But each time he'd managed to fight down the urge and gone back to the kitchen for another beer.

He'd been talking with Walt Lowenstein on a more or less daily basis, but on that end not much had changed. As far as Lowenstein could tell, nothing new had developed on the investigative front. Ron kept looking out his window or glancing both ways when he got into his car, half expecting somebody to be trailing him. And he kept waiting for the knock on the door that would herald the Lipscomb woman standing in the hall, armed with another warrant for another search. Or, in the worst case, a warrant for his arrest.

But so far nothing.

Although on the bright side, the local news media also seemed to have completely forgotten him.

****

"But don't they have to do something sooner or later," he'd asked Lowenstein about a week before. "They can't keep me hanging out like this indefinitely, can they?"

"Technically, they can. Some investigations go on for years and years. Actually, though, if I were you I'd be counting off days on the calendar."

"Why?"

"Because the longer they go without coming up with something, the more it looks like there's nothing to come up with. The more it stretches out, the more likely that you'll never face charges."

"At least in court."

"Come again?"

"I said at least in court. In terms of public opinion, I'm already guilty. The adulterer who slaughtered his former lover in her bedroom."

"Doesn't matter what the public thinks, as long as the cops and courts don't have anything to go on."

"You sure about that, Walt? Why don't you tell that to my colleagues, or the trustees of the university, or my students or neighbors. All those people who won't look me in the eye, won't acknowledge my greetings. Tell them that I'm looking more and more innocent."

Lowenstein didn't even try to hide his heavy sigh over the phone.

"Sorry about that, guy. It's my job to worry about the legal end of things. Sometimes it becomes a forest and trees kind of deal. Any luck on the job front?"

Ron knew what his lawyer meant. Had he been looking for a new job? The truth was, he hadn't been able to find within him the energy to even try, but he didn't want to admit that. Might make him look just a wee bit on the edge.

"Not so far," he said, "but I've got packets out and I'm hopeful."

"Okay well, hang in there. And look at it this way. No matter what you may think of the cops, no matter how much you may think they're screwing with your life, remember the Lisa Willard angle, how they're looking at you for her too?"

"Yeah."

"Well, I know you're staying away from the news, but trust me on this one. There hasn't been word one of that in the media."

"You saying they're looking out for my feelings on that end? 'Cause I've got to tell you, I find that really difficult to believe."

"Not saying that at all. But think how much worse things would be if that part of it did get out."

Ron experienced a momentary surge of vomit, which almost, but not quite, made it up his throat.

Would there ever be an end to all the angles and possible entrapments?

****

So here he was, days later, camping out in a coffee bistro and drowning his sorrows in foam-laden, barely liquid junk, when the person at the table next to him got up and headed out the door.

Leaving their newspaper behind.

It was one of those random events that, by all rights, shouldn't have in any way influenced a life, but the simple act of his fellow patron leaving the newspaper on the table turned out to profoundly influence Ron's future.

With the natural curiosity of an academic, not to mention a business professional in the current economic climate, Ron found it somewhat difficult to avoid the local news. As the days went by, he found it easier, so much so that eventually he'd more or less stopped following national news as well.

But today, with nothing to do and too much time on his hands, the abandoned newspaper became something of a temptation. After all, he rationalized, what harm could it do? Enough time had gone, especially with nothing new to report, that coverage of Diane's death had surely all but faded away.

The person at the next table had left the paper neatly creased and folded to the front page.

With nothing better to do, Ron decided what the hell and picked it up.

After a few minutes' perusal of the A section, he realized just how little he'd really missed by not keeping up with current events. Stories on the economy, politics, and a new food safety threat could have been written two months ago, or two years ago, with little difference between now and then. He learned interest rates had bottomed out, one political party was accusing the other of negotiating in bad faith on some bill, and while the stats for assaults, robberies and rapes were all down in this part of the state, those for homicide seemed to be on an increase.

Here, here.

He also learned that some Hollywood star had been served with papers for being a delinquent parent and things in Afghanistan were going downhill.

Then, just as he'd decided to toss the paper aside as a worthless exercise, he happened to turn to the next to last page of the front section and saw it.

Had the story been text alone, Ron would have

missed it. Had it been a busier news day, with less of a hole to fill, the newspaper wouldn't have run a picture with the story. Had it been a day or so later, the story would have dropped out altogether. However, it just happened on this day that it was still a story, albeit a minor one basically reporting nothing new to report, with enough space on the next to last page that the layout editor had decided, what the heck, go ahead and run the guy's picture again.

A shiver ran through Ron, so violent he almost dropped his cup. Leaning over, he peered closer at the page. Such a small story, barely two inches, and the picture rather blurry and ill defined. Looking back on it later, Ron figured his subconscious brain had pinged on something that the conscious would have skipped.

But his subconscious did in fact ping, and Ron leaned closer to make sure he'd seen correctly.

His eyes hadn't been fooled, and beside the picture the headline, in fairly small font, bore further witness to something so fantastic he almost couldn't grasp it.

INVESTIGATION STALLED IN CALDWELL SLAYING

Jonathan L. Caldwell, according to the story, had been found dead in his home nearly two weeks before. A retired Navy captain, Caldwell had lived alone ever since his wife had died a little over a year ago.

Jonathan L. Caldwell. 72. US NAVY Retired.

Or, as Ron remembered him, Johnny.

"Call me Johnny," the older man had said on first meeting Ron. Despite his wife having recently passed away, the old man had seemed like a happy-go-lucky person for the day and a half that Ron had worked with him.

After all, a man had to feel seriously okay with the world to wear the seventies-style, polyester leisure suits and Hawaiian print shirts Johnny had worn.

Johnny had been the oldest person in the focus group.

The same group which had counted, as members, Diane Brewster, Lisa Willard, and Ron himself.

And now Johnny was dead as well.

Another thought, even more morbid, caused Ron to shiver all over again.

By any chance, he wondered, were there any others?

CHAPTER TWENTY-SEVEN

April 16

Ron hadn't entered this particular office complex in nearly a year, and the last time he'd assumed he'd never enter it again. As he turned the Focus off and sat listening to the engine tick down, he wondered, for about the fiftieth time in the last day and a half, whether he was being incredibly clever and cunning or indescribably stupid.

The office building, kind of a split one-story affair composed primarily of brick and glass, sat towards the rear of an industrial complex on the city's far east side. From his vantage point in the parking lot, Ron could just make out the letters "AK" ornately scrawled into the brickwork over the front door.

AK—Amos-Kettering Public Relations. The firm once heavily involved in the reelection campaign of State Senator Lucy Rawlings.

The firm that had, among other activities, conducted the focus group Ron had taken part in.

That same group of which three members had been murdered within the last two months.

Maybe someone actually would call it indescribable stupidity on his part, but Ron had finally decided to take matters into his own hands.

After reading the short newspaper account about

Johnny's death, he'd gone home and done some serious thinking. His first thought, naturally, being to call Walt and dump the thing in his lap.

But it seemed like for months now Walt had done nothing but preach caution and waiting. And quite frankly, Ron was tired of waiting for something to happen. While his attorney kept him sitting on the sidelines, his entire life had fallen apart, and he was just about through being a passive observer.

He'd also considered, briefly, bypassing Walt entirely and going straight to the cops with his story. Two or three minutes of sober thought had knocked that possibility out of contention. He'd thought telling them what he knew about Lisa Willard would serve to exonerate him. Instead, it had made them even more suspicious. So what would happen if he came to them with a story about a third member of the group ending up dead?

His third idea had been to hire a private investigator and dump the entire thing in his (or her) lap. But a quick mental tally of his personal finances had ruled that out as a viable option.

Three people dying in a relatively short period of time, all with the same tenuous link to each other, seemed to stretch the concept of coincidence just a bit too far.

It would have helped if they'd all been killed in the same manner. That at least would have given the cops something tangible to latch onto. But other than all three victims killed in their homes, Ron could see no parallels.

Just to make sure, he'd gotten on the net and dug up everything he could find on Johnny's death. Most of the stories, at least over the first few days, had carried a few details of his personal life, including the death of his wife a few years back, but didn't really reveal anything Ron hadn't already known.

Before he went to either his attorney or the cops, he had to have something more than just wild suspicions and far-fetched coincidences. Which left him, as far as he could see, with only one viable approach to take.

Walking through the front doors, he came immediately to a long, polished receptionist counter behind which a young Asian lady was speaking into a headset while at the same time taking notes on a legal pad.

"Yes, sir," she said into the mouthpiece, "I'll see that he gets it as soon as he gets back. Let me make sure I have this correct." She rattled off an address, waited a moment and, having evidently received an affirmation, said good day and flicked the switch on the headset.

Then she looked up at Ron and gave him a brilliant, no doubt practiced, smile.

"Yes, sir. May I help you?"

"Hi there. My name's Ronald Green, and I was wondering if either Mr. Amos or Mr. Kettering were in?"

"Uhmm–well, sir, there is no Mr. Amos. At least not for several years. But we do have a Mr. Kettering."

Ron smiled, doing his best to appear as non-invasive as possible, a pose he hoped he could hold all the way through.

"Does Mr. Kettering have a partner, or is he the sole owner?"

"Yes, sir. He's the sole owner."

"Okay, then. Is he available at the moment?"

"Well," she drawled out the single syllable, "he doesn't usually see anyone without an appointment. But

I'll see if someone can help you. Mr. Green did you say?"

"Yes, Ronald Green. I really need to speak to him if at all possible."

"Can I ask what this is about?"

Ron took a deep breath. He'd tried to prepare himself for this moment. If he told her what he really wanted to see someone about, he'd come off as a flake. But if he kept it too understated, his inquiry may come across as trivial.

"I was here about a year ago," he said, "doing some work on the Rawlings campaign. Something's come up concerning that campaign and I wanted to discuss it with your boss."

"You worked for us at that time?" Her cheerful expression, designed to greet anyone coming in and put them at ease, was becoming somewhat strained.

"Well, I was–involved–with the campaign so I was wondering if…"

Her brow creased even further, and Ron thought perhaps he'd overstayed his welcome, when she reached down and stabbed a button on a desk set phone.

She turned half away from him and spoke briefly, almost too briefly, into the phone. A crawling sensation went up and down Ron's spine, and he almost expected to see a couple of security guards come around the corner.

Then the receptionist hung up the phone and turned back to him, her expression a bit more relaxed than it had been a second ago.

"Mrs. Baxter will see you in a minute, sir."

"And Mrs. Baxter is?"

"One of our vice presidents. I'm sure she can help you out."

At that instant her headset buzzed, and she reached up to it, taking hold of her pen with the other hand.

Ron turned away from the counter and walked over to stare out the windows, his back to the reception area.

A few minutes later, he heard movement behind him.

"Mr. Green?" a woman's voice asked.

Turning around, he found himself looking at a slim, fairly pretty brunette woman in her mid forties.

"I'm Amy Baxter," she said, holding out her hand.

"Ron Green," he said, returning the shake.

The woman seemed to do a double take, but a moment later dropped his hand and was all business.

"Why don't we come to my office and we can talk?"

He followed her down a long, carpeted hall to a door which, to his eyes, seemed to be made of maple. The interior furniture was all tubular chrome and muted colors, and the outer wall seemed almost entirely windows.

"Please, take a seat." She gestured towards an array of chairs in front of her desk.

As he sat, she walked over to a wall cabinet.

"Would you like a drink?"

"No, thank you."

Shrugging, she poured a small glass of what looked like bourbon for herself, then left the cabinet and returned to her desk.

"I've worked here for eight years, Mr. Green. Been vice president of independent projects for the last three. And I've got to say I don't remember either your face or name working for us, either as an employee or independent contractor, in all that time."

Although the words sounded normal enough,

something about the lady's tone, an unnatural tightness to her voice, put Ron even further on edge.

That crawly feeling returned to his backbone, now combined with a sour taste in his mouth, and he still expected a security guard to show up at any minute and whisk him away.

"So you're familiar with Senator Rawlings's re-election efforts, right?' he asked.

Amy Baxter pulled a sour face of her own, then took a sip of her drink before answering.

"Not exactly our best moment," she said. "We did a fairly decent effort for the senator, but even so…"

"She lost."

"Yes." Another drink, and Ron began to wonder if she wasn't a closet lush, or maybe one not so closeted. "So what exactly does that have to do with you?"

His stomach muscles tightened. This was the moment of truth.

"Actually, I never worked for you guys as such."

"Do tell."

Ron wondered if it was only his nervous state that made the statement come out in such a sarcastic, strained way.

"But early last March, your company had just completed some copies of new television ads for the senator."

"Yes, I remember that. So what?"

Before Ron could answer a slight knock sounded at the door. Without waiting for a response, a young man wearing a pin-striped suit and suspenders entered the office, crossed the room and placed a file on Baxter's desk. He waited only long enough to receive a slight nod from her, then turned to leave.

But just as the kid turned, he came even with Ron's chair, and as the two looked at each other Ron saw a start of recognition on the kid's features.

No doubt his own face showed something similar. Not too many years back, the efficient young man in suspenders had been one of his own students. Try as he might, Ron couldn't remember the kid's name.

The youngster gave him just the briefest look before he crossed the room and went out the door.

Turning back to the desk, Ron saw Mrs. Baxter perusing the file.

"Yes," she said a moment late as she slapped it shut. "Sorry about this, just double-checking. I'd already done a check on our computer system, but every now and then something slips through the cracks. So I just had to make sure."

"Make sure?"

"That my memory was right. That you never worked for us. So I'm sorry for the interruption, but please get with it and tell me what you want."

That sour feeling flooded his entire digestive system now, but he was in too deep to go anywhere but forward.

Ron tried to marshal the best way to proceed, but was distracted by the woman in front of him repeatedly opening and shutting the folder.

A moment later, he felt like kicking himself for not realizing the natural cause of her discomfort. Regardless, at the moment his own need for answers took precedence.

"I didn't work for you, as such, but I was selected to participate in a focus group involving the Rawlings campaign. You had a dozen people out here for a day or two, showing us several series of commercials and getting our opinions on them."

"Yes, that's a standard practice in our business."

Another sip of the whiskey.

"I was wondering if I could get a look at whatever records you have on that group."

The Baxter woman seemed to blanch at that.

"Excuse me?"

"The records. Concerning that particular focus group, and the campaign as well. I was wondering if I could see them."

Keep smiling, Ron told himself. Ingratiate yourself as much as you can. Don't let her see you as a threat. Obviously, for whatever reason, she hadn't recognized either his name or face from the news, and he hoped to keep it that way.

Back before he'd stopped watching or reading the local news, there'd naturally been a lot of coverage of his affair with Diane. But only once, in passing, had Ron ever seen it mentioned where the two of them had met. While at the time he hadn't exactly been in the mood to devour and analyze the news, he hoped any other mentions of their meeting had been just as slight.

At the same time, he felt something like an old-time circus performer putting his head in the open jaws of a lion. Had the cops bothered to come down here and question people about the time he and Diane had spent here? On the one hand it seemed like it should have been a natural move on their part.

On the other, he had never made any secret of when and how they met, had in fact volunteered the information, and the info hadn't done anything whatsoever in the form of exonerating him, so there was a chance the cops had dismissed with checking his story.

After all, what could it have to do with the fact that Diane was dead and they were sure they knew the murderer?

Still, that head in the lion's jaws image wouldn't leave him.

"That's an unusual request, Mr. Green. And I've got to admit I'm a bit concerned. Exactly why do you want that data?"

Ron had rehearsed this scene in his head a dozen times, and now he hoped he could pull it off. The most important thing, he knew, was to present as much truth as he could comfortably reveal.

"Actually, it was rather fortunate you picked me for the group. I'm a business teacher, and I've been working on a book project concerning focus groups and their dynamics. As I was working the other night, I realized what my book really needs is some firsthand accounts, and with several people in this city who've taken part in such an activity…"

A momentary frown creased Mrs. Baxter's forehead.

"I don't quite follow, Mr. Green. Wouldn't your own experiences serve just as well? After all, you were there?"

Ron started to provide a pat answer, concerning academic objectivity and such, when a flash of black through the windows caught his eye.

The office he sat in was towards the back of the building, and as Ron had sat there talking with her, it hadn't registered on his mind that he was looking out at a parking lot. Obviously, the parking lot from which he'd entered the front of the building was not the only one, and in the lot her windows faced out onto a police squad car had just pulled up.

He looked back at the woman behind the desk and noticed her pale and quivering face.

"Thanks a lot, lady. I came here peacefully enough, not intending to bother you people, and you…"

"Don't take me for a fool, mister." Ron marveled that even in her obvious state she managed to retain her composure. "Did you think I wouldn't recognize your name? As soon as Marilyn buzzed me from the desk I was on the phone with the cops. And you should know that…"

A knock at the door interrupted her. Without waiting for any kind of invitation, the door opened and two young uniformed officers entered.

"You okay, ma'am?" one of them asked.

"So far. But if you would please…" She gestured towards Ron, sitting quietly in place.

"Mr. Green?"

Ron turned around.

"Yes, officer?"

"The lady wants you to leave. Would you come with us please?"

Trembling, Ron had never felt so humiliated in his life. Even over the last few months, with his name and story plastered all over the local media; even when he would walk into his classrooms and see one or two students there, if he was lucky; not even when the dean of the business school had informed him of his termination, had he felt so personally degraded as now.

He'd set out be a big hero, Richard Kimble from *The Fugitive*, and he'd fallen flat on his face. Even worse, for all the letdown he hadn't acquired a single piece of information.

Head hung down, trying but failing to muster some

shred of dignity, he stood up and followed the cops out the door.

"Mr. Green," Amy Baxter called out to him. All three men at the doorway turned to look back.

"Just so you know, I'm intending to file a restraining order with the county. I don't want you coming around these offices again. Understand?"

Still bowed, more humbled than even a second ago, Ron turned back and let the officers escort him outside.

"Where's your car?" one of them asked.

"Out front."

"Let's go then."

They took him down the long middle hallways, past an assortment of offices and rooms, a few of which he vaguely recognized from his prior visit the year before, and out into the front lobby. As they passed by several firm workers and clients, some individually and some in small clusters, Ron saw all of the shocked looks, the whispered questions, the sudden turnings away.

It felt almost like the kind of perp walk you sometimes see on TV, and Ron now understood why all those famous people, even the ones already famous, tried to turn away from cameras, tried to cover their faces with jackets, coats or scarves.

It wasn't so much the fear of being recognized as that they didn't want the public to see the shame and humiliation etched across those features.

Yeah, Ron understood so much of it now.

As the final capping degradation, just as they got to the outer lobby they passed the young man from a few minutes before, Ron's former student, who now had the experience of seeing his former professor being hauled out of his current place of business by two cops.

Cullen. The name leaped into Ron's head. Andrew Cullen. A smart kid, not the brightest Ron had ever had, but smart nonetheless.

What must the kid be thinking now?

The patrolmen took Ron all the way to his car and made sure he was behind the wheel before they relaxed a bit.

"You heard what the lady said, mister." This from the one who had yet spoken. "My guess is that she's on the phone to her lawyers now. So if I were you I'd steer clear of this place."

"No problem," Ron said as he fired up the engine, feeling a bit of confidence coming back to him. "For what it's worth, you may want to also make sure word of this gets to Detective Lipscomb. I'm sure she'll get a kick out of it."

In a juvenile burst of anger, one he could hardly afford, Ron peeled out of the parking lot and left the cops standing there staring after him.

CHAPTER TWENTY-EIGHT

"So did he say what he wanted?"

This late in the afternoon, nearly six o'clock, Helen wanted nothing more than to go home, flop on the couch and order a pizza. Yet here she sat, trying to wrap her head around just what the hell Ronald Green could possibly be up to.

"He wanted records on the panel he served on last year," Amy Baxter said.

"This would be the panel in connection with the Rawlings campaign?"

"Yes. Mr. Green wanted a look at the records of that panel and, although we didn't quite get that far before your people showed up, I'm assuming he wanted to look for personal information on the participants."

"And he said this was in connection with a book he was writing?"

"Yes, but I recognized his name right away and well…"

Helen frowned.

"Tell me this. If his story had been legitimate, would you have given over the information? If you didn't know what he was accused of?"

The lady executive hesitated, and Helen could have sworn she saw some inner turmoil march across the woman's face.

"I doubt it, for two reasons. One, we're not in the

habit of operating like that. We use testimonials, focus groups and candid discussions quite often, and it wouldn't be very ethical to release private information about the people involved. Beyond just the squeamishness of it all, we could conceivably open ourselves up to all sorts of legal liabilities."

Helen tapped her pen against her knee for a moment as she let that explanation roll around in her mind.

"I can see that," she finally said, "but in this particular situation, since he'd spent almost two days with the people anyway, would it really be that big of a deal? After all, the man's a trained academic, and these days anyone with a modicum of common sense can find out almost anything they need to know on the net."

"True. If he had their names."

"Excuse me?"

Before Baxter could answer, a knock sounded at the door. Without waiting for a response, the person outside came right on in.

Tall man, really, really tall. Helen guessed his height at nearly six four. Full mane of silver hair, even though judging by his features he wasn't much over fifty. As for his clothing, while neither Helen nor any of the men she knew made a habit of shopping in the exclusive shops around town, she was experienced enough to recognize a hand-tailored suit when she saw one.

"Amy? I came right back as soon as they phoned me."

The Baxter woman stood up, and to Helen she looked faintly guilty, like a kid caught sneaking gum out of mom's purse.

"Mr. Kettering." She smoothed her skirt down, then turned to Helen.

"Detective Lipscomb, this is John Kettering."

Kettering nodded to Helen then moved up to the front of the desk, using the three foot wooden expanse as a solid barrier between him and his employee.

"Are you all right?" he asked. "Your people?"

"We're fine, sir. No one got hurt."

"I was filled in on my way here." He turned to Helen now, a decidedly unfriendly look on his face. "Is it true that the man who bluffed his way in here is a murder suspect?"

"Suspected, not accused. Yes, sir. It's true."

"So why is he running around loose? Why are you allowing him to bother my company?"

Helen felt herself bristling a bit at his implication.

"Suspected is not the same as charged. While he's a strong suspect in the death of a young woman, we can't just hold the man with no evidence."

"Well, when do you plan on finding some evidence?"

Helen's slight bristling had turned into a full-fledged dislike, so she turned back to the other person in the room.

"Mrs. Baxter, a minute ago you were telling me why Mr. Green wouldn't know the names of the other participants in this panel. How could that be if he spent two days with them?"

The woman seemed to be trembling as she slumped back down in her chair.

"I meant he probably wouldn't know them. When we first meet with a group, we assign them name tags. But first names only. Sure, some of them will get to know each other a bit more over the course of time, and some last names will be exchanged, but it's not a given that one member of the panel will know everybody else's names."

"What's the other?" Helen asked.

"I'm sorry?"

"A minute ago, before Mr. Kettering came in,"—the businessman had by now given up his perch at the desk and sunk down into another chair—" you said there were two reasons you wouldn't have given Green the names. What's the other?"

"Well…" The lady looked even more nervous than before, glancing first at her boss, then back to Helen, leaving Helen with the sudden feeling the woman's jitteriness had nothing to do with what had happened earlier in this office.

"Mrs. Baxter?" Helen repeated. "What's the other reason?"

By this point, Kettering was perched forward in his chair, looking for all the world as if he wanted to pounce on something.

"Amy," he said, and beneath the polished tones Helen caught the barest trace of impatience, "what's this about?"

She didn't look like a smooth business person now, nor like a little kid caught snatching cookies. Instead, she had the appearance of a teenager nailed in the act of her first shop lifting experience. Her shifting eyes and constant hand movements, plus a slight uptick in her breathing, all became noticeable.

"Amy," this from Kettering once more, "what aren't you telling us?"

Helen waited, figuring the boss man was doing as good a job, maybe better, of interrogation than she could have.

"We–we couldn't have given out the information."

"Couldn't?" Kettering said. "Not wouldn't?"

"Right, couldn't. Because…"

Helen suddenly had the feeling of standing right on the edge of something that could turn her whole case upside down.

"Why not?" Kettering prodded as the Baxter lady's uncomfortableness made her pause. "Amy, why couldn't you have?"

"Because we don't have any of that data. From the focus group for the Rawlings campaign."

"Don't have?" Helen interjected.

"Names, addresses, e-mails, or phone numbers. I tried to pull it up before you got here, detective. And we've got nothing. All of that info's missing from our files."

CHAPTER TWENTY-NINE

"You want to explain to me what you meant back there?"

The two of them were alone in Kettering's office, with Amy feeling less like a recalcitrant schoolgirl and more like a professional woman who saw the end of her career barreling towards her. The tone in John Kettering's voice clearly conveyed him holding his temper back by the thinnest of threads.

"John, I…"

"How the hell do you manage to lose all of the records from an entire account? Please explain to me, Mrs. Baxter, how that's even possible?"

Amy bristled, slightly, but managed to keep herself in check. His tone now shifted to the same in which her ex-husband had talked down to her, especially during the final year of their marriage.

"It was a closed account," she said.

"Yes? So?"

"So no one has bothered looking at it since last fall. If you remember, Senator Rawlings discontinued our services around the first of October."

"Of course I remember." He seemed to be working hard to keep the disdain out of his voice. "I also remember the one saving grace in that whole affair."

"You mean that she ended up losing anyway?"

Kettering seemed a bit taken aback by his

subordinate's tone, but a second later he actually broke into a slight grin.

"Alright, so I deserved that. You're saying that after the account wrapped, everything got filed away and dropped."

"Well, not right after. But as soon as we got our final payment for services rendered."

"Which came approximately when?"

"End of October? Something like that. I remember being surprised when financial called and said they'd gotten it. Considering how things ended up, not to mention the state of her campaign in general."

"You thought we'd be stiffed?"

"Well, let's say that I thought payment would be extremely delayed."

"So let's nail this down," Kettering said as he walked over to a liquor cabinet recessed into the east wall of his office. "The last time anyone did anything official with the Rawlings account was when?"

"First of November at the very latest, possibly a week or so before then."

"And under ordinary circumstances,"—he turned his back to her and began mixing a drink for himself— "we could look in the files and check the date."

"Right."

He turned, drink in hand, and lifted it up to her in question. She shook her head.

"But in this case," Kettering continued, "we can't look in the files for the date because no one can find the files."

"Unfortunately, John, that's the way it is."

Kettering reached up and tugged the knot of his tie loose, as if he felt a little smothered.

"Who was the primary on this account?"

"Mike."

"Howerton?"

"Yes."

"Well, crap. That doesn't help matters any."

"That's one way of putting it." Amy worked hard to keep any hint of elation out of her voice.

"What about his subordinates? Any of them still around?"

"Maybe one or two. I could check tomorrow. It's been rather difficult lately keeping track of who's…"

Kettering looked up from his drink, and Amy caught a flash of a look that had become increasingly common around the offices in the last year or two.

"This is no time for lip, Amy. You know I've been doing everything necessary to keep this place afloat."

"I know, John, but—"

"And don't think for a minute that you're high enough up the ladder that you're indispensable."

"I wouldn't dream of—"

"Good, just so we get each other. Now, first thing in the morning track down anyone we have who worked on that account and, goddammit, find those records."

"John—" Amy paused, hesitant about irritating her boss any further— "do we really need to worry about it? The cops probably scared Green off, and even if they didn't—"

Sighing, her boss set his glass down on the desktop.

"I expected faster thinking from you, Amy. I'm not concerned about Green as such. I'm worried about liability."

"Liability?"

"Yes, this Brewster woman. The one Green killed?

What will her friends and family do if it becomes common knowledge that the two of them met each other here?"

"You're joking, right? You're worried about a lawsuit?"

"I'm worried about keeping the reputation of this company intact, and I'll do whatever it takes for that to happen. Are we clear, Mrs. Baxter?"

She looked down, realizing, possibly a bit too late, that she'd done the one thing no one in this firm ever wanted to do.

She'd pissed off the boss.

"Yes, sir. First thing in the morning. Surely there's at least one person still around here who worked on the account."

Kettering shot her a look, his face twisting in such a way that indicated he contemplated taking that last remark as a personal dig. "Make sure it gets done," he said before leaving the office.

Amy slumped down into a chair, hand over her mouth in a mental effort to keep down the gorge threatening to rise inside of her.

How much more of this tension, she wondered, could any of them take?

CHAPTER THIRTY

"What kind of fuckin' bone-headed move was that?"

Ron had never heard Walt Lowenstein either curse or yell, and his doing so showed just how on edge he was. Ron figured if he didn't do something to defuse the situation quickly, on top of everything else, he would have to start looking for a new lawyer.

"Walt."

"No! I don't want to hear it, not right now. I told you to let me handle this. For God's sake, you're paying me to handle this for you, and I've been working like hell behind the scenes to do just that. And so far, despite the fact that you're the main target in their crosshairs, for two murders no less, I've managed to keep you from being charged. The last thing we need right now, the very last thing, is for you to go playing Batman on your own and screw up the whole damned thing. Jesus!"

Lowenstein kicked a small metal trash can next to his desk, sending it flying across the room and papers rolling out of it.

Then, seemingly deflated, he plopped himself in the chair behind his desk.

"Why, Ron? For chrissakes, just tell me why you would do something so unbelievably stupid as that?"

"Because of Johnny," Ron replied, almost in a whisper.

"Who?"

"Johnny Caldwell. An old retired Air Force guy. Somewhere in his seventies. His wife…"

"Waitaminnit. I don't get what you're—"

"His wife died a couple years back, and since then he spent most of his time just puttering around his house, feeling useless. Just marking time."

"What are you…?"

"Then, a little over a year ago, he got an invitation to join a bunch of other people and take part, for a few days, in a political campaign. At first, he almost refused. Then he figured, what the hell, it would get him out of the house for a few days, introduce him to some new people, and who knew, maybe…"

"Ron," Lowenstein said, his own voice a near whisper, "you're talking about this guy in the past tense."

"Yes, I am." Ron's eyes snapped, and the almost-dreamy monotone left his voice. "A few days ago, someone attacked Johnny in his home. A seventy-two-year-old widower. They beat his head in with a hammer, so many blows that, at least according to the newspapers, the coroner may never be able to figure out exactly how many."

"And this Caldwell fella, I'm guessing you knew him from the PR place."

"That's right."

"My God." Lowenstein slumped low behind his desk, his eyes assuming a glazed expression.

"So that's why I went out there," Ron said.

"Three of them. Your friend Brewster, the Willard woman, and now this–what was his name?"

"Caldwell. Johnny Caldwell."

"Three people from your group. All dead? That's–that's—"

195

"Yeah," Ron said. "It's nuts, is what it is. But seems to me that it should be phrased as 'at least.'"

"Come again?"

"At least three. Diane, the Willard woman and Johnny. Three out of the twelve dead within a year of our group meeting. At least."

"You're thinking there may be more."

"Right."

"Which is why you went to Amos Kettering trying to get the records?"

"Yeah. I really don't remember any of those people. Diane and Johnny were the only ones I got to know at all, and it's just a fluke that I recognized Lisa Willard. But as far as I know, none of those three had anything in common, so I wanted to get the records, get the names and contact info of the other people."

"And see if they were all alive?"

"Well, putting it that way sounds kind of gruesome, but yeah."

"But instead you made a total and complete mess of the whole situation," Lowenstein concluded.

"Well–yeah."

The two men stared at each other. A fly buzzed in the room and a tractor trailer drove through the street below.

"I'm really not sure how to proceed with this, guy," Lowenstein finally said.

"Yeah," Ron said, "I know."

"You know criminal law has never been my specialty, let alone of the felonious nature. Even if it was just a matter of defending you in a homicide case, at some point I'd be ethically bound to turn you over to someone who knows the field better than I do."

"Right."

"But what you're suggesting here…"

"Yeah."

Another few shards of eternity ticked away in silence.

"You really think there may be more? Other than the three you know about?"

"Hell if I know," Ron said with a sigh, "but here's what I do know. I know for a fact that I didn't kill Diane. Despite what the cops think. And I know I didn't kill Lisa either. Again, despite what the cops think. And if I point out to them that Johnny was also a member of the panel, they'll probably just go on thinking in their rutted manner that I'm doubling down on this whole 'throw suspicion off myself' nonsense of theirs."

"Probably think the same thing if I tell them," Lowenstein said.

"No doubt."

"But if they find it on their own?"

"Why would they? It's not the kind of connection that just pops up. Hell, if Diane and I had only known each other for that day and a half, there would have been no reason for them to connect the two of us."

"So you may have, in the most inadvertent way possible, done yourself some good here. You've forced the police to look into what happened at Amos Kettering, and they'll be on the lookout for any more connections."

"I think, Walt, that you've got more faith in the cops than I do. Can you help this newfound wisdom of theirs by passing on the news about Johnny?"

"You're not listening to me, Ron. That's the beauty of it. I won't have to. After you stormed in there today, asking for the group records, the cops will want the same

197

thing, wondering what you were so interested in, and they'll find the connection. It's even better if they find it on their own. Like you said, if we bring it up, they may dig their heels in even more. And there's another angle to this."

"Which is?"

"If there is something weird going on here, the other people will get police protection, and they'll be okay."

"If?"

"Huh?"

"If there haven't already been other victims we haven't heard about yet. You watch the news, Walt. We usually average over a hundred killings in this city each year."

"So?"

"So it would be fairly easy to have an obvious pattern, but thrown in with such a large number, who's going to notice it?"

"Okay. First thing I'll do is make a few phone calls. If this thing breaks like we're imagining, you're going to need better representation than I can give."

"I can't afford some hot shot, Walt. Can barely afford you as it is."

"Don't worry about that. The thing I need you to do is call a guy I know."

Lowenstein pulled a pad of paper out of his desk drawer and began writing on it.

"Why?" Ron asked. "Isn't there a chance I'm about to be in the clear?"

"From the cops," Lowenstein said as he consulted something on his computer, then continued writing.

"Yeah from the cops? Who else?"

The lawyer stopped scribbling and looked up, and

for just a second Ron thought he detected actual fear in his attorney's eyes.

"Ron," the man said, "worst case scenario. Let's say this is all correct, and there is some loony out there knocking off members of a short-lived advertising panel group from over a year ago. Who's to say he or she's done yet? Who's to say you aren't on their list as well?"

CHAPTER THIRTY-ONE

"So let me get this straight," the lieutenant said. He looked grizzled and irritable, and Helen could only guess at the cause of his bad mood. Lately, it seemed that every time she saw her superior he appeared more and more on edge.

She wondered, for a moment, if someone in the department had gotten a call about her from John Kettering. For the life of her, she couldn't see anything she'd done out of line at the AK offices the evening before. But with some of those business types, you could never tell what would set them off.

And the air of tension when she'd left Amy Baxter's office the evening before had been damned near palpable.

"So let me get this straight," he repeated, "our suspect shows up at this advertising place and bluffs his way in."

"Right," Helen affirmed.

"And he's trying to get a contact list on all the people who served on this survey thing with him last year?"

"Correct."

"At least two of those people we're looking at him for their murder."

"True."

"Even though we don't seem to be able to make any

progress whatsoever in either of the cases."

Helen knew that he intended the growled criticism to make a point, so she took it without responding.

"Which leaves one huge question dangling out there, doesn't it?" said Jarvis.

"Yes," Helen said.

"What the hell does he want the other names for?"

"One obvious reason comes to mind."

"Sure it does," said the lieutenant, "and it's so obvious that it's damned near ridiculous. Was he trying to get a line on the other people in that group in order to off them as well?"

"That would be my first guess," Helen said.

"But you don't think so?"

"Not really. Our initial theory was that he killed the Willard woman as a blind, to make us think that someone was going after this group."

"Yeah."

"But there's a couple of things wrong with that. If that's so, then he already had, at the very least, her name and contact info. And if he intended to throw us off the scent by killing some of the others, he wouldn't necessarily have planned on stopping at one."

"You've been reading too many mysteries, Lipscomb. That's the plot of every other murder story I've ever read."

"I know, which is another reason I doubt it. It's too well known of a ploy, at least from the movies. But again, let's assume for a moment that he planned to kill at least a few of the others so that we'd think him innocent in the Brewster killing. That would mean he already had the info on how to get a hold of them, so why would he have to go to the source at this late date?"

A short silence descended over the office while the two of them stared at one another. Helen sincerely hoped her supervisor would come up with some sort of rationale, something she had overlooked to make the whole thing make sense.

And he didn't disappoint.

"Maybe he wanted to make sure we made the connection. After all, if he plans a string of these things, he couldn't come traipsing in here after every one and saying 'hey guys, guess what.' So maybe he thought if he made a big enough stink of it all that we'd go back and double check."

"On all our unsolved homicides?"

"We're dealing with a civilian here, Helen. All he knows about cop work is what he sees on TV. When fifty-five minutes went by and we hadn't pinged on anything ourselves, he may have figured we needed a push."

"I guess." She still wasn't convinced.

"And when you were there, according to that company woman, all the records of that group of theirs have disappeared?"

"Right." Helen grimaced as a slow, steady throbbing began at her temple.

"Their records for the entire campaign?"

"Not all of it, but a goodly portion, among which are any records anyone had on that focus group."

"But not their memories," the lieutenant said.

"Huh?"

"There's still people who work at that place, right. And yeah, it's been over a year, but surely some of them will remember the details of the campaign, if not of the focus group itself."

"True," Helen said, "but I can tell you now that the main guy out there isn't going to take much to having us snoop around."

"Too bad. We've got two homicides here that—" He looked up as Jack Hollis knocked on the door.

"Yeah?"

"Sorry to bother you, sir, but I just came across something I thought you'd want to know, maybe Helen too."

Helen glanced up at her sometime partner's earnest, intense face.

"What?" the lieutenant asked.

"I caught that case a few weeks back, the old navy guy killed in his home?"

"Yes?"

"He was a note-taker, lieutenant. Had all sort of letters, memos, calendars with notes on them, even a set of old-fashioned journals that he jotted stuff down in almost every day. So I started going through that stuff, thinking maybe there'd be something for us, some indicator of who may have done him in."

"This the guy with the hammer?" Helen asked.

"Yeah. A really bloody job there. Never know for sure, but ME figures at least twenty or so blows."

"Lots of hatred there," Helen said.

"Seems like."

"Anyway," the lieutenant brought the two back around to him, "these notes you found. What about them?"

Hollis's hands nearly trembled as he glanced down at the paper in his hands.

"The thing that jumped out was a notation from last May. It says: Go to AK tomorrow."

"AK?"

"That's what it says."

"Amos Kettering," Helen whispered. "The date?"

"The fifteenth."

"Anything else written down about that date?" Helen asked, barely breathing through her constricted throat.

"Yeah, something written down at the bottom of the page, with a notation that looks like a time—8:30 pm."

"What does it say?"

"Says 'didn't really care much for the first sequence they showed us, though the second and third were pretty neat.' Also says something about 'met a couple of interesting younger people. Want to talk to Ron and Lisa more tomorrow.'"

"Oh my God," Helen said, her breath now almost entirely gone.

"I've only gone through this stuff once," Hollis said, "and this is almost too much to swallow, but it sure sounds to me like this guy was part of the same political group as Green and Brewster, plus the Willard woman, were involved with."

"And he's dead now," the lieutenant interjected.

"Yes, sir."

"Beaten. Viciously."

"Yes, sir."

"Helen," the lieutenant said, turning back to the woman seated in front of him, "this makes how many that we know of?"

"Three, sir. Diane Brewster, Lisa Willard and now Caldwell. Different methods, though."

"Say what?"

"Different methods in each one. If it's the same

person doing it, Green or someone else, why aren't they sticking to a pattern? Especially if it's Green and he wants us to connect the dots, why isn't he making it more plain?"

"Well, all three took place in the victims' homes," Hollis said.

"Yeah, but—" she trailed off for a few moments, then seemed to snap back into focus. "Intensity."

"What's that?" the lieutenant asked.

"It's a matter of intensity. Look at it, Diane Brewster is hit a few times, probably to quiet her down, then strangled, about the first of March. Some weeks later, Lisa Willard is beaten to death with, as much as can be told, bare fists. Now we have someone who takes a hammer to an old man? And probably kept hitting even after the killing blow?"

"You're saying it's getting more violent with each one," the lieutenant said.

"Right."

"But if," said Hollis, "it's Green just trying to fool us, why would he keep amping it up?"

"On the other hand," Helen said, "we can't discount that this all may just be an outlandish coincidence. That in fact we have three totally random and separate crimes here."

"You two," the lieutenant said, "go back to where it all started. Get all your notes together, get everything lined up, then get back out to that firm and find out what the hell's going on."

CHAPTER THIRTY-TWO

The two of them entered the Amos Kettering office building at 9:30 the next morning. They presented their badges to the receptionist, who seemed a bit flustered at the idea of facing down two actual, honest to goodness police detectives, and within three minutes had ensconced themselves in Amy Baxter's office.

The lady herself wasn't there.

"Mrs. Baxter is in a meeting right now, but she should be free in just a few minutes. Please make yourselves comfortable. May I get you anything? Coffee? Juice?"

Both Helen and Hollis waved the offer away, and the nervous young thing immediately scampered out of the office, leaving the door open behind her.

Helen and Hollis sat down in two chairs facing the lady's desk.

"You know," Hollis said, "this only makes sense if the killings are connected. If they really are just coincidentally random, we're just wasting time."

"I know," Helen replied. "What's your gut tell you?"

Hollis breathed out an exasperated sigh.

"Same as yours, I'm guessing. That they're connected some way, but damned if I can figure out how."

"Sure. And if they are—"

Helen stopped herself in mid sentence as Amy Baxter walked into her office. She nodded to both of the detectives, then sat down behind her desk. Placing a folder she'd been carrying into one of the drawers, she looked up at her visitors, smoothing the sleeves of her pale blue jacket as she did so.

Helen had the distinct feeling the lady had been buying time for some reason.

"Detective–Lipscomb, is it?"

"Yes," Helen said. "And this is Detective Hollis."

Baxter gave Jack just the quickest inspection before turning back to Helen.

"What can I do for you? I'm guessing this has to do with Mr. Green's *visit* of the other day?"

"In a way. Have you been able to find any of the records on the group he participated in?"

"I'm afraid not. Things have been kind of topsy-turvy here the last several months and—"

"Topsy turvy how?" Hollis interrupted.

The lady looked at him, and for a second Helen got the impression she wasn't going to answer the question. She did, directing her answer to Helen.

"We've had an unusual turnover in personnel lately, lots of people coming and going. We've done the best we can to keep up but…" She spread her hands in what she no doubt intended as a placating gesture.

"Is it unusual for you to lose nearly all the records on a client's account?" Helen asked.

"Of course it is. If this wasn't an aberration we couldn't stay in business. But I'm afraid that I just don't know—"

"What about personnel?"

"Excuse me?"

"Your people who worked on the account," Hollis said. "Could we talk to them?"

"Well, of course…but…well, you see, everyone's very busy here, and I don't think—"

"Mrs. Baxter," Helen said, "we're investigating a couple of homicides here, quite possibly several. Do you have records of who works on which accounts?"

The woman's eyes flashed anger.

"Please don't talk to me like a child, detective. Of course we keep records."

"And as one of the vice-presidents, you can access that information, right?"

For a moment, the lady executive looked as if she wanted to snap out another harsh reply, but then the harsh light faded from her gaze.

"As I said, we've had an unusual amount of turnover in the last year or so, much more than is normal, and everyone around here is very busy. I really don't think it would be wise to bother them."

"Lady," Hollis's voice took on a somewhat nasty edge, "point us to the right people and we'll be out of your hair. We're trying to save some lives here."

"I understand that. But I need you to understand that I can't divulge company business without Mr. Kettering's approval."

"Then call him in." Hollis's face, Helen noticed, was starting to turn red. "Call him up and get his okay."

"He–he had to leave town this morning for a meeting upstate. I really don't—"

"How about his cell?" asked Helen.

For a moment, the lady looked almost ashamed, as if she couldn't believe she hadn't thought of that.

"He–he left instructions with his secretary that he

didn't want to be bothered while he was out," she finally said. "So you'll just have to wait until he returns to ask your questions."

The two detectives glanced at each other.

"You know we can get a warrant, force you to comply."

Baxter leaned all the way back in her chair, which usually would be seen as a posture of confidence. But to Helen, the woman looked more nervous than ever.

"So get your warrant," she said. "There's nothing I can do about that. But until then, please leave us alone."

Helen and Hollis looked at each other, a whole new raft of suspicions crossing the space between them.

By unspoken agreement, they turned without another word and left her office.

****

With each of them struggling to collate their own thoughts, it wasn't until they got to their car and snapped in their seatbelts that they began speaking.

"She was awfully nervous," Hollis finally remarked.

"No," Helen said, "not nervous, scared. I got the feeling she was about to jump out the window to get away from us."

"Why?"

"Her boss?"

"Well, he does seem the kind to heavy hand things."

"Maybe."

"Or it could be…" Hollis paused as he turned the key and shifted the car into gear. Glancing behind him, he backed out of the parking space and headed towards the parking lot exit.

Helen looked at him, realized he was still working something through in his head, and left him to it. Her own mind contained such a jumble of possibilities and theories that she was beginning to wonder if she would ever think straight again.

"Maybe we're not thinking big enough," Hollis finally said. By now, they were heading away from the AK building and towards the central part of the city. If traffic was at all kind, they'd be back at the central station, where the homicide division was located, in under half an hour.

"What do you mean, not big enough?" she asked.

"Let's say there is something going on having to do with that focus group. That it's not just a big coincidence and is more than just this Green character playing games."

"You think he's innocent?"

"I said 'let's say.' If there is something going on with that group of people, it's a logical assumption the PR firm is hiding something."

"Right. I thought that's what we were assuming."

Grinning, Hollis glanced over at her.

"Come on, partner. We can think more than two thoughts at the same time, can't we?"

"I'd hope so."

"So let's assume," he continued, "that it's not Green, not some random nut, and not anyone at the PR firm. Who else would potentially have a grudge against the members of that group? Who else is involved in this whole thing?"

They continued down the road, managing to hit three green lights in a row, as he let Helen mull it over. Actually, she got it within about three seconds but had to take a little extra time to come to grips with the idea.

"The senator," she finally said.

"Bingo. State senator, or rather former state senator, Lucy Rawlings. We actually should kick ourselves for overlooking it back there."

"You mean we should have asked Baxter if someone from the senator's campaign team was in on their work?"

"Yeah. We should have, but we didn't think of it."

"We could turn around and go back," Helen said.

"We could."

Their luck finally ran out, and Hollis stopped at a red light.

"Or we could wait," he said.

"Because," Helen said, "we may be about to implicate a former state official in multiple homicides."

"It's a possibility. At the very least, someone associated with her."

"But what about motive?" Helen asked. "If in fact someone on the senator's staff, or at least in her orbit, is involved, for what reason? What could be gained? Especially since the election's long done?"

The light turned green and Hollis accelerated through the intersection.

"So what do you think?" he asked after a few minutes.

'I think we'd better go talk to the boss."

CHAPTER THIRTY-THREE

April 20

His phone rang at some point during the night. It rang a second, then a third time as Ron hauled himself off the couch.

But as he made his way upright, the room started to spin. He clutched his stomach with one hand and his head with the other. He didn't have to look at the bottle of bourbon canted on its side on the coffee table to know it was empty; his insides were screaming to him.

Meanwhile, his phone had stopped ringing.

Ron glanced around the room until his eyes lighted on the television set. How his cell phone had ended up there he had no idea, but it looked to him as too far of a distance to go just to check the message.

Then, as he once more began to sink into oblivion, the damned thing started ringing again.

Sighing, he somehow managed to make it to the phone before the fourth ring.

"Yello," he slurred, not really giving a damn what the caller on the other end thought of his diction.

"Professor Green?"

"Yeah." It was a male voice, kind of youngish, but beyond that Ron didn't recognize the caller.

"I wanted–I wanted to talk to you, sir."

"Who is this?" Ron managed to get those three

words out with fair enunciation.

"It's Andrew, sir. Andrew Cullen. I don't know if you remember me but—"

"Andrew?" Ron felt his head rapidly clearing. He stood up a little straighter.

"Yes, sir. I saw you several days ago down at—"

"Yes, Andrew. What can I do for you?"

"Well, professor, I've been following your *troubles* in the news. Kind of hard to avoid it."

"Yes?"

"So when I saw you at AK, I–well it kind of blew me away."

"Andrew," Ron said, his head now almost entirely clear, "I appreciate your calling, but it's kind of late and I was just—"

"Professor, sir. The reason I'm calling you is–I think you're being done wrong, and I think I can help."

As he processed that last sentence, Ron knew the smart thing, the rational thing was to thank the kid for his concern but tell him to keep out of it. It was what his lawyer would tell him to do.

But Lowenstein had been on this thing for months, and in that time Ron's life had only sunk deeper and deeper into the crapper.

So okay. His stint at playing cops and robbers hadn't turned out so well.

But that, he figured, only counted as strike one.

So okay.

He took a couple deep breaths, forcing his head to clear and his faculties to engage. "Thanks for calling, Andrew. You got some free time tomorrow we can get together?"

CHAPTER THIRTY-FOUR

In another time, he would have felt bad about roping some young kid into his problems. But it was becoming clear to Ron that he stood, more and more, on his own, and if he was going to get out of his predicament he would have to do so himself.

"You know, sir," Andrew said between sips of coffee, "you really stirred things up the other day."

"That wasn't quite my intention."

The two of them had agreed to meet in another of the city's mushrooming downtown coffee shops. Ron had deliberately picked the far and away busiest of these shops, figuring the more people around the less chance of them being picked out of the crowd. Immediately after making that decision, he'd grimaced internally, wondering if he was really beginning to think like a criminal.

Now, watching Andrew's hands shaking as he lifted his cup to his mouth, Ron started to get an idea of just how much stress the kid was under.

"Intentional or not," his former student continued, "you left quite a show behind."

"How so?"

"Well, for one thing the cops didn't leave for hours. Mrs. Baxter was running around frazzled as hell, and Mr. Kettering almost looked like he wanted to punch someone. So whatever you did, it sure had an effect."

Ron wracked his brain, going over the entire encounter in his head. For the life of him he couldn't figure what he had done to antagonize the situation so much.

"And the cops looked pissed as hell," Andrew continued.

"Come again?"

"The cops. They were all over the place and one of them, that lady detective, she looked pissed as all get out."

"About what?"

Andrew took a long sip of his drink, and when he put it back down on the table rotated it around a few times, making circles on the dark wood.

"I got to be careful here, Professor."

"I know."

"I mean, I called you because I think you're getting kind of a raw deal. For what it's worth, a lot of us former students do. I hear you're kind of being treated like a leper at the college these days, but believe me when I say that not everyone thinks that. Do you have any idea when they're taking you to trial?"

The non sequitur threw Ron for a moment, but he decided that if he wanted the kid's help, he had to be as up front as he could.

"Hell, Andrew. I haven't even been charged yet. It's why I'm still walking around free."

"So they're just letting you twist in the wind?"

"Something like that. My lawyer says to be patient, that the system will eventually work itself out, but I'm telling you the longer this drags on the less I believe it."

Andrew shifted in his seat and looked back and forth around the coffee shop. His shoulders bunched, then loosened, then he looked around some more.

Nearly holding his breath, Ron gave him all the time he needed.

"This is a good job," he finally said, "especially considering it's right out of school and the state of jobs right about now. I got pretty lucky."

"They treat you well?"

Andrew shrugged.

"Probably as good as most places. Pay isn't that great, at least to start, but they're kind of committed to the new people learning as much as they can about the business. They move you around a lot to give you as much experience as possible."

"Does sound pretty good," Ron said.

"And I'd hate to screw that up, especially in today's economy. Especially with…"

"With what?"

"Well, it's just that…"

Ron gave the kid some more time to gather his thoughts.

Finally, Andrew sighed and pushed his cup away.

"When you first showed up, nobody knew much of anything. We were all walking on eggshells around there, not sure what exactly was coming down. It's not exactly common at AK to have someone escorted out by the cops, and to then have several hours of commotion, well, we just didn't know what to think."

"Understandable."

"But within a day or so, stuff started floating around."

"You want to be careful with workplace rumors," Ron said, "they're usually at least halfway wrong."

"Yeah, so I hear. But the thing is–well–in the time

I've been here, it seems like a lot of people have quit AK."

"Quit?"

"Well, probably more like let go. I mean, I've only been there a few months, but already I've noticed several people just suddenly not there. Actually, sir, I don't think the company's doing so hot."

"Lot of that going around these days," Ron said.

"Right. And like I said, it's been a good opportunity, but I'm not sure how long it's going to last. So I'll just pass something on to you, and you can decide whether it will help you or not. Okay?"

"Okay."

"Well first, after you and the cops left, and after those other cops left even later, Mrs. Baxter got a real yelling at from Mr. Kettering. I'd stuck around late that day, trying to finish up some reports that had to go out the next morning. I had to go by Baxter's office and, even through those thick walls, heard Mr. Kettering carrying on. Something about incompetence."

"Incompetence?"

"Yeah, well, see, that's the thing. From what I heard, seems like after they booted you out that lady cop wanted to see the firm's records on that political campaign."

"Senator Rawlings."

"Right. Don't know why she wanted to see all the paperwork, though."

"Probably," Ron mused, "wondering what was in it, wondering why I wanted to see it."

"Maybe, but…" For a moment, Andrew looked as if he wanted to ask something, then he shook his head and went on. "But the thing is, as far as I can see, there are no records."

217

"What?" Ron didn't quite think he'd heard the kid right.

"That's what I hear. Mrs. Baxter and one or two others went through every file, both paper and computerized, looking for the records of who was on that focus group with you. And there's nothing there."

Ron stared out the window for a moment as he tried to digest it all.

"There's no record of any kind?" he finally asked.

"From what I hear. And it really has Mr. Kettering in an uproar."

"With Kettering as the main boss?"

"Yeah, and since Mrs. Baxter can't find any files on the Rawlings campaign, even though everyone around the place knows damned good and well we worked on it, it's causing something of a problem."

"But how would—" Ron paused, his brain beginning to hurt.

"Professor Green, if you don't mind my asking, just what is it you wanted out there? Why'd you come to AK?"

Ron hesitated, then decided what the hell. It wasn't like he'd been intending to keep things secret.

"I wanted to get a list of names and addresses for the people who were in that focus group with me."

"But why?"

"Because there were twelve of us, and at least three of them have been murdered in the last few months."

"And you think–oh, I get it. You're thinking someone in that group is knocking off the rest of you?"

"What?"

"You know. Somebody who was with you all has some kind of grudge, or thinks he does, and he's out to get the rest of you."

Ron almost trembled at the sudden realization and began to wonder if he hadn't been looking at it all wrong.

"You may have something, Andrew. But that wasn't what I meant. I wanted to get the list to warn the others. If it's actually one of us doing it–no, wait. That doesn't quite add up. If it was someone in the group, how is it that all the records are missing?"

The kid's face had gone a couple of shades paler than normal, and as he reached out to pick up his cup again his hands trembled even more than before. Ron felt suddenly ashamed at putting this kid, just starting out in life, in the middle of this.

Whatever the hell "this" turned out to be.

He stood up.

"Thanks for your help," he said as he held out his hand to the youngster. "As far as I'm concerned we never had this talk. Don't bother contacting me again, and for God's sake don't jeopardize your job."

"Doesn't feel like I've done much for you, sir."

"You've done more than you may realize, Andrew."

And indeed the kid had.

Now, Ron had at least a few more directions in which to go.

CHAPTER THIRTY-FIVE

When Helen entered the squad room the next afternoon, she noticed right off that Jack Hollis's desk appeared more cluttered than usual.

The three desks adjacent to his, including hers, were messier than the norm. Hollis was a youngish guy, and a bachelor, so it was only to be expected that he would keep his working area, to put it charitably, untidy. It was not uncommon to see at least three half-empty coffee cups, scattered pages of typewritten notes, and a stray napkin or two on his desktop.

Today, however, someone had piled a lot of his usual jumble on her desk, not to mention Larry Anderson's and Janey Turner's. Looking at the piles on her desk, Helen couldn't see any remote area where she could get any work done. Fortunately, the other two detectives whose territory had been appropriated were out. Helen had no doubt that Janey, at the least, would go ballistic when she saw what had happened to her work area.

Helen approached Hollis' desk. Crime scene photos, along with accompanying notes and file folders, stood in piles. Actually, upon close inspection, the array was, for Jack, rather meticulous. What looked like a couple of dozen piles of folders and papers, each with a grainy photo on top. Further, as Helen peered over his shoulder at the material, she saw what she'd expected. The photo on top of each pile was a crime scene photo of a dead body.

Furthermore, while the department's photogs meticulously took pictures from all angles and dimensions, the top photos were all of a kind: drawn back, full length shots of the various bodies. On top of that, Helen could easily tell that Jack hadn't been at all discriminatory in his selection of material. A mixed bag of male and female, young and old, and all races, his-cobbled together work area looked like a haphazard cross section of the city's population.

Bent over his desk, Hollis stared intently at the array he'd laid out, so engrossed in whatever had caught his attention that he didn't notice her come up.

"Whatcha doin'?" she asked.

Hollis looked up at her.

"Any luck with the lieutenant?" he asked.

"It took quite a bit of arguing, but he finally agreed to let me question Rawlings and her people. But he looked like I was making him swallow Drano while he did it."

"Figures." Hollis chuckled. "When you going over?"

"Probably tomorrow. I called her office today, but they said she's out of town."

"Hmm." Hollis looked back down at the jumble on his desk. "You want me to tag along?"

"Actually, I thought I'd have Janey go with me. It's looking like she has a part of this case too. So what is all this?"

"Something I'm working on," he said. "I got on the computer, went back over records for the last year or so, ever since that focus group met."

"Yeah?"

"Yeah, and these are the files on all the current unsolved homicides."

Helen moved her arm in a sweeping gesture that took in the material on the various desks.

"Just these?"

Hollis grimaced.

"Didn't phrase that very well. I should have said these are all the dead end cases."

Helen nodded. With most murders, even if they didn't have an actual suspect on hand, the police at least knew the main category the crime fell into: domestic situation, gang work, sexual attack, street crime, or robbery. What Hollis meant, of course, was that the piles on his desk represented those homicides over the last year or so with absolutely no open avenue of investigation.

"Looks like a couple of dozen," she said.

"Twenty-three to be exact. And three of them you know."

Helen bent closer.

"Diane Brewster, Lisa Willard, and John Caldwell. They were, at least according to Green, all participants in that group."

"Right," said Hollis. "But what about all these others?"

He swept his arm over the desk in an inclusive gesture.

"You're wondering if some of these others may be related?"

"Yeah."

"And," Helen said, "I'm going to take a guess that you have them arranged in chronological order?"

"Right."

"Any other connections at all between them?"

"Not that I can see." Hollis pointed at the third pile from the top left.

"Take this one, for instance. I caught this one right at the end of the year. Name's Randall Cummings, managed a furniture store. Shot with a single round in the back of the head."

"A mugging?"

Hollis grinned. "You'd think so, wouldn't you? Problem is that nothing was taken from him. Shot once, left for dead, and that was it."

"I'm still not tracking though, Jack. You're not saying that all of these unsolveds are connected to our case?"

"Of course not. But isn't it possible that at least some of them are? I got to wondering what if. Let's assume for a minute that Green's wild story is correct, that someone is out there killing off members of that bunch of his."

Beginning to feel weak, Helen snagged a chair over to the desk and sat down in it.

"What you're suggesting is that some of these earlier victims are connected to our vics. That some of them may have also been members of the group?"

"Wouldn't it be wild if they were?" Hollis asked.

"Shouldn't be too difficult to find out. Let's just question their families and…"

"Well, see, Helen, that's part of the problem. Some of them have friends and family we can ask, but some don't. Like this Cummings guy. A divorcee who has two kids who live out of state. And, as I found out when I did the initial groundwork, not much in the way of close friends who would know something like that."

"Still, some of them would have people we could ask. But seems like there's an easier way. All we have to do is go down to the Kettering place and ask."

"Sure, but there's something you're forgetting."

"What's that?"

"How would they know? According to the people over there at Amos Kettering , they've lost all the records on that campaign. So we don't have a master list to check these other victims off against."

"Well, maybe and maybe not," Helen replied. "If we think outside the box a bit, we just might have a master list available."

The two of them locked eyes for a moment, Hollis trying to read her mind, before he got it.

"You mean Green?"

"Sure. Why not call him in, show him the photos, see if he recognizes anyone."

"Helen," he said, his eyes fixed on her, "he's your primary suspect in at least two killings."

"I know. But at the same time he's the only person we know for sure was a part of that group. If the firm still had their records, we'd just have to check the paperwork to find out. But since they don't, we've got to go with the next best thing."

"But if he's our man, why would he conceivably incriminate himself?"

"He probably wouldn't."

"So what…"

"But what if he's not our man?"

Helen broke her gaze away from her partner's, not wanting him to see in her eyes any trace of the doubt she'd lately begun to harbor. It had seemed so simple at first. A young woman is killed, with the likely suspect her former lover. Then another woman is killed, one with the same vague connection, and it still seemed simple, if overwhelmingly ghoulish. The lover trying to confuse the issue, to make it seem as if there were some maniac out there and thus divert suspicion from himself.

Except that now they were up to three, possibly more if Jack's speculation turned out to be correct, and would anyone be deranged or perverse enough to kill a bunch of innocent people in order to cover up his guilt in a single one? Well, yes, they would. Helen knew of people walking the streets who were demented or calculating enough to do just that. Except…

Except that for some reason Ronald Green didn't strike her that way. Her training and intellect said one thing, but her instinct told her something else entirely. And even if Green was their guy, or even somehow remotely connected to the real killer, how did that explain the confusion over at Amos Kettering?

"You really think he's not our guy?" she asked Hollis.

"I didn't say that. If I had to put money down, I'd say he's still the most likely. Though I admit I'm questioning that more and more each day. But in the interest of complete thoroughness, why don't we bring him in and see what he says?"

"There's one other angle you may not have considered."

"Such as?"

"Who's to say that his attorney will let him talk to us, even if we present it as an effort to help him clear himself? Lowenstein will probably see it as some kind of a ploy."

"Quite possibly. But the same condition holds true regardless. Do we really have anything to lose by trying?"

Helen looked down again at the piles on Jack's desk. It was possible they'd been wrong, and if so something really heinous could be at work here.

On the other hand, Jack could be barking up a wrong tree completely, and all those others could be totally random killings, having nothing whatsoever to do with the Brewster and Willard deaths.

Again, though, what did they have to lose?

"I'll give Lowenstein a call," she said, "see if I can set it up."

****

On one level, Ron knew he was being incredibly stupid. More than anything else, a person in his position should never, but never, ignore his lawyer's instructions. And yet here he was, not twenty minutes after his last conversation with Lowenstein, climbing the steps of the central division police building and heading into the enemy's lair.

Walt, as was his duty, had contacted his client immediately after hearing from Detective Lipscomb, and had made it clear to Ron that they were not, in absolutely no freakin' way, going to waltz in there and start looking at photos from other crime scenes in an attempt to identify victims.

"I don't know what they're up to," Lowenstein had said over the phone, "but it stinks from here to Chicago."

"You think it's a trap?" Ron had asked.

"I know it's a trap, dammit. The only thing I haven't yet been able to figure out is what kind of snare it is that they're laying."

"But I thought it was part of the rules that cops have to play straight. You know, let my counsel know ahead of time of anything they plan to do concerning me?"

"That's the courtroom you're thinking of. The advocacy part of the system, not the investigative part. The cops can't out and out violate your civil rights of course, such as the right to keep your freaking mouth shut at all times, but there's nothing to say that they can't trick you into providing information against yourself. Assuming that you're dumb enough to give it. Which we aren't. So not only no, but hell no, are we going to go down there and offer you up on a platter for whatever dumbass stunt they're trying to pull."

And that sounded like it should have been the end of it. Except that after Lowenstein had hung up, Ron had sat there, alone, at the dining table in his empty apartment, drumming his fingers on the wooden surface and staring at the half empty bottle of Scotch on a shelf over in the corner.

The more he thought about it, the less he saw it as some sort of trap. And even if the cops did have something nefarious in mind, wouldn't the fact that he voluntarily walked into their offices and offered to help them go a long way in convincing them their suspicions were off base?

It seemed like clear reasoning at the time, but as the elevator took him closer to the homicide squad room, the second thoughts began creeping in.

As the elevator doors opened, he wished Walt stood by his side to yank him out of there at the first sign of trouble.

But it was too late. Helen Lipscomb and that other detective, Hollis, were heading his way.

"Mr. Green, thanks for coming." This from the lady detective, no doubt taking the lead, just as she had in their previous interactions.

Both cops looked around, Hollis looking rather bewildered.

"Where's your lawyer?" Lipscomb asked.

"Uh–Walt isn't here."

"We can see that," said Hollis, a slight edge of peevishness to his tone. "But where is he?"

"He–well–he advised me not to come. Thought you guys were trying to trick me in some way."

Ron rubbed his suddenly damp palms on his pants legs as the two cops glanced at each other.

"Mr. Green," Lipscomb finally said, "are you telling us that you came in here against the advice of counsel?"

"Well, yeah, I guess you could say that."

They looked at each other again, longer this time, before turning back to Ron, whose heart began to beat faster.

"Then we really need to be clear on this," Helen said. "You have the absolute right to walk out of here. You're not under arrest, and we really didn't even bring you in for questioning. There's no legal reason for your lawyer to be here, but it would be better all around if he was."

Ron worked to get his breathing under control. In the last few moments, he'd changed his mind entirely and now wanted nothing more than to bolt through the door, not bothering with the elevator, and run down the stairs and out of the building.

Yet at the same time, his rational mind told him that bolting now would make him look even guiltier than they already considered him.

"Okay," he said, hoping they wouldn't hear the quaver in his voice, "so what did you want to ask me?"

"Again, Mr. Green, you're not being questioned. We just need your opinion on something."

His throat tightening up, Ron nodded.

"And you can leave whenever you want," Detective Hollis interjected. "Is that clear? Whenever you want?"

"Got it," Ron managed to croak out.

The detectives glanced at each other one more time, and Ron thought he saw a faint nod pass between them.

"This way," Lipscomb said.

He followed them to a desk on the other side of the room, where Lipscomb motioned him to sit down at a desk covered with all sorts of file folders.

"We'd like you to look at the photos on the tops of these folders," she said, "just the top photos, don't look at any of the material below."

"Who are they?"

Lipscomb hesitated just the slightest beat before answering.

"They're pictures of crime victims."

Ron glanced at her, realizing even more how idiotic he'd been to come here on his own. If they were trying to trap him somehow, as Walt had seemed convinced, this was the moment at which it would happen. He knew they suspected him of multiple murders, and now his contention that coming and volunteering his help would further the idea of his innocence seemed beyond naive.

But not seeing an easy way out of the predicament he'd gotten himself into, he looked down at the pictures.

At first, he saw nothing but a mélange. The photos, all the same size and black and white, just seemed to blur together into a mass of bodies and faces from which he couldn't discern any specific details.

From the corner of his eye, Ron noticed the two cops had backed off. He turned his attention back to the desk top, and as he sat there scanning back and forth, the blur of images slowly began to resolve into distinct pictures.

It was a collection of all sorts of people. For some reason, Ron had expected it to be mainly whites, but there were multiple races, and the preponderance of the pictures were of women. One was of a small child, probably no older than ten, while another was of an elderly Asian woman.

And as he bent over and peered closer at the specific features, recognition slowly came to him.

Most of the photos were of strangers, and no matter how hard he looked he couldn't recognize them. Of course, part of that was no doubt due to the circumstances of the pictures. Ron saw the whole mélange spread out before him: shooting, stabbing, blunt force and a few of them seemed to have died in some way that, at least from the pictures, his inexperienced eye couldn't quite make out.

But after a while, from the entire jumble swarming before his eyes, three of the photos caught his attention.

All three were men, one young and two rather middle-aged. He bent even closer, his concentration so deep by now that he'd almost forgotten the two detectives standing behind him.

He knew these men, at least their faces.

Yes, beyond any doubt he recognized the three.

Though to be honest, the fact that he'd guessed ahead of time the possible connection the cops had in mind probably helped somewhat.

One was named Randy, although Ron had never

known his last name. Another one, a middle-aged black man, had called himself Josh. And while Ron couldn't recall the name of the third, he easily recognized the face.

All three of them had been members of the Rawlings focus group at Amos Kettering.

Yet in the same instant as he recognized the three, Ron knew he could in no way let Hollis and Lipscomb know.

He could do simple math, and as the two cops edged a little closer to him, no doubt concerned as to his protracted silence, Ron understood that, out of the twelve members of his group, at least six were now dead. But even as he stood there absorbing possibly the most frightening knowledge of his life, an even more basic truth surfaced.

He had to get out of this place. Walt had been right. It was a trap of some sort, and while being suspect in two murders seemed about as bad as things could get, being suspected of seven, and counting, was beyond worse.

"Well, Mr. Green," Helen Lipscomb asked, "do you recognize any of those people?"

"No," he said, using his hands on the table to push himself to a standing position. At first, he kept his hands in place, afraid that if unsupported his legs would give out on him.

"Sorry," he said, "but I've never seen them before."

"Are you sure?"

Hollis was now staring at Ron with a thinly-disguised suspicion.

"I'm sure," he said. "Never seen any of them."

"Mr. Green," interjected Helen. "Could you concentrate for a minute here? Is there any chance that any of these people were part of the same focus group as you were last year?"

"No," he said. "Trust me, if they were part of that group I'd remember. And they weren't."

"Maybe a closer look…"

"No!" he snapped, louder than he'd intended. "I'm sorry, but I have to leave."

Without looking at either of the detectives, afraid they'd read something more than plain fright in his face, he turned and walked towards the door.

He kept expecting to hear footsteps behind him, feel the clap of a hand on his shoulder and hear an order for him to stop. Somehow he made it through the door, to the elevator, down to the main floor and out of the building.

The entire way, he couldn't stop trembling. Up there in the squad room, confronted with those pictures, an aspect to this entire nightmare that his attorney had already pointed out suddenly became much more plausible.

How long, he wondered for the first time, before the killer came for him?

CHAPTER THIRTY-SIX

Lipscomb and Hollis stood looking at the door to the squad room, through which Green had fled just a moment before.

"You believe him?" Hollis asked.

"About not recognizing any of them? Not even close."

"We hadn't told him what we wanted him to look at, so he had no way of knowing that we'd made a possible connection between him and some of those people."

"Still," Helen said, "he must have sensed something was up."

"So why'd he come? And why'd he freak out when he saw the pictures?"

"The second one's easy. He thought we were investigating him for two murders, three at the very most. When we confronted him with evidence of possibly more victims, it's no wonder he took off."

"So why come here at all?" Hollis asked

"Think about it, Jack. We've all heard the stories about serial killers who dare the police to catch them. Lots of these guys think they're so much smarter than the cops, and they love flouting it. Maybe that's what we've got here."

"Maybe, but when he high-tailed it out of here he sure looked frightened."

"So maybe he's just not very good at the game,"

Helen said.

The two of them stood quietly, their personal thoughts racing through what had just transpired.

"Then again," Helen said a minute later, "there's another possible angle."

"Which is?"

"One way or another, we can be fairly certain that Green's mixed up in this."

"Well sure, but—waitaminit–what do you mean one way or another?"

Helen turned to her partner.

"Think about it, Jack. If he's not our guy, if he's not the killer, he is, at the very least, on the list to be another victim."

"If he is just another innocent person, he may have recognized some of those faces."

"Right. And he's a highly intelligent man, that we know for sure."

"So maybe if he knew some of the folks in the files, it didn't take him long to put it together."

"Right. In which case, he may consider that he's next on the list."

"So why hightail it out of here, why not…"

"Because," Helen said, a rueful grimace staining her face, "he considers us the enemy."

CHAPTER THIRTY-SEVEN

Leaving the central station, Ron felt as if his heart would explode at any moment. Sweat dripped off his face, and his vision blurred in and out of focus. It took everything he had to walk the sidewalk in a straight line, and he didn't dare go back to the nearby parking garage and pick up his vehicle. Fainting behind the wheel was the last thing he needed.

About three blocks removed sat a small park, and he managed to make it there and collapse onto an empty bench. Afraid someone would mistake him for a wino or a junkie, he still didn't allow himself to completely let go, but after some time managed to regain partial control of his senses.

Stupid. Stupid and more stupid. Of all his actions in the last few months, since this seemingly-unending nightmare had begun, walking into that squad room and offering himself up to those cops had been the flat out most moronic thing he'd done.

It took several minutes more for him to realize that, idiotic as the maneuver had been, it had at least allowed him to finally come to grips with his situation.

No possible way to avoid it now. Someone was killing off members of the focus group. Not just Diane, and not just the women participants. Someone had actively targeted all of them. For whatever reason, sane or crazy.

And with six down there were, at most, only six to go.

And as he sat there on a park bench, watching idle people pass him by, the ultimate truth hit home for Ronald Green.

He was one of those six.

The old cliché of living on borrowed time had always seemed hackneyed to him, but now he fully grasped the meaning of the phrase.

And he had absolutely no way of knowing how much time he had left.

CHAPTER THIRTY-EIGHT

April 25

Howard and Lucy Rawlings had their offices on the top floor of the Fifth National Bank building, located in the downtown area just a few blocks from the police station. As Helen entered through the building's glass doors, she found her queasiness amping up with nearly every step.

She stopped at a far wall to double check the building's directory, even though she'd made a note of the floor number before leaving the station. Realizing she was deliberately stalling a potentially uncomfortable encounter, she silently chided herself and turned to the elevators.

When the doors opened on the twelfth floor, Helen had managed to get her nerves somewhat under control. She would have felt better if she had another cop with her, strength in numbers and all that, but Hollis had been out of the shop doing some witness interviewing on another case; Janey Turner was testifying in court; and all the other day shift detectives had been scattered hither and yon. Even so, the lieutenant had suggested she hold off until someone came in, but Helen had decided to go ahead on her own.

The former senator's office sat all the way at the end of the hall, giving Helen even more time to question the wisdom of her move. Before she knew it, she had the door open and had stepped inside.

The young woman manning the receptionist's desk was swift and efficient, and in record time Helen found herself in a private office, confronting former state senator Lucy Rawlings.

Rawlings looked about as one would expect a successful female politician to appear. Her hair a somewhat frosted blonde, age anywhere from thirty-five to forty-five, but Helen knew the lady was a couple of years older than the outside figure. Peering closely, you could barely make out the faintest traces of a little bit of eye work, and the trimness of the figure in the light green business suit hinted at more than a little nipping and tucking going on in other parts as well.

"Detective," Rawlings greeted Helen as she got up and walked from behind her desk with one hand outstretched, "please take a seat."

Helen sank down into a chrome and black leather contraption that quite possibly cost as much as her monthly rent.

"So what can I do for you?" the former senator asked as she ensconced herself again behind her desk. "You said on the phone this had something to do with my campaign?"

"Well, actually it—"

Before she got any further, the office door opened and a nervous looking man in a blue pinstriped suit scuttled in.

"Sorry I'm late," he said.

Helen looked quizzically at Senator Rawlings.

"John Irvin, my attorney," the politico said.

"Attorney?" Helen wished even more she had

someone else there on her side, for moral support, if nothing else.

"Of course. I learned long ago that any time I'm talking to someone about legal matters, it doesn't hurt to have a lawyer with me."

"Legal matters?"

Helen felt herself flushing like a fifth-grader called into the principal's office. What the hell was the matter with her?

"Detective Lipscomb, when a police officer calls my office and wants to set up an appointment, I can only imagine it's for some kind of legal issue, am I right?"

"Actually, you are, but I don't see any reason for your—"

"Maybe you don't. But I haven't survived in politics as long as I have without being prepared."

Helen discovered a new level of irritation underneath the unease she'd been feeling. For a brief instant, she was tempted to make a catty comment about how the lady hadn't survived politics all that well, considering that she'd lost her first shot at reelection. But she decided to play it as cool as possible.

"If you say so," she said, hopefully sounding more flippant than she felt. "And you're right, I do have some questions to ask, but I believe the matter involves you only indirectly."

"Even so."

"What exactly is all this about?" Irvin asked.

Taking a deep breath, Helen bit the bullet.

"We believe there may be some connection between your campaign and a series of recent deaths around the city."

If Helen had hoped for a reaction of totally shocked

silence, that's exactly what she got.

After several heartbeats, Senator Rawlings herself broke the silence.

"Deaths?" she said.

"Murders, actually."

"Now see here," Irvin began before his boss cut him off.

"You said a series?"

"That's right."

"How many are we talking, exactly?"

"Lucy, please," Irvin tried to interject.

"At least three. Possibly more."

"Excuse me?" the former legislator stood up behind her desk, her face pale but eyes flaming. "Are you accusing me of three murders?"

"No, she's not," Irvin finally managed to butt in. He turned then to Helen. "You're not, are you?"

"Of course not." Helen placed her hands flat against her thighs to hide their trembling. She hadn't been prepared for Rawling's mercurial temper. "But we do think there may be some connection between the senator's campaign and the killings."

The lady took a moment to visibly compose herself, then sat back down at her desk.

"What kind of connection?" she asked.

Helen, despite knowing the case details by heart, pulled out a small spiral notebook. If nothing else, she needed to hold something to keep her hands from quivering.

"We have a number of local residents who have been murdered in the last several months."

"Yes," interjected Rawlings, "those of us in public life have noticed things are a lot more dangerous around here the last year or so. And we've been wondering just what the police department is doing about it."

Helen, hoping the lady wasn't about to break out in some sort of campaign speech, bit her tongue. It was true that the area, especially the metro, led the nation in violent crime stats, but she really didn't need a lecture on it from a politician.

"Yes," she replied as noncommitally as she could. "But these particular victims were connected to your campaign."

"Members of my staff?"

"No, but—"

"Volunteers? I can't possibly be expected to keep track of everyone who—"

"I'm not following this," Irvin piped up. "Just what is this connection you're going on about?"

Taking another deep breath, and hoping they wouldn't interrupt her again, Helen proceeded to lay out the story. Once or twice, the lawyer opened his mouth, but a look from his client shut it without saying anything. When she was done, Helen sat back and waited for their reaction.

It wasn't long in coming.

"Are you telling me that you suspect someone from my staff is doing these killings?"

"It's a possibility," Helen said. "One of several that we're looking into."

"So you don't actually suspect Mrs. Rawlings?" the attorney piped up.

"No, sir, we don't. As I said, one possibility is that someone on her staff, or in some way connected with the campaign, for some reason has it out for these people."

"But what possible reason would that be?" Senator

Rawlings asked, a distinct edge creeping back into her tone.

"Well, for one thing, you did lose your reelection. When that happened, how many people ended up losing their jobs?"

"This is ridiculous." She popped up from her seat again. "People in public service lose their jobs all the time. Usually gain a new one before the ink's settled on the severance check. What would be the point in doing something like you're suggesting?"

"Mrs. Rawlings," Helen began.

"Senator, if you don't mind. It's customary to use the honorific, even when out of office."

Not really, Helen thought. At least not at the state or local level. Maybe federal officials, but even at that they didn't usually insist on it. She was beginning to believe that the good senator wasn't as resigned and accepting of her defeat as she'd seemed in public comments.

"Senator Rawlings," she began again, deciding to mollify the woman. "Would you happen to know of anyone on your staff who didn't land a job easily?"

"Someone who would be deranged enough to go around killing innocent people, you mean?"

"Well, yes."

"Even if we accepted your absurd premise," said Irvin, "what would be the reason for seeking out those people? There was a lot of activity in the campaign, a lot of moving parts coming together to make it work. So on one small part, what difference would the opinion of twelve people matter?"

"Maybe it wasn't such a small part to someone," Helen said. She turned to the woman behind the desk. "Surely you had a portion of your staff allocated just to advertising and media?"

"Of course."

"So that's where I'd like to start."

"Start?"

"Yes." Helen had thought she was being obvious, but clearly this was going to be tougher than she'd anticipated. "I'd like your personnel records on everyone associated with the media aspect of your campaign."

For a second, Helen had a strong sense of déjà vu. It puzzled her, till she realized that only a few days back she'd gone through the same routine over at Amos Kettering.

"Detective," came from Irvin.

"Now just a minute." The former senator was in snapping mode again.

"I'll need to examine their backgrounds and also question each of them. So if you could just supply me with..."

"We're not going to hand over anything." Irvin himself was developing a bit of fire in his tone.

"At least not without more discussion," Mrs. Rawlings interjected. "For instance, do you have a warrant or court order or anything like that?"

"Why would I need a warrant?"

"Really, detective," Irvin said, "do I need to give you a primer on unreasonable search and seizure?"

"No," Helen said, more in Mrs. Rawlings's direction than his. "But I was hoping you would cooperate with me. We have several people dead, more possibly to come, and I need to track down whoever's doing it as quickly as possible."

The former senator took on a look of reflection and briefly drummed her fingers on her desk top.

"You said that this was only one avenue of your investigation?" she finally asked.

"Yes. And to be frank, not the most likely. But the quicker we can eliminate each line of inquiry, the quicker we can find our culprit."

"Lucy," Irvin began.

"Be quiet, John." She turned to look out the window, and after a moment Helen realized she was holding her breath.

Along with beginning to seriously consider the possibility that the good senator had something to hide.

"Okay," Rawlings said without turning to look at either Helen or her lawyer. "Miss–Lipscomb–go get your warrants."

Irvin stood up and motioned Helen out of the room.

CHAPTER THIRTY-NINE

April 28

"His name's Jonathan Wilder," Hollis said.

It was some days later, and he, Lipscomb and Janey Turner were seated across from the lieutenant's desk. It had been an intense couple of days, with one judge turning down their request for a warrant before they found another to grant it. Even then, the Rawlings people had proven obstinate, to say the least. Eventually, though, with a lot of brow beating, threatening and more patience than Helen had ever dreamed she possessed, they got what they wanted.

And one person jumped out of the pack and right into their laps.

The head man reached out his hand and took the photo Hollis handed over to him. The picture depicted a youngish man, probably no more than thirty-five, with a badly-receding hairline.

"And I'm looking at his picture why?" the lieutenant asked.

"He was the head media coordinator for the senator's campaign. Synchronized all their various media operations with the overall campaign."

"Synchronized?"

"Sorry, lieut. A few days of arguing with those people and, before you know it, you start to sound like them."

"And so?"

"And so Wilder was particularly involved with the arm of their operation run by Amos Kettering. From what I understand, he was actually on site for the entire day and a half that this survey group was active."

"So he saw how much they panned his product," the lieutenant said.

"Not his product, but the firm's, yes. He was the man in charge of turning thumbs up or down on the various commercials."

"Which means that he was the one who finally turned down all of AK's ideas?"

"Yes."

"I still don't get it," the lieutenant said. "If he flattened AK as far as the account, why would he have a grudge against the people in that group? I assume this is where you're going?"

"It's like this," Helen piped up. "And please bear with us, boss, 'cause this is kind of complicated. We started looking at him because he was the only person on the campaign who had any direct involvement with the PR firm."

"Meaning if there's any connection at all between the campaign and your cases, he would have to be it?"

"Right. So he looks at what the firm managed to come up with, and maybe he likes it and maybe he doesn't."

"Actually this plays a little better if he likes it," Janey put in.

"True. So let's say he likes it, and he thinks the senator has a kick-ass campaign coming up. You with us?"

"Sure," the lieutenant said. "Just get to it."

"Alright. So then, just because this is the way things are done and for no other reason, they convene this focus group and run the commercials by them."

"Which they then tear apart."

"Right, boss. So, with the bad reviews from the group, Wilder has to scratch it all, dump AK and start over again."

"Why? If he thought the commercials were okay, what did he care—"

"Because if he went ahead and ran them, and the senator bombed out, someone could at least partially blame his incompetence when it came to picking effective advertising."

"And they could prove that because of the documents left behind from the group," the lieutenant said.

"Right," Hollis put in. "And after he nixed that particular campaign, he eventually approved one from another agency."

"And how did that one go?"

Almost on cue, the three detectives shrugged.

"Rawlings lost, didn't she?"

"And what happened to this Wilder?"

"When Rawlings lost her bid, he ended up on the unemployment line."

"So?" the lieutenant asked. "Probably lots of people did. That doesn't mean—"

"I checked it out," Janey said. "He's been out of work since. According to a few friends, been trying like hell to get a new job. But no luck so far."

The lieutenant leaned back in his chair and stared up at the ceiling for a minute.

"I got to tell you, kids. I think you're reaching with this one. Lots of people lose their jobs every day. Doesn't turn them into serial killers."

"Well," Helen said, "there is one other little thing."

"Which is?"

"Our boy Jonathan has a record."

****

The address they had for Jonathan Wilder was a fairly nice home, split level, at the end of one of the ritzier cul-de-sacs in town. As Turner and Lipscomb pulled up into the driveway, they gave each other a look.

"Living pretty good for unemployment," Helen said.

"Yeah, but you know how these types are. They'll borrow whatever they need, max out their credit cards like nobody's business and do whatever it takes to keep up their flashy lifestyles. After all, if he looks and acts like he's down on his luck, who's ever going to hire him again?"

"Maybe, but from what we know nobody's hiring him now."

"I've been thinking about that, and it may not be as significant as we think."

"Meaning?" Helen asked.

"Meaning that last year was the election year, so who would really need his services right now? If he was still out of work this time next year, maybe it would mean something."

"Maybe. Then again, are politicians ever not running for office?"

"Yeah, got a point."

Helen turned off the engine and the two of them got out of the car.

Helen rang the bell, waited a few minutes, then rang

it again. Less than five seconds later, they heard a lock click and the door swung open.

Helen had her hand wrapped around her shield case hanging by her side. Had Wilder opened the door, she would have whipped it up right away. But as she looked down at their door opener, she felt her heart sink.

A little girl, no more than ten with her head covered in blonde curls, looked up at them.

"Hello?"

Both Lipscomb and Turner had noticed the light of expectation on her face as she swung the door open, and the sudden darkening of that same face. Helen, long accustomed to reading people's body signals, felt her abdomen tense.

"Is your father home?" Helen asked.

The kid's face screwed up and reddened, but she managed to keep the tears at bay.

"He is, but he doesn't want to see anybody."

Helen and Janey looked at each other, their bad vibes of a moment ago worsening.

"It's okay, honey," Helen told the now-trembling little girl. "See what I'm holding?"

Helen flipped open her badge case and held the shield down to the girl's eye level.

The kid's face relaxed, but only barely.

"You're policewomen?"

"Police officers," Helen said, she being the one, by silent consent of the two of them, to keep talking to the girl. "And we really need to see your daddy about something. Do you think you could tell him we're here?"

The girl's face relaxed even more, the redness of a moment ago dissipating, and something close to a smile almost crossed her face.

But her next words caused Helen's heart to momentarily stop.

"Did you–did you police officers find my mommy?"

****

Jonathan Wilder did indeed look like a man on the edge. Unshaven, with sallow eyes and wrinkled clothing, Helen's suspicions perked up the moment she laid eyes on him.

The three grownups were situated in the living room, the two detectives on a couch and Mr. Wilder perched on the edge of a La-Z-Boy. The little girl, Laurie, he'd introduced her as, almost nine years old, had been sent to her room while the adults talked.

"I'm sorry about your reception," he said to the two of them. "It's only been about three weeks, and I haven't yet figured out how to explain to Laurie that Julie, her mother, has gone and isn't coming back."

"What do you mean gone?" Hollis asked.

"Gone, left, took off, couldn't take it anymore. Pick whatever phrase you want, it all comes to the same thing."

"And do you know where she went to?"

"Not specifically. She called once, to talk to Laurie. The caller ID showed an out of state area code, but with cell phones that doesn't mean a whole lot."

"And do you know–" Janey glanced over at Helen before turning back to Wilder "—if she left with anybody?"

Wilder's expression darkened and he began clenching and unclenching his fists.

"I have a pretty good idea, especially since the bastard won't answer my phone calls."

"What bastard?" Janey asked.

Helen had sat back against the couch cushion, making herself as unobtrusive as possible.

In a situation like this, it was usually better to have only one person do the questioning, and Janey had, by nature, a bit less edge to her personality.

"A bastard who I once called my best friend. Name's Tim Kellerman. He and I went to college together. Both settled in this state, and over the years we must have worked on half a dozen campaigns together. One of these good-hearted guys, made you think he would tear his kidney out with his bare hands if a friend needed it. Over the years, I saw him charm his way into more women's pants than I can count, but I always thought he had his limits. That he wouldn't go after a friend's wife. Looks like I was—"

Wilder halted in mid stream, and his countenance took on a rather contrite look, as if he hated the idea of so easily spilling his guts to total strangers.

"Wait a minute. Exactly why are you two here? Has something happened to Julie?"

Janey flicked her eyes to Helen, who gave her the slightest of nods.

"Not that we know of, Mr. Wilder. We're actually here on an entirely different matter."

"Great, that's just wonderful!" The guy punched his fist into the armrest of his easy chair. "And here I went blubbering on like some sort of hungover college kid."

"It's okay, Mr. Wilder," said Helen, sensing the time had come to assert her presence. "Sometimes you've just got to get things out of your system."

"Sure. To family. Or friends. But not to total strangers. So if you're not here about Julie, and since she left on her own, what are you here about?"

"We have some questions," Janey said, picking up the thread again.

"What kind of questions?"

"About your work for Lucy Rawlings reelection campaign."

He laughed, a short, almost startled sound, got up and went over to a wet bar in the corner. Without even considering asking the two detectives if they wanted anything, he began mixing himself a Scotch and soda.

Helen and Janey waited while he mixed the drink, then knocked back about half a finger, before looking back at them.

"Rawlings," he muttered. "Christ, things just keep getting better and better."

"You worked for her re-election campaign, right?" Hollis asked.

"Yes I did. Marks the twentieth campaign I've worked on. Started out as a two-bit speech writer for a city councilman and worked my way up. Media relations is my specialty."

"So you were a spokesman?"

"Not even close. The spokesperson is the one who stands up in front of the press and pretends to answer their questions while not really saying anything. For the last few years, I've been a media coordinator."

"Meaning you're the one who gets all those press people together so the spokesperson can do his thing?"

Wilder took a sip of his Scotch, then glanced at Helen.

"That's about the size of it," he said." and most people would tell you I'm damned good at my job. Or at least, they used to say so."

"They don't anymore?" Janey asked.

"You saw what happened to Rawlings last year, right?"

"Well, she lost."

"Uh huh. Not even close. She bombed, she flatlined, she was shellacked, to use our current chief executive's euphemism."

"I'm sorry," Helen jumped in. "I don't quite follow."

"Of course you don't."

He took another, longer sip.

"You'd have to know Lucy Rawlings to get what I'm saying. But let me just put it this way. Nothing that happens, directly or indirectly, is ever the good senator's fault."

"Lots of politicians are like that," Janey said. "Probably most of them."

"True, my friend. But the honorable former senator is damned near pathological when it comes to never accepting blame. And since in the nearly twenty years of her political career this was the first election she ever lost, naturally somebody had to take the fall."

"And that someone was you?" Helen asked.

He finished his drink, set the glass down on the bar top, glanced over at the bottom sitting a few inches away, then finally shook his head.

"Yes," he said, "that someone was me. And ever since the campaign folded, let's see, how can I put this politely, the goddamned bitch has hounded me out of any possible employment. From what I understand, at least according to the few people who are still talking to me, she's made it something of a personal mission to see I never get hired again."

Helen glanced at Janey and could see her own

thoughts mirrored in her partner's eyes. It had been a long time since she'd met such a whiny, self-pitying drunk. If he'd been like this for very long, it was no wonder the wife had left. And yet...

"Mr. Wilder," she said, "we have some questions to ask you about the work you did with the Amos Kettering firm."

"Ouch." This time he did reach for a refill. "You really know how to rub the salt in, don't you, lady?"

"We understand the focus group session AK put together didn't go very well."

With the first sip from his second glass, his eyes began to glisten, and a looseness developed in the lower half of his face.

"Didn't go well is something of an understatement, isn't it? But I don't get this. Why are you interested in something like that? What's this all about anyway?"

"Routine investigation," Janey said.

The euphemism, a long-standing habit with the detective squad when they didn't want to reveal their true motives, satisfied most people, in most circumstances. But a guy like Wilder had been around the civil service/political arena for a long time.

And Helen could tell it didn't satisfy him.

"Routine, huh? Well I'll take that for what it's worth, which ain't much." He paused to take another, even longer, sip of his drink. "So what exactly do you want to know?"

"We're interested in contacting the members of the focus group that AK put together. But it seems the firm has somehow lost most of their records from that time. So any information you could give us about the group, the members, and what they were like would help us a lot."

Wilder, in the middle of another drink, began to chuckle. Then, setting the glass down on the counter, he laughed out loud.

"You want to track them down?" he asked, still grinning.

"Yes."

"I get it now. This is about the Brewster chick, right?"

"Excuse me?" Helen asked.

"That one gal. What was her name? Donna, or something like that. The one that college guy murdered a few months back."

The two detectives looked at each other. If Wilder was acting, their glances said, he was damned good at it.

"Is that it?" Wilder continued. "Do your 'routine' questions have to do with her? You thinking some of the people on that group may be suspects?"

Helen nearly held her breath, her mind working overtime to come up with some way to keep Wilder in the dark concerning their suspicions.

"So what can you tell us?" Janey asked, no doubt stalling for time.

"Unfortunately, not a lot." Wilder's hand drifted over to the Scotch bottle, then paused, hand hovering in midair. After a moment, he dropped his hand to his side and turned back to his visitors.

"I was there for that week."

"We heard the group only met for two days."

"Sure. But you don't just walk in first thing in the morning and set these things up. We had to plot everything out ahead of time, go through the actual process, and then debrief over everything once they'd done their job and left. I actually was more in the background than anything, around but not really visible for most of the time."

"So you didn't ever interact with the participants?" Helen asked.

"Oh, I popped in once or twice, checked out how things were going, but I never talked with them or anything. Actually would have been self defeating. If you want to get their true feelings about campaign material, you don't want anyone identified with the campaign hanging over their shoulders."

"Makes sense."

"Sure. And despite what some people, including Lucy Rawlings, may say, I know my job. So I really don't remember much about those people, except for the Brewster woman. Let me tell you, even from the background she was hard to miss. I actually thought about getting in touch with her afterward, maybe take her out for drinks, but just about then the wife and I were doing okay, so I decided not to screw things up."

He rubbed his chin for a minute, his eyes holding a faraway look.

"Seeing as how things ended up between me and the missus, maybe I should have gone ahead and made a play for her."

It seemed to Helen as if practically all the men she'd met recently were having marital problems, and she wondered for a moment if she hadn't been fortunate in not, at least so far as she knew, having to deal with that during her former marriage.

"So you don't remember anything about the other participants?" Janey asked again.

"Nope. But I still don't see what you need me for.

AK should have all the records you need."

"But they don't. That's the problem. We're trying to track down the other people in that group, and we don't have any leads at all."

"Sure you do."

Janey and Helen glanced at each other, both managing to convey their puzzlement.

Had they missed something obvious?

"We do?" Helen asked.

"Sure. That college guy. The one that the paper's saying killed the Brewster babe. He could probably point you in a few directions. 'Course, I'm not sure I'd trust a guy like that, but hey, he's better than nothing."

A look of firm determination settled on Wilder's face, and almost instantaneously he turned and began making himself a fresh drink.

No doubt, he considered his civic duty done.

But when, several swallows later, the two cops were still there, that look of determination turned to one of concern.

"Was there something else, officers?"

"Yes," Helen said. "We'd like to ask a few questions about your activities of the last several months."

"Activities?"

"Right."

"Why?"

"Well, this is a pretty high profile case."

"It is? I thought the gal was just a student teacher or something at the university. What's so high profile about that?"

"Well for one thing," Janey took over, "if her lover killed her, and considering how much hell's come down in his personal life since he became a suspect, and the fact of how they randomly met at the Kettering place, it's pretty spicy stuff."

A quick swallow of nearly a finger of Scotch seemed to not even faze the man.

"True. Which still doesn't explain why you want to ask me some questions. As I said, I barely knew either of them. Unless you're thinking…"

Helen jumped in right away to cut that train of thought off.

"Not at all, Mr. Wilder. It's just that our lieutenant, who's kind of a hard case when it comes to procedure, wants us to interview everyone in any way connected with the case. The more people we can absolutely rule out, the more we can focus solely on bringing Ronald Green to justice."

She could tell the political worker didn't entirely believe them, but he was already three sheets to the wind, if not four or five, so he nodded his head in acquiescence.

"So," Janey picked it up once again, "what have you been doing to occupy your time for the last several months?"

Wilder drained the rest of the glass and, without even looking at them, turned for another refill. If he kept on at this rate, Helen figured, he'd pass out before he could tell them anything.

But the man seemed to have acquired the talent of becoming plastered and talking at the same time, and as he squirted soda into his glass, he began answering Janey's question.

"Mainly," he said, "I've been looking for work. Which isn't easy, considering how badly bitch Rawlings managed to blackball me."

"We figured you were taking some time off. After

all, the political season doesn't exactly get going for several months yet."

"Spoken like a true civilian." Wilder raised his glass in a mock toast. "The problem with your analysis, honey, is that while the political season doesn't truly start until about the first of the year, or possibly late November of this year, when it does start everything has to be in place and ready to go. Which means, especially for all those congressmen, that as soon as each election's over they begin hiring staff, letting contracts, and ordering toilet paper for the next go round."

"So people like you, the nuts and bolts of the operation …"

"Are never truly out of work. If he's lucky, a guy will have a week or two off before he's hired for another campaign. Three weeks tops. And I've been idle for more months than I care to count. Actually, idle doesn't really tell the tale. I've been on job interviews, believe me. Probably more interviews in the last few months than I've been in my whole life put together. And the net result?"

"Not good?" asked Helen.

"Bust out all the way, man. All the freakin' way. But, hey, all of this is really beyond the point, isn't it? I can't help you with your problem, honestly I can't. Other than the Brewster babe, I don't remember any of those people that AK roped in."

"Maybe someone else who served on Senator Rawlings's staff?" asked Helen.

"Nope. When it came to media stuff, I was *numero uno*. If I didn't have the info, no one did. Besides, there never was any reason for the campaign to have that stuff. We'd hired AK to do a job, and it was their obligation to handle the details. So sorry. I really can't help you."

****

"Well?" Janey asked.

The two of them sat in their car, having driven only a few blocks from Wilder's house before finding a quiet place to park. They wrote down their individual notes on the encounter while it was still fresh in their heads.

"Long shot," Helen said as she scribbled away in her small spiraled book.

"Why? He's got motive, at least in a twisted way."

"What motive? His anger, and God knows there's a ton of it percolating underneath his skin, is with Rawlings as much as it's with anyone. He sees her as the reason for his downfall, not the group."

"Yeah, but who's to say…" Janey paused, her mind clearly working overtime, before she mentally shrugged her shoulders.

"And besides," Helen said, "even if he had any inclination to go after those people, he doesn't have access to them. AK kept the only records on the group."

"According to him." Janey pointed back in the direction from which they'd just come.

"True."

"Which if he was our bad guy he would naturally lie about a little thing like that."

Helen grimaced.

"This damned case is starting to fry my brain. I'm not even thinking straight anymore."

"For what it's worth, I agree with you."

"Yeah?"

"Yeah. I know his type, and he's not a man of action. He'll talk your head off all day and all night, get as plastered as he can, all while carrying on about how unfair life has been to him and what he'll do to make it right, but he'll never actually get around to it."

"But what about if he's got a big enough jolt? His wife left him, after all."

"Yeah, but we only have his side of that story, and who the hell knows the exact what, where, when, why and how of it?"

"So you think we can cross him off our list?" Helen asked.

"I would."

"Which leaves us exactly where?"

"Right back where we started."

"You mean Ronald Green."

"Wouldn't you say he's still the most likely?"

"For Diane Brewster, sure. No argument there. But even so, all these others, including Willard? I just don't see him doing that."

"Why not?"

Helen hesitated, working through exactly how she wanted to frame her argument. The truth was, more and more every day she felt her gut whispering to her that Green wasn't their man.

All cops had to go by their intuition more often than not, even in this day of high-tech forensics. "I just don't read him as a total nut. He seems more like a heat of passion guy than a cold calculator."

"Heat of passion?" Janey's voice raised nearly an octave. "From what you told me, he's a dry, dull professorial type. Where's the passion?"

"Look at Diane Brewster. Would a woman like her have fallen for a stodgy old dullard?"

Janey half shrugged.

"You're old enough to know, Helen, that there's no

rhyme or reason to why anyone falls for anyone."

True enough. In her time, Helen had seen much more unlikely pairings than an attractive young woman like Brewster falling for a middle-aged teacher. Whether the couplings were motivated by love, money or just plain old fashioned lust, in romance, or its close equivalents, the old line about books and covers usually held true.

"Don't forget," she said, "that I've talked to the man, sat across a table from him, more than once. Laugh if you will. But I just don't read him that way. Flying off the handle in a fit of rage or denied hormones? Sure. Once. I can even see him in desperation and panic killing the Willard woman to try to mask his fooling around. I could buy that. But more than that? Sorry, I just don't read him that way. I think we're off the beat somewhere."

INTERVIEW OUT OF STATE

May 7

It had turned into desperation time now. As chaotic as life had been recently, he'd actually lost track of the number of job interviews he'd gone on. Five at least, maybe more, and as he fell a little bit short on each one, his prospects became more and more dire.

The last one had been the most demeaning. A no-count town in the far northern part of the state, jutting up against the Iowa border, a town so small that he'd never dreamed a firm of any repute resided up there. Yet it had, and in desperation he'd applied for a junior level position.

Humiliating beyond belief, especially at his age and with his years in the business. But there you had it and, with the bank accounts completely dry and retirement savings half depleted already, he had no choice but to apply for it.

Of course, he didn't get it.

This most current possibility, just over the state line in a town almost as small as the last one, felt like his final chance. He was down to beans and rice six nights a week, and if he didn't get a job soon he'd have nothing left at all.

And the mortgage on the house still had about six years to go.

He started doctoring his resume as well as he could before sending the damned thing off. Did everything possible, all the tricks the old hands taught you, to try and cover up the fact that he hadn't worked in months. Considering the current job climate, no one would look twice at someone who'd been out of a job for just a month or two.

But over half a year? Even in this environment, such a gap would raise red flags.

Still, he'd done the best he could, and his best had at least gotten him considered at several places, even if he hadn't yet been offered a single position.

This latest one was so far away from home that he'd had to leave the afternoon before, driving nearly five hours to arrive at his destination. Once there, he'd secured an affordable room at a Motel 6, and asked them to wake him up at six in the morning.

His interview, with the company located right down the street, was set for nine. After showering, shaving, and grabbing a quick breakfast (thank God there was a Denny's on the corner), he needed all that extra time to ensure he looked as presentable as possible.

Which wasn't easy.

He'd lost a lot of weight in the last several months, and the suits originally tailored to his body now basically hung off of him. He also hadn't been able to afford dry cleaning for a while, so he spent several minutes brushing out the light-weight wool he'd brought along on this trip. Shoes also required shining, even though it had been some time since he'd worn dress shoes on a regular basis, and it took several minutes with a steam iron to make the plain white shirt he'd recently bought (two sizes smaller than most of his shirts to fit his shrunken frame) presentable.

Finally, he stood in the small motel room, fully dressed and literally praying that this time, this place would be the difference.

If not, if this opportunity ended in the same manner as all the others, he wasn't sure if he could keep it together any longer.

****

As he walked into the conference room, sparsely outfitted with a single wooden table and a total of eight chairs, his heart sank. His last few interviews had been at some bargain-basement firms, but nothing like this.

Three people were seated on one side of the table. The thirtyish man in the middle stood up, shook the interviewee's hand and gestured him to a chair facing the three of them. After a quick round of introductions, too quick for him to capture the names of either the young black woman on the right or the older guy on the left, the man in the middle got down to business.

"So," the interviewer said with what he probably considered a charming smile, "tell us a little bit about yourself."

Staring, he froze at the banal idiocy of the question. It was the sort of thing you asked college students looking for an internship, or at job fairs with 5000 people lining up for a 100 slots.

It was not, dammit, the kind of thing you asked a seasoned professional, one with probably more years in the business than at least two of the interviewers, and for damned sure not something you asked of someone you had personally called up. Someone who, by the way, had just driven over five hours to interview for your no-account job.

"Excuse me?" the middle man said. "Are you okay?"

He continued to stare at the three of them, at their blank, plastic faces and their rigid postures, at their fifteen-dollar haircuts and J C Penney business suits, and knew that he'd sunk too low, that there was no going back to his own life.

Without a word, he stood up, turned on his heel, and left. As he shut the door of the conference room behind him, he could hear their confused buzzing, but it didn't matter.

Four minutes later, climbing into his car, he decided not even to stop at the Motel 6 to pick up his things. There wasn't enough in that small suitcase to make it worth the trouble of stopping.

Ten minutes later, he found himself on the Interstate and heading home. It wouldn't be home for long, he knew that now, but hopefully at least long enough to conclude his business. He'd begun the business nearly a year ago, shortly after he'd lost out on that first job, and he now knew that his old existence was as dead as his victims.

It was time to finish things up, wrap it all up once and for all, and if he was lucky he'd survive just long enough to finish the last job he'd ever have.

CHAPTER FORTY

May 10

When, by his count, the forty-ninth commercial in four hours came on promoting the new remake of *Dallas*, Bobby said to hell with it and clicked the power button on the remote. As the television screen faded into black, he sat back on his couch for a minute to luxuriate in the near total silence. Except for the slight hum of electrical appliances, his home contained no noise.

Quite a contrast with the house he'd lived in for most of his life.

Most of the time, Bobby preferred silence. It was a passive vice that, because of his upbringing, he'd never experienced until the twentieth day of January. The day, forever etched in his memory, when he'd turned on the TV in his mother's living room, leaned back on her plastic-covered couch and, tickets clutched in sweaty hand, waited to hear the week's Powerball numbers.

When it had finally sunk into his momentarily-uncomprehending brain that he'd actually won the top prize, Bobby knew his life, somewhat forlorn up to that moment, would never be the same.

First, he quit his job down at the Dunkin' Donuts. Should have left there long ago, it was no sort of job for a twenty-five-year-old. Next, he bought his mom a house down in Key West, about as far from their home in the

Midwest as he could geographically get her, and found himself a nice condo smack dab in the middle of a downtown neighborhood undergoing massive gentrification.

Not that Bobby knew what gentrification was or whether it was desirable. No, all he knew for sure as soon as he saw the top floor unit, complete with balcony overlooking the city, ornate brick fireplace and hard wood floors, was that it was the quietest of the twenty places he'd looked at.

It had taken him and his realtor nearly three weeks of searching but, with an after tax total of nearly a hundred million dollars in his pockets, Bobby hadn't intended to stop until he found the place of his dreams.

And at the end of that third week he found it. Not exactly the best value on the market, and it didn't have the finest view of the city. The amenities weren't the most up-to-date, and the parking situation was far from desirable. But it had the one thing Bobby was looking for more than anything else.

Silence.

As soon as his realtor unlocked the door and stepped aside for him to walk in, Bobby knew he had found his place. When they entered, all of the sliding doors and windows were closed and, despite the fact it was the middle of the morning in the heart of downtown, Bobby could barely hear anything. The condo, unfurnished at the time, was absolutely the most silent place he'd ever been in.

As the realtor came in through the door, already launching into her spiel about the wonders of the place, Bobby turned and asked for the keys.

When you've got a hundred mil in your pockets,

things tend to get expedited like crazy.

So here Bobby sat, over four months since moving in. No more cars racing up and down the streets at all hours; no more Hairy Tony, his manager at the Dunkins', yelling at him to get his lard ass to work; no more girls giggling as they walked by the store and looked in at him mopping the floor or wiping down tables; and for damned sure no more mom screeching at him to grow up, lose weight, get a real job and, before she died and left him, find a nice girl.

Sitting alone in his spacious living room, with the clock clicking steadily towards 10 p.m., it came to him, for nowhere near the first time, that he could do whatever he wanted, yet didn't really know anything he wanted to do. He was probably the only lottery winner in history who hadn't been besieged with friends and family seeking loans, investments in killer deals or basking in his limelight.

Bobby had no friends.

And his family never had wanted to have anything to do with him.

So here he sat, in the quiet, wondering what to do with himself.

He could, of course, go down to any of the infinite number of bars or clubs in the downtown area and look for female companionship. But again, even with his wealth he found most women didn't want to be around him.

He could go on a trip. Head out to the airport tonight and take a flight for the first place that looked interesting. Or he could take another stab, via the net, of hunting up some of the people he met last year, back before he got his money, and make contact with them. A couple of the women in that bunch had at least treated him decently. Like a real human being instead of a lard ass.

Or he could…

A knock on the door interrupted Bobby's train of thought.

Getting up from the couch, he glanced at the new Rolex on his wrist.

Awful late for visitors, and when it came down to it, Bobby never had many visitors anyway. In fact, he realized as he made his way to the door, this was the first time in the months since he'd moved in that anyone had come to his place.

Curious, he glanced through the peephole, then leaned up against the panel for a closer look. He didn't recognize the man on the other side of the door, but the fellow looked like someone in dire trouble.

He threw open the door.

"Can I help you?" Bobby asked.

The man swayed for a moment before managing to steady himself.

"I need some help, please. My girlfriend… she…she"

For a moment, Bobby stepped back. The stranger almost resembled the television depiction of junkies going through withdrawal. Hunched over, face kind of pale and trembling, he seemed like he'd collapse at any moment.

"Your girl?" Bobby asked. "What about—"

"Please," the man said, "I just need…"

He swayed again, almost stumbling forward.

Worried, Bobby moved back another step.

"Stay there, buddy," he said, turning to the coffee table which held his cell phone.

"I'll just…"

Bobby turned his back to reach for the phone. "So tell me," he said as he turned back around, "what's up…"

Bobby got no further. He gasped in midsentence as the pressure formed in his gut. A shock of cold swept over him, he glanced downwards. It took him a moment to register the blade sticking out of his midsection or the stream of red blood running down his front.

Bobby looked back up at the visitor. The trembling, nervous man of a few seconds before was gone, replaced with a stone-faced, fiery-eyed demon.

With a sudden lurch, the blade popped out of his gut, releasing an even fiercer cascade of gore. Bobby's knees buckled, bringing him to the floor.

"You bastard," the man with the blade said. "You unspeakable bastard. You're going to pay for what you did."

And the blade moved towards Bobby once more.

CHAPTER FORTY-ONE

May 18

Ron considered it fairly ironic that probably the best day to clean out his office was graduation day. On the other hand, it made a logical kind of sense.

With everyone, both graduating students, staff and other faculty, occupied with the commencement ceremonies, and all the other students done with finals and out for the semester, the halls of the business college were virtually empty, allowing him to get in and out with, hopefully, no witnesses.

This wouldn't be the official severing of ties, of course. That would only happen after a trip to the HR office to sign forms, make arrangements for final pay and securing of retirement funds, and drop off any university-related paperwork. All of which could be handled another day, maybe in a week or two.

For today, he was making his own personal goodbye to his workplace of the last seven years.

He'd brought four storage boxes along, assuming that would constitute more than enough. Naturally, the greatest amount of his own paperwork was safely stored on various flash drives, and he had steadily turned in any student-related material over the last few weeks. Despite the simplicity of the task, he couldn't bring himself to do it. Instead, he'd spent the last twenty minutes or so slumped in his chair, facing the desk top, and wondering just when and if this nightmare would ever end.

"Word is they're letting you use the office until the end of June," came a voice from the doorway.

He turned and saw Ed Turner, one of the associate profs in the department, leaning against the door jamb.

"Ed? Why aren't you down at the ceremony?"

The tall, fortyish black man smiled. "Pulled a fast one. Told them I had to go out of town to a non-existent niece's grad ceremony. But right in the middle of my free weekend, I remembered some papers I'd left behind Friday. So figured I'd sneak in and get them."

His former colleague looked around the office, then settled his gaze on the four boxes stacked in the corner.

"Sorry about what happened to you, guy."

"Thanks," Ron said, not bothering to remind Turner of all the times over the last several weeks that he'd avoided meeting Ron's gaze as they passed in the halls.

After all, what the hell difference did any of it make now?

"So why aren't you stretching out your use of the facilities?" Turner asked.

Ron shrugged.

"Doesn't seem like much point to it. Anything I could do has been done, so what's to keep me?"

He knew what Turner really wanted to ask, but it took the man another several hemms and hawws before he got around to it.

"Have you found a position yet?"

With such an inherent bias in the question itself, Ron felt like laughing out loud.

"Seriously, Ed? A position? Don't you think if I had that you and everyone else in the department would know about it already?"

Turner looked a little chagrined, which made Ron decide to back off a little. After all, everything that had happened to him wasn't his colleague's fault, and even if the guy had made a point of avoiding him the last several weeks, he hadn't behaved any worse than anyone else had.

"Sorry, Ed. Guess I'm feeling a little sorry for myself lately. But no, I haven't found a new place yet, and I probably won't as long as all this mess is hanging over me."

"You haven't been around much lately, so some of us have been wondering. Have you had some interviews?"

Again, Ron couldn't help but be struck by his co-worker's ingrained bias. Although he hadn't come out and said it in so many words, clearly Turner thought the only kind of job Ron should consider would be another university teaching gig.

But Turner, like any stalwart academic, couldn't conceive of any job other than a professorship in a college.

"No interviews," he told Turner.

"Applications? Any feelers at all?"

"Come on, Ed. Get realistic. Once I leave here, I'll probably never set foot on a campus again."

Turner fidgeted for a moment, no doubt thrown off by Ron's directness.

"So what comes next?" he finally asked.

"Meaning?"

"Meaning—well, you know."

"Meaning am I going to be charged with anything? Has my lawyer heard anything from the district attorney?"

"Well, yeah. After all, it's been how many months now?"

Ron wasn't sure exactly how to answer. For some time, he'd been worried about what had happened the last time he'd encountered the detectives. He'd barely stirred out of the apartment, living in fear of someone coming after him as well. Lately, Lynda's phone calls and e-mails had become more insistent, wanting to know when he would be leaving so she and the kids could move back in. On top of that, he'd been served with the preliminary papers for divorce proceedings.

Just a total freaking mess.

"I don't know, Ed. My attorney says the longer they drag it out, the less likely of any sort of action. But it's just guesswork on his part, and until it's all taken care of…"

Ron shrugged, wanting to drop the conversation.

"Well, it's sure been a tough one," Turner said. "I saw your door open and just wanted to stop in and wish you the best."

Ron took the proffered hand, even though he didn't feel much emotion behind the gesture.

Without saying anything else, Turner backed out of the office and walked away.

About twenty minutes later, Ron had finished his collecting and trudged the boxes out into the hallway. He stopped at the door and looked around one more time, telling himself he just needed to make sure he hadn't forgotten anything.

Had he been over in the humanities department, he realized, he would have some profound thought about the new emptiness of the office mirroring the ongoing emptiness in his life.

But since he wasn't there, he merely tossed the keys on the desk and shut the door behind him.

CHAPTER FORTY-TWO

May 19

She was a youngish-looking woman. Not actually young, just working hard to give the impression. In a phrase that popped into Helen's head from some old movie she'd seen years ago, "forty-five trying desperately to look thirty-five." The blond hair was a good job, but a closer look revealed the darker roots. Her clothes fit well, hugging a fairly trim figure, except they looked like something a woman in her twenties would wear. The skirt was a little too short and the blouse a little too revealing. Even though, Helen had to admit, what both skirt and blouse revealed was pretty damned impressive.

The woman had come off the elevator and stood just inside the squad room door, looking around. Helen, who'd received a call from the uniform manning the desk downstairs, got up and walked over to her.

Within twenty feet of the visitor, Helen could tell by her body language that she wanted to bolt. Although not an unusual reaction from civilians visiting a police station for the first time, Helen detected something beyond the normal uncertainty in the woman. The wild flickering of her eyes and the jitteriness of her limbs revealed more fear than confusion.

"Mrs. Henderson?" Helen held out her hand, and

after a second of hesitation the woman took it.

"I'm Detective Lipscomb. Why don't we come over here?"

As Helen steered Rachel Henderson toward her desk she saw the visitor throw one last, longing look towards the exit before going along.

"Would you like some coffee? Something else?" Helen asked as the two of them sat down.

Rachel Henderson mutely shook her head.

"Well then, what can I do for you?"

"I wanted to talk about–ask about—" Without finishing the sentence, the woman opened her purse, rummaged for a second, then came up with a newspaper clipping.

Placing it on Helen's desk, Mrs. Henderson immediately looked away.

Helen picked up the clipping, noticed it was several weeks old, looked at it more closely, then set it back down.

While she'd had some idea of what to expect, she still had to mentally force herself to keep on breathing.

"John Caldwell," she said to her visitor.

"Yes." The woman stopped glancing around the room and focused her gaze on Helen. "John Caldwell. I knew him."

"How?"

"I met him some months back, last year in fact."

Helen realized she was holding her breath again but at the moment didn't really care.

"How did you meet him?" she asked. "Where did you know him from?"

"He and I were members of a sort of panel thing for a politician."

Breathe, goddamnit, Helen told herself. *You won't do anybody any good if you fall over in a faint.*

Glancing around the squad room, she saw the normal, sluggish late night activity, and the total surreality of the moment hit her. Probably none of the half dozen people sitting at desks, talking on the phone, or tapping out reports had any clue of the tiny, encapsulated moment of high drama going on over here in the corner.

"A panel," she finally said.

"Yes, and…" That look of haunted fear came back into the woman's eyes, and to Helen it almost looked as if she were going to bolt out of there.

My God, Helen thought, *she's figured it out.*

"Mrs. Henderson? What is it you started to say?"

"I think–oh my God, this can't be happening." Her shoulders hunched, and a new level of fear clouded her eyes.

"What can't be happening?" Although Helen wanted to reach over and give the woman a hug, tell her it would be okay, she had to stay objective with a possible witness.

"I've been worrying over this for weeks. I tried to push it away, figured it was just my imagination going wild. But the more I thought about it, the less I could let it go. Do you understand?"

"Mrs. Henderson? What can't be happening?"

The lady looked up, a nervous twitch jumping in her cheek.

"Detective Lipscomb," she said. "I think someone's going to kill me."

CHAPTER FORTY-THREE

Walt would kill him if he knew about this.

As Ron approached the south entrance to the park across from the city building, he couldn't help but wonder if Walt would be right and he'd entirely lost his mind. Maybe it was merely a delayed reaction to his awkward leaving of the university two days before, but what he was about to do broke nearly all the rules.

And yet here he was, rapidly striding down the curving sidewalk, heading to meet the enemy.

At least, that's how Walt would describe her, but Ron was beginning to think that there may be more to Detective Helen Lipscomb than merely a cop doing her job.

Whatever, he'd finally reached the point on the curve where the dense cluster of bushes would open up, revealing the assorted benches scattered around a central fountain. At the moment, as far as he knew, he remained undetected. He could stop here, turn around and leave with no one the wiser. However, even as he had the thought he'd reached the break in the bushes, and the lady cop had come into view.

Ron paused for a moment, far too late to escape detection, and scoped out the area. As far as he could tell, Lipscomb was alone. Looking up, she spotted him and waved him over.

Mentally shrugging, he walked the rest of the path

till he stood next to her bench.

"My lawyer would hate this," he said in greeting.

"Probably. Actually, the DA wouldn't be all that happy either. I'm probably breaking about a dozen different regs by meeting with you like this."

"So why did you call?"

"Because I needed to see you. Jack and another detective, Janey Turner, would be here too, but they're tied up at the moment."

"But why call? Why not just show up and haul me in like you did the first time?"

"We didn't haul you in, Mr. Green. If you recall, at the time you were offered the choice of coming with us or not."

"And if I hadn't come along, then you would have hauled me in?"

The lady cop puffed in exasperation.

"We have our procedures to follow, Mr. Green."

"Procedures."

"That's right. And usually they work fairly well. You've got to understand that your relationship with Miss Brewster, plus some of your actions since then, made you one of our prime suspects."

"Still?"

"Excuse me?" She looked up shading her eyes with her hand.

"Am I still one of your suspects? Do you still think that I've killed–however many people–just to cover up the business with Diane?"

Helen motioned with her hand.

"Sit down, Mr. Green. I've got something to show you."

He tensed, expecting some sort of trick. But when

she sat patiently without making any sort of move, he took a seat about a foot away from her.

"So show me," he said.

"First, a question. Does the name Rachel Henderson mean anything to you?"

He thought about it, rolled the name around in his head a few times, before finally shaking his head.

"Okay, then." Lipscomb reached into her jacket pocket and pulled out her cell phone. She flipped the phone open, punched a few buttons on the keypad, then held it out to him.

"What about this? Do you recognize this person?"

By this point, Ron had gotten the idea that something very important, possibly even critical, was happening here. So he took the phone from the cop and looked closely at the picture.

He studied it silently for several heartbeats before a faint tendril of memory crawled forward.

Lipscomb sat quietly and let him do his thing.

Several minutes later, he sighed and flipped the phone closed, then handed it back to the cop.

"Well?" Lipscomb asked.

"I remember her," he said. "Please don't tell me she's dead as well."

"Quite the opposite. She's very much alive, and she came in to see us."

His heart skipped a couple of beats.

"Came to see you?"

"Yes. She heard on the news about your friend Caldwell. And pieced it together with one or two of the others, and–*voila*–guess what conclusion she reached?"

"Someone's killing off members of the group."

"No stretch there. If it was only that I could have

listened to you at any time. No, she came up with quite a bit more."

He forced himself to look steadily at the cop, not wanting the mounting nervousness inside of him to show itself.

"What more?" he asked, keeping his voice as firm and modulated as possible.

"She thinks she knows who the perpetrator is."

"Not–me…" he asked, nearly terrified of the answer.

"No," she said, "not you. Hollis and Turner are getting a statement from her now. If you want, we can go on up and you can listen in, maybe give us some kind of corroboration."

He sat silently for a moment, almost not daring to hope it was all about to end. But before he could allow himself to hope, he needed to know more.

"Who does she think it is?"

Lipscomb grimaced.

"Actually, it's kind of ironic if she turns out to be right. She thinks it's another member of your group."

CHAPTER FORTY-FOUR

It was an odd feeling, almost as if he'd stepped into an alternate world. This time he was the one who sat behind the one-way glass, quietly observing. Observing a–well, not quite an interrogation but more like a–hell, he didn't know what to call it.

Ron realized that, more likely than not, he'd only recognized Rachel Henderson's picture on Lipscomb's cell phone because the lady detective's leadup had conditioned him to look for something special. Watching the middle-aged woman sitting at the table in the other room, being quietly questioned by the three cops (when they got into the squad room Helen had gotten Ron settled then joined her partners) he knew that if he'd passed her on the street, he wouldn't have recognized her. Hell, had it not been for his attention of the last several months being focused so much on the group, even if she'd come up to him and explained where she knew him from, he probably still would have had no memory of her.

During the day and a half spent at Amos Kettering, which seemed so damned long ago now, almost in another life, only two things had occupied his attention: the ads they'd been reviewing and Diane.

Well, and Johnny of course. Good old Johnny Caldwell, who everybody had liked so much. Which included, according to the background Lipscomb had given him as they'd walked over here from the park, the lady sitting in the other room.

"I think the person you want is a man named Latham," she'd told the detectives. "Robert Latham."

Latham? It took Ron a moment, but in no time the memory came flaring back at him.

Oh God, of course.

Latham.

Christ. Why didn't I think of him before?
****

It had been the first morning of the group's meeting. Somewhere right around eight, and slowly but surely the focus group started to come together. As the participants continued arriving, they spent their time waiting in AK's reception area, outfitted with a white cloth covered table which held an assortment of pastries, fruits, bottles of water and assorted juices. Although Ron had had breakfast before coming over, he figured what the hell and indulged in a bear claw and half a bottle of grapefruit juice.

As more and more of the participants filtered in, Ron took a seat in the corner and looked them over. Purely a time-wasting exercise, seeing as how he never figured to see any of these people after the next day. Naturally, he remembered most clearly the moment when Diane walked into the room, went over to the small corner table, wrote out her name tag and plastered it above her left breast. After that, he paid little attention to anything else, not even to the older, vaguely military-looking guy who was walking around glad handing everybody. He'd get to know the guy later if the opportunity presented, but for now he wanted only to check out the little thirty-something brunette, the one who looked a bit lost and unsure of herself.

Several minutes later, a man wearing a light grey suit stepped into the room. He scanned the clipboard he held in his hand, then looked up and counted the number of people in the room. Without thinking, Ron found himself counting heads as well and, including his own, came up with twelve.

It sounded like the right number. He knew, from his time in private business before entering academia, that panels of this kind usually had an even number, most often ten or twelve, occasionally twenty.

Clearing his throat to get everyone's attention, the suited guy began calling off their names. When he called Ron's as the second name, Ron gave him a perfunctory wave in acknowledgment. He'd leaned forward a bit, hoping to catch the name of the cute brunette.

"Latham," the man called. "Robert Latham?"

"Over here."

Ron looked over and for the first time noticed the man sitting in the corner. Really looking at the guy for the first time, Ron felt a vague uneasiness.

On the surface, he looked normal enough. In his twenties, with slightly reddish hair and maybe a light dusting of freckles. His clothing, rather shabby and mismatched, seemed to fit him kind of oddly. Sitting down, his olive cotton slacks came to about an inch above his shoes, and his pale blue shirt looked rumpled and half askew.

The kid looked fairly plump. Not to the point of being actually fat, probably just overweight enough to make him feel awkward around other people.

After making a mark for Latham, the suited man continued checking off their names until he had everyone accounted for. Through the entire exercise, almost everyone was looking around the room, checking out all these people who they'd spend the next day or so with.

Everyone, that is, except for the man identified as Robert Latham. He continued to sit crunched in his chair, eyes downcast to the floor.

****

"Latham," Detective Lipscomb repeated.

"Yes."

"You said Robert. Is that the name he went by? Not Bob or Bobby?"

"I don't think it mattered to him, just as long as someone was talking to him. But most of the time he was referred to as Robert."

"And he was a member of your panel?"

"Yes."

Through the glass pane, Ron could see the woman shudder. He remembered her now as probably the meekest, most soft-spoken of their group, so it was understandable that Latham had left a strong impression on her, strong enough that all these months later she was offering him up to the cops as a potential murderer.

Ron's own jury was still out on that, but he definitely wanted to hear more.

"And why do you think he may have something to do with the murder of Mr. Caldwell and the others?" Lipscomb asked. So far, Hollis, sitting off in a corner, hadn't said a word.

"Because," Rachel said, "because he was–he was just so weird."

Weird, Ron thought, was certainly one way to phrase it.

****

287

Before they went into the panel room to begin screening commercials, the man who seemed to be running things had them go once around the room and introduce themselves, giving a little bit of their background.

It was a standard practice Ron often used in his classrooms, especially in lower level classes; however, he saw now the futility of the whole thing because after each person introduced themselves, he promptly forgot what they'd said. Except, of course, for the young brunette, Diane Brewster. Ron perked up a bit when she mentioned that she was a teaching assistant in the sociology department of his own university.

Also, he couldn't help but focus on the Latham guy in the corner. He looked so much like the clichéd socially-awkward nerd that he seemed to have been plucked from some sort of casting lineup.

Ron did notice one thing, though, during the introductory go-round. Every time one of the women spoke up, Latham would wait until they were done saying their piece and the group's attention had shifted to the next person. Then he would, quietly and subtly, let his gaze linger on the one who'd just spoken.

****

"What do you mean by 'weird'?" Helen asked.

Rachel clasped her hands together and stared down at the table for a minute before answering.

"He was just a–odd–I guess you'd call him. He dressed tacky, hardly talked to anyone, yet so many times I seemed to feel his eyes on me when I wasn't looking…"

Ron watched as Helen laid down the pen she'd been using to take notes, then shifted around so that she was within Rachel's line of sight.

"Are you sure you couldn't have been imagining that?" she asked. "After all—"

"But it wasn't just me," Rachel interrupted. "During the breaks, several of the other women were talking about it as well. Eventually, on the second day, Johnny realized something was up and tried to talk to Latham about it."

"He did?"

"Yes."

"How did that go?"

"Not–not very well."

****

Ron remembered now, and he wondered how he could have possibly forgotten it. Good old Johnny, who everyone liked so much, had started off that second day by taking Latham aside with the intention of having a man to man with him.

It was the first thing in the morning, and they were hanging around in that outer reception room, sipping from either juice or water bottles, and waiting for the project director to show up and get them started.

Ron had taken a seat next to Diane, talking to her about something trivial, when he looked up and saw Caldwell heading over to talk to Latham. The older man crouched down next to Latham's seat and began whispering to him. Intrigued, Ron divided his attention between focusing on Diane as much as possible while still watching the small drama unfolding in front of them.

****

"What do you mean by 'not very well'?" Helen asked.

"Mr. Caldwell–Johnny—just wanted to talk to him,

289

let him know how uncomfortable some of us were with his ogling and his oddity."

"Why didn't someone tell the people at AK that they were uncomfortable with this Latham person?"

"Well, we didn't want to cause him any trouble or single him out in any way. We just wanted him to stop. And Johnny was such an easygoing guy that you couldn't imagine anyone getting upset with him."

"But Latham did?"

Miss Henderson nodded her head, almost too vigorously Ron thought.

"Oh yes. They started out whispering, at least Johnny did. Then they began talking in normal tones, and before long they were almost shouting at each other. It was odd because, up to then, no one had seen hardly any emotion out of Latham. Finally he stood up to confront Mr. Caldwell and, I don't know how to say it but there was something in his eyes. Something that was just– terrifying."

****

Despite himself, Ron had become interested in the scene over in the corner. Obviously, Caldwell was trying to keep things calm, but that Latham fellow was getting more and more agitated by the moment. Glancing over at Diane, he noticed her getting a little pale.

"I don't like that man," she said.

"Which one?"

"Which do you think? He's just so odd. Last night, when we left, he followed me all the way to my car."

Ron raised an eyebrow at that.

"Did he actually bother you in any way?"

"Asked me if I wanted to go out for a drink. I turned him down."

Ron looked back over at the corner scene. Johnny was backing off now, raising his hands a trifle. The geeky little guy was standing up and, despite his wimpish appearance and mismatched clothing, Ron got the idea he wouldn't want to meet him in a dark alley.

"Did he do anything after you shot him down?" he asked, turning back to Diane.

"Not really. Just gave me a kind of creepy look. Sort of a 'this isn't over yet' look."

Ron started to say something more, but just then their group monitor came back into the room, apologizing for his lateness and, pausing only to glance with concern at the two arguers, ushered them on into the viewing room.

Four hours later, their work done, the group broke up and went their separate ways.

****

The door behind him opened up, and Lipscomb, Hollis and the other lady detective came into the room.

"What do you think?" Hollis asked.

"Actually," Ron said, grimacing, "I'm a bit embarrassed. I should have thought of Latham before."

"Well, it's not a sure thing," Lipscomb commented, "only a possibility at the moment. But Mrs. Henderson seems fairly positive, not that that means anything in the real world."

"He bothered Diane," Ron said.

"'Scuse me?"

So he told them the story about Latham asking Diane out for a drink and getting kind of wiggish on her when she said no.

"Okay," Lipscomb said, "so he's got a personality type that may fit. And despite no record over at AK, with a first and last name, plus approximate age, we can find him easily enough."

"So what happens now?"

"Now," Hollis said, "you go home, Mr. Green, and let us deal with it. Thanks for coming in, we'll keep you updated as need be."

"Can I take this to mean that I'm no longer a suspect?"

The two cops paused, playing it cagey as hell, and for once this gave Ron some reassurance. Despite their earlier encounters, he was seeing these two as more and more professional.

"Go home, Mr. Green," Lipscomb said. "We'll let you know what happens."

Ron turned to walk away, but paused after only a few steps. For a moment he fought an internal battle with himself, then decided what the hell and threw his chips in.

"I recognized a few of them," he said.

Both Lipscomb and Hollis glanced at each other before turning their gazes on him.

"Say what?" Hollis asked.

"I recognized a few of them. Those pictures you showed me the other day, when I bolted out of here? I knew some of those men. Three of them, to be exact."

"Three of the people that were in those files on my desk?" Hollis said.

"Right. Three of the men, actually."

"And you knew them from where?" Lipscomb asked, though her expression clearly showed that she already knew the answer.

"From the group, of course. Got to admit it freaked me out more than you can imagine."

"Freaked you out so much that you decided not to let us in on it?"

"No. Freaked me out so much that I was convinced my lawyer was right, that you were trying to trap me somehow. Plus, I can do simple arithmetic. And adding three more to the number I already knew about, well, sorry but right about then I just didn't know what to do."

"Except run," Lipscomb said.

"Tell me, detective. If you were in my place, not as a law enforcement person but as an ordinary citizen, what would you have done?"

The two cops looked at each other again.

"He has a point there, Jack," she said.

"Maybe, but would you mind taking a few minutes and pointing out to me just which ones you knew?"

"Sure. Now that you've got someone other than me shaping up into a bona fide suspect."

"Okay, let's go. I've still got most of those files on my desk."

"One thing," Ron said as he and Hollis headed out of the room, "if it is Latham, if he has anything to do with this, how did he find out how to get a hold of everyone? They never gave us that information."

"Well you see, Mr. Green, that's one of the things we're going to ask him as soon as we find him."

CHAPTER FORTY-FIVE

All three of the various primaries, Lipscomb, Hollis and Turner, had two patrol cars meet them at Latham's condominium. A quick computer check had yielded all relevant info on him including, naturally, his last known address. The first three floors of the building were set aside as parking lots, and as Hollis wheeled their car into an available space, regardless of the fact all the slots seemed to have assigned numbers, he looked over at Helen.

"Won the lottery, huh?"

"What Records told me," she said. "There wasn't any hit as far as any run-ins with the law before, but there was a ping from the state revenue guys as to his upward mobility."

"A serial killer who won the lottery? Doesn't add up. When did he luck out?"

"Right about the first of the year," Helen said, her face suddenly drawing tight. She glanced at her partner and could tell that he'd caught it as well.

"Uh huh," Hollis said. "Just about when the killings started."

"Let's go on up and see what he has to say," Helen said.

As the three of them got out of their car, Helen looked the place over while Hollis and Janey walked over to give instructions to the two patrol cars. With it the middle of the afternoon, most of the parking slots were empty. Of the occupied ones, she spotted several Beemers, a handful of Mercedes, and one or two Jags. Impressive, she thought, provided the building's occupants weren't living off of credit.

One patrol unit did a quick U turn and came to a stop, its nose pointed towards the entranceway. The other one pulled into an empty slot, the two men inside getting out and coming over to the detectives, looking more than a little nervous.

Janey scurried off around the corner to scope out the back side of the building.

"See an elevator anywhere?" Hollis asked.

"Northeast corner," Helen said.

"Okay, then. Let's go talk to the man."

****

Just as the four of them stepped off the elevator onto the twenty-sixth floor, a young redhead stepped out of one of the apartments, a laundry basket in her arms. She froze, a panicked look in her eyes when she saw the cops. Helen motioned her on, at the same time placing a finger to her lips.

The girl nodded, then scurried on.

By unspoken consent, Helen placed herself to the side of the door, where she wouldn't be visible from a peephole, while Hollis stepped forward to knock. Seeing as they didn't have any sort of firm proof of Latham's culpability in anything, neither Helen nor her partner had drawn their weapons yet.

They waited a minute for an answer to Hollis's knock, and when they didn't get one he rapped twice more.

Silence. Dead and utter silence.

Lipscomb and Hollis looked at each other.

"Go on in?" Hollis asked.

"Got no warrant."

"True."

A long moment of silence went by.

"Probable cause?" he said.

"I'd hate to sell it to the lieutenant, let alone a judge. We just want the guy for questioning, don't even have any hard and fast evidence against him."

"Couple of eyewitnesses."

"Who said he may have done something. Not even witnesses when you get right down to it."

Hollis shrugged.

"So you got any ideas?" he asked.

"Jack," Lipscomb said, "if he's not home why are we whispering?"

An odd look crossed Hollis's face, and in that look Helen could see the answer to her question. But she hadn't really needed an answer because she thought she already knew.

"How about trying a compromise?" Hollis said. "Let's see if we can split the difference."

He reached out and twisted the doorknob.

The door swung open on slightly creaky hinges.

"And there's our probable cause," he said as the stench hit both of them at the same time.

They went in and saw the corpse laying in the living room.

"Oh geez," Hollis said, taking a step back.

"I'll call it in," Helen said as Hollis began slipping on a pair of latex gloves.

He only nodded as he gingerly stepped towards the body, working his way around the solidified puddles and splatters of blood to gently grasp what was left of the head and turn it upwards.

"Yeah, that's him," said Helen, who had taken a good look at Latham's driver's license photo before they left. She finished talking to the station house and flipped her phone shut.

"Haskins! Josephs!" she yelled to the two uniforms they'd left standing outside the elevator.

As their footfalls came down the hallway, Hollis stepped backwards so he was out of the splatter zone.

"One thing about it," he said as he looked around the room, which appeared as if a horde of kindergartners had been allowed to go wild with cans of red paint, "at least we can cross him off the suspect list."

CHAPTER FORTY-SIX

"You can't be serious," Amy Baxter said.

"We're very serious. Here's the paperwork," Helen said, handing her the warrant.

Helen looked over her shoulder at the five detectives standing behind her as Mrs. Baxter glanced over the warrant.

Better late than never, she thought.

****

The incredibly violent murder of Robert Latham and Green's subsequent revelations, which brought the grand total, at least as far as anyone knew, to seven, had convinced the lieutenant the time had come to assign a full task force to the string of murders. A hastily-convened meeting with the chief of detectives and a late afternoon conference with the police commissioner himself had sealed the deal. And while the lieutenant had cautioned Lipscomb and Hollis that he'd be keeping a close watch on them, he'd made the various assignments, which now gave them a total of eight detectives (including themselves and Turner), five uniforms and two clerical staff at their disposal.

But there was one other factor.

"Time," the lieutenant had said. "This Latham thing is as bloody as all get out. Hell, I guess I don't have to tell you two that. Couple the brutality with the fact that the victim recently hit easy street with the lottery, and you've got one hell of a story. The media's already got a handle on the Latham angle, and you can bet in no time at all they'll be connecting all the dots themselves. If nothing else, this much manpower devoted to what's technically one case isn't going to escape notice for very long. So get your keisters in gear and get it done."

****

"You actually want to look at all of our employee records?" Mrs. Baxter asked her, as if she didn't believe the writing on the warrant.

"That's right."

"But what are you looking for?"

"It's in the warrant. We want to start with the paperwork on anyone either connected with the Rawlings campaign or who had access to your overall database."

Watching the woman closely, Helen caught something in her attitude. She wasn't sure what because the lady managed to keep herself under pretty good control, but something that Helen said had gotten to her.

"I'm not sure I can do this without clearing it with Mr. Kettering."

"So clear it. In the meantime, these two gentlemen,"—she motioned two of the backup plainclothesmen forward—"want to start going over your records."

Now the woman's facade began to crack, a slight shiftiness showing in her eyes.

"I really need to check with Mr. Kettering on this," she repeated.

"Check with whoever you want to," Helen said, her patience with the entire case coming to an end. "But any more stalling and I'm taking you in and charging you with obstructing police officers in the performance of their duties."

****

As it turned out, the lady didn't check with her boss right away, for the simple reason that he hadn't yet shown up that morning. With no other way to stall, she went ahead and told her staff to cooperate with the cops in any way possible.

And yet, as the morning wore on and the team of detectives pored over the employment and work records of the AK staff, Helen couldn't shake the notion, growing stronger by the hour, that the Baxter woman was hiding something.

As it turned out, four people had directly worked on the focus group aspect of the Rawlings campaign. Another eight had designed and produced the actual ads, with the film work itself done by a small outside firm that AK had used fairly regularly for the last three years.

"What's the name of the firm?" Helen asked Baxter at one point during the morning.

"Seriously, detective, why do you need that? All of their work was done before the focus group was assembled. They didn't even have a representative here while the evaluation was underway. How could they possibly have any connection with—"

"I don't know, and I won't know until I or some of my people can talk to them. What's the firm?"

Even with Baxter sitting behind her desk, which should have been her power position, Helen could see the woman growing more agitated by the moment.

Then again, having a horde of cops swarming all around would make almost anybody wilt.

"What's the firm?" Helen repeated.

Baxter sighed, then shrugged her shoulders.

"What the hell. It's all just a waste of your time anyway. Louis Feldstein and Associates."

"Associates? I thought you said it was a small firm?"

Baxter grimaced.

"Louis is a whiz with film. He also just turned twenty-nine and looks like he's sixteen. If he didn't have a major sounding name for his business, he wouldn't have any. He does eighty percent of the work himself and hires out the other twenty percent on a for-hire basis."

Helen just managed to smother a groan. It was beginning to look as if this simple little task of questioning the people involved in the Rawlings account was mushrooming beyond control.

"Get me his number," she said before turning and leaving the office.

****

Hollis hunted her up shortly before noon. He found her sitting at a small desk in a back office.

"Hey."

"Hey," Helen said, looking up from some phone logs from May of the previous year. "What's up?"

Hollis snagged a chair with his foot and sat down next to her, leaning in.

"Have you noticed anything odd around here?" he whispered.

"Odd?"

"Yeah. Something just doesn't feel right."

"How so?"

"Well, for one thing they don't seem to have a whole lot of people working around this place."

Her vantage point in the back gave Helen a fairly good view of most of the office suite. It was true that, at the moment, she saw only a few employees moving around in the front part. Then again, many of them could have ducked out for an early lunch.

"I hadn't really noticed," she said.

"I've been keeping an eye out, making a rough count, and I get around forty people. I don't know anything about this kind of business. Still, for a supposedly major firm that seems a bit low."

Helen leaned back, closed her eyes and tried to visualize the various people she'd seen coming and going during the morning.

"And on top of that," Hollis continued, "most of them seem kind of young."

"Under thirty for the most part," Helen said as she opened her eyes.

"So you noticed it too?"

"Not consciously. But now that you mention it, yeah."

"Mean anything?" Hollis asked.

"Damned if I know. Like you, I don't know that much about this line of work. Forty may be normal."

"But shouldn't they have some older, more experienced hands around? And as far as the number, last spring how many people did the Baxter woman say they had working on the Rawlings account?"

Helen took a moment to dredge her memory.

"About twelve, not counting the outsourced stuff."

"Which means, if the numbers are consistent, they had over a fourth of their staff working on one account."

"What are you suggesting, Jack?"

"I don't know, maybe nothing. Then again, we've been here nearly four hours, and the boss man hasn't made an appearance yet? With a team of cops tearing up his place of work?"

"Yeah," Helen said, somewhat somberly. "I'd noticed that too."

****

John Kettering showed up shortly after one, a half roar from the reception area the first indication Helen had of his arrival.

"What the hell is going on around here?"

She stood up from her desk and headed towards the reception area, wishing Hollis was here with her, but as far as she knew he hadn't gotten back from lunch yet.

By the time Helen made it to the reception area, Kettering was clearly just getting warmed up.

"I said, what's going on around here?"

He directed his second roar specifically to two youngish detectives, one on each end of the room, engaged in interviewing two of AK's account representatives. As Helen came into the common area, it was clear the two plainclothesmen weren't about to be intimidated by the businessman. Both of them merely looked up, scoped the man out for a second, then turned back to their respective interviewees.

Helen couldn't keep from grinning. Kettering was the kind of hot shot who could ordinarily bully and stare down most people, even most cops. However, when stacked up against a serial murder investigation, his importance shriveled to almost nothing.

Nevertheless, the amenities having to be followed, Helen strode over to the fuming executive.

"Mr. Kettering," she said, "I'm Detective Lipscomb. We met a while back."

"I know who you are. You were here the day that lowlife broke in here and tried to intimidate my staff.

Before we get down to business here, could you please tell me why that man hasn't been arrested yet?"

"He hasn't been arrested," said Helen, "because he didn't kill anybody."

A bit of a premature leap, and the lieutenant would no doubt have wrung her neck if he heard her say it, but it managed to set Kettering back for a minute.

"He's not? But according to the papers he—"

"Mr. Kettering, we're here because we're currently investigating a series of killings that seem linked in some way to your company. We'd appreciate the cooperation of you and your employees in answering our questions, but regardless, we have a warrant and we're executing it."

Helen watched Kettering closely as she spoke, and for an instant he seemed to wince. He recovered almost instantly, but the slippage was there. She filed that along with Baxter's earlier nervousness and Jack's concerns about the staffing.

"Okay," he said, "what exactly do you need from me?"

"Right at the moment, just a few things. First, are you currently at full staff?"

"What do you mean, detective?"

"I mean are you currently carrying a normal complement of employees?"

That slight flinch returned, and this time the man didn't do quite as good a job of concealing it.

"We've experienced some retrenching recently. You may have noticed, detective," he put a noticeable emphasis on the word, "that we've had a rather rough economy for the last several years."

"True, but according to what we've found, you

stayed fairly stable through '09 and '10, and it's just been in the last year and a half or so that you've begun reducing in force. I was wondering why."

He shrugged, and now Helen definitely felt as if the man was acting.

"I don't know what to tell you. There's always ebbs and flows. We're probably just in a particularly long ebb."

"Okay."

"You had something else?" he asked.

"Yes. We're primarily looking into anything having to do with the Lucy Rawlings account."

"Yes." His tone sounded damned near withering. "I've been informed of that. I'm telling you, that damned account's been more trouble than it ended up being worth."

"Right. But it seems that one of your 'retrenchments' was a gentleman named Mike Howerton."

"That's correct. Mr. Howerton is no longer with us, along with probably a third of the people who worked on that account."

"No doubt." Helen had to work at it to keep her own tone neutral and professional. "Do you keep in touch with the people who leave here?"

"Not really, Miss Lipscomb. After all, I do have a business to run."

"Right. And doing a fine job of it, it seems."

****

Hollis got back from lunch about half an hour later, looking somewhat rumpled and out of sorts. Helen could sympathize. They weren't strictly partners and each had their different case loads to work on. At the moment, she was working two other cases besides the spree, and last she'd known Hollis had three different investigations he was pursuing. Janey Turner was supposed to have shown up by now, but she'd called an hour earlier. Something had come up downtown, and she didn't know when she would be able to join them.

"Anything new?" Hollis asked as he walked into the room.

Without a word, Helen took him by the arm and hustled him into a small, empty anteroom, shutting the door behind them.

"They're definitely hiding something," she said.

"For sure?"

"Well, probably not the entire company, but for damned sure Baxter and Kettering are keeping something from us."

"Still no trace of the records on the group?"

"No."

Hollis got up and went over to look out the window. Nothing to see there, just a half-filled parking lot, an assortment of cars with several trees offering shade.

"This is a crock," he said. "You know, Helen, we screwed up a few weeks back."

She grimaced at his back.

"I know, when they told us their records had been deleted. We should have gone after their computers right then and brought them into the tech guys."

"Too late to do anything about it?" he asked.

"Don't know. But I've already got a call in, and the lieutenant's working on a new warrant."

"Let's only hope they haven't swapped out computers since the last time."

"Well, if they have, the techies will be able to tell us

that real quick, so it won't waste a lot of time."

"And in the meantime?"

Before answering, Helen threw open the door and looked out into the office area. The activity out there had died down a bit, by now probably most of the questioning was winding up. She needed to check with the detective overseeing the actual employment records, but before then they had something else to do.

"Let's go," she said, "and take one more shot at finding out what the two top dogs are hiding. You want the girl or the guy?"

CHAPTER FORTY-SEVEN

It was nearing 7 o'clock, and everyone else had gone home for the night. Amy Baxter sat on a small couch that lay along one wall of her office, drinking. Only one light illuminated her office, a small night light recessed behind her desk. Had anyone been in there to see, they would have had to squint into the shadows to make out her form on the couch.

A minute later, someone was in there to see.

"Hello, Amy."

"Wondered if it would be tonight or tomorrow." She paused to take another sip from her glass. "Guess this falls under why put off, right?"

The form standing in the doorway moved all the way in and stood just in front of the couch.

"So you've expected it?" he asked.

"Sure," she looked up. "Had to happen sooner or later anyway, didn't it? Seems to be the way things go around here lately."

John Kettering sighed and walked over to sit down behind her desk.

"Make yourself a drink, John. After all, you own everything in here. So you might as well enjoy it while you can."

Her boss sighed.

"I did my best. You know that," he said.

She took time for a good, long swallow before

answering.

"But your best doesn't seem to have been good enough, does it. What would your dad think, John? What would his partner, old man Amos, have thought of the way you ran their firm down?"

He spread his hands out on the desk, preferring to look at them instead of his employee.

"Times are tough all over. They would have understood."

Draining her glass, Amy sat up a bit straighter.

"Sure, times are tough. And you tried every trick in the book, didn't you, John?"

"Yes, I did. And who knows? In the end, it probably would have worked."

"Probably. But not now."

"No, not with this Rawlings mess. Once this gets out, no one within a hundred miles will want to hire us for anything."

"And just think," she said, "it if hadn't been for you trying to cut corners…"

"We don't know that," he snapped.

"Don't we? How long before the cops figure it out? You know as well as I do how much material they yanked out of here today. When it comes down to it, it's just a matter of crossing names off a list until they eventually come across…"

Kettering abruptly stood up.

"Regardless, as of right now none of it is your concern."

"Discussed it with the board already?" she asked.

"First thing tomorrow. Why don't you take a personal day?"

She stood up, smoothed the wrinkles out of her skirt

and picked her jacket up off the floor where she'd dropped it earlier.

"Do I at least get the same deal you gave all the others?" she asked.

"No. End of the week."

She slipped into her jacket, took about six steps to the door, then turned back to her boss.

"Just like that?" she asked. "How do you know I won't go blabbing to the cops?"

Kettering shook his head and lifted up his palms in kind of half shrug.

"Like you said, in another day or so is it really going to matter?"

"Guess not."

She opened the door and stepped out.

"Good luck, John," she said, with her back to him. "When word of this gets out, you're really going to need it."

CHAPTER FORTY-EIGHT

He waited until 9 o'clock to call Lipscomb.

The last time Ron had talked with the lady cop, she had, probably contrary to regulations, updated him on the progress, what there was, that she and Hollis had made. She'd told him to give them until 9 o'clock, and if he hadn't heard from either of them by then to call.

Which he did. And got no answer.

He'd never contacted Hollis by phone, didn't even have the man's direct number, and he barely knew that other woman, Turner, and didn't trust reaching out to her. So he sat in the dark of his apartment and tried to figure out what to do next.

Lipscomb had said they had to run some things down. Ron didn't know what things she'd meant, but it was a safe assumption they had something to do with the time spent that day at Amos Kettering. So...

It took him about ten more minutes before he figured out how to proceed, and when it came to him he snatched his phone up and began dialing as quickly as he could.

After two rings the person on the other end picked up.

"Hey, Andrew, it's Ronald Green. Yeah, sorry to bother you. Look, there's something I need to know, and I feel really awkward about asking you, but it may be important. I can find out some other way, but I thought it may be quicker to ask you."

He listened to the response from the other end, then began breathing a bit easier.

"Okay, thanks. Actually, I don't know why I think you would know this off the top of your head, but I was wondering if by chance you could tell me…"

CHAPTER FORTY-NINE

He pulled his car into the driveway, looking down at his cell phone one more time to triple check the address. It was still early, just past 10 o'clock, and the light shining from behind living room curtains indicated someone was home.

The question, which Ron couldn't possibly answer without getting out of his car, was how many people were home. According to the address listing, the occupant wasn't married, but that didn't mean she lived alone. She could have a man in there, or a few kids, or even a damned Rottweiler.

As far as that went, considering the state of the economy for the last few years, she could be living with her parents or her grown children.

Only one way to find out.

He got out of his car and walked up the driveway to the front door. He hadn't consciously planned on being as quiet as possible, but about halfway up the drive realized that he was walking nearly on tiptoe.

Worse than that, his palms were sweating like crazy, and a dull pain in his lungs made him aware that he'd spent the last several seconds holding his breath.

What he was about to do was probably not very smart. It was, in fact, about the stupidest thing that anyone in his position could possibly contemplate.

On the other hand, despite the fact things seemed to

be breaking Ron knew he wasn't out of his jam yet. And if by chance anything happened to either Lipscomb or Hollis…

Once on the porch, Ron could hear the faint murmur of a television from behind the door, and while he couldn't make out the individual sounds, he got the impression someone inside was watching a game of some kind.

Get it over with, he told himself. *Just lift up your hand, extend a finger and ring the damned bell. What's the worst that could happen?*

Especially compared to what already faced him.

He rang the bell, took about half a step back and waited.

About ten seconds later, he reached out and rang again. A moment later, a half of a shadow passed across the curtained window, and he detected a momentarily faint darkening at the peephole.

At that moment, Ron realized what a total incompetent he was.

No woman, alone in her house and in her right mind, would open the door at night to a strange man standing alone outside. Even worse, if he wasn't a stranger, if by chance she recognized him, she most definitely wouldn't open the door. Would, in fact, probably be on the phone in a flash, dialing 911.

Ron stood on the porch an instant, weighing options and possibilities. The easiest thing would be to turn tail and run, chalk it up to a moment's idiocy and hope that this wouldn't be another black mark against him.

On the other hand, the more rational part of his brain knew that, compared to what he already faced, bothering a woman at night was practically insignificant.

And in that case, in for a penny....

This time he didn't ring the bell, but instead pounded on the door.

Her voice came from behind the panel.

"I've called the police, Mr. Green. They're on their way."

So that answered that question.

"Call them back and tell them you made a mistake, Mrs. Baxter. I'm not here to hurt you."

"Get away, now. They'll be here any minute, and you'll be in even more trouble than you are. So just go."

"Mrs. Baxter, stop and think a minute. If I wanted to hurt you, I'd already be breaking down this door. I'd be able to do whatever I wanted and be gone before the cops showed up. I honestly don't mean you any harm. Would you please open up?"

Several moments lagged by, with Ron beginning to think he'd lost his bet with himself. He decided to give it another minute before giving it up as a lost cause, and at that point the lady opened the door.

Just as far as the security chain.

"Mrs. Baxter?"

"What do you want?" She no doubt intended her voice to sound firm and in control, but the words came out as more of a croak.

"I have a few questions, mainly about some of your employees. Can I come in?"

"You're not any kind of cop," she said.

"No. What I am is a basically ordinary guy whose life has blown apart on him. And dammit, I need some answers."

"What makes you think I have them for you?"

He looked down, noticing she had an open cell

phone in her left hand. He couldn't see the right one, but presumed it was clenched around the knob. For an instant, he had the rather paranoid idea that the phone was on and she was transmitting their conversation to the cops.

Well, he thought, *what the hell*. Let them hear him trying to clear himself.

"Because everything that's happened to me, everything that's gone wrong, began when I was asked to be on your focus group. That's where it started, and I figure that's where I have to find the answers."

"I'd think it would be more accurate to say your troubles started when you began screwing Diane Brewster."

Ron noticed the wording, figured that the solid-businesswoman was gone, leaving in her place nothing but a frightened creature.

But frightened of him, or of something or someone else?

"May I come in," he repeated, not knowing what else to say.

Her face twisted, then she shut the door. Before he could plan his next move, or any move, he heard the swick of a chain, and the door opened up all the way.

Her right hand hadn't been grasping the door knob, after all. Instead, it held a shiny, new-looking pistol trained right on him.

"My father was military," she said, "and he taught me about guns from an early age. So if you've got any ideas of pulling something, forget it. You can come in, but if you get closer than six feet to me, or if your hands make an idle move I don't like, you're finished."

For an instant, Ron couldn't move. The sight of the

metallic object, focused on him and him alone, had taken away not only his breath but practically any sort of conscious feeling. At that moment, he wanted nothing more than to turn tail and run like hell, but figured this crazy lady would take his sudden movement as antagonistic and drill him where he stood.

"Come on," she said, waving the pistol in a half motion, "come in and ask your questions."

Only after he'd gotten inside, and somehow stumbled to a sitting position on a small loveseat in one corner of the living room, did Ron notice that Amy Baxter wore a plain white cotton robe, cinched all the way to her throat. Plain white slippers on her feet helped contribute to an image of icy control and competence.

For the moment, Ron couldn't get his tongue untied, but a harsh glare from the lady managed to loosen him up.

"Your staff at the company," he finally said.

"What about them?" She hadn't moved from her position beside the door, and her posture and expression showed she had no intention of getting any closer to him.

"I wondered if–if there's any of them that the police should look at."

That got to her, making that icy expression flinch a little. He hadn't meant to put it so bluntly, and yet…

"Look at," she repeated. "You mean that the police should look at my staff instead of you?"

"Well, yes."

Another flicker crossed that stern demeanor. An expression of something, but Ron wasn't sure exactly what.

The gun wavered, fractionally, as she moved over to a small recliner and perched on its edge.

"They're not my staff anymore," she said.

Ron looked at her.

"After the police left the firm this evening, I got a visit from John Kettering. And, well, to put it mildly—"

"He fired you," Ron said.

She grimaced, for the first time something other than harshness appearing in her eyes.

"Yeah, he did. It's not official yet, but John made it fairly clear that I'm not wanted around the office anymore. Fact is, they've been cleaning house for a while, and it finally got around to me."

Ron wondered for a moment if she was on something. Hardly anyone could be as cool and collected as her when their life had just blown up in front of them. And yet, she appeared, at least on the surface, to not be affected at all.

"So now we have something in common," he said.

"Excuse me?"

"Unemployment." He attempted a weak smile.

A quick spurt of annoyance appeared on that glacial countenance, then she scooted herself around to ease back into the recliner.

"Not very funny, Mr. Green. As I said a moment ago, the way I see it you brought all of your troubles on yourself. It was just my bad fortune to get caught up in it."

"I'm sorry you feel that way." As she seemed to relax, Ron felt some of his own tension easing. Even so, he couldn't completely tamp down the qualms that her gun gave him.

"You can be sorry all you want," she said, "but it doesn't change the fact that you've managed to completely screw up my life."

"Not me. Sorry, but you can't throw that on me. I'll admit to my share of culpability in my own fuckups, but you're taking the rap for somebody else's actions."

"Somebody else?" Her body tension seemed to ease by another iota or two.

"Yes. Come on, Mrs. Baxter. Let's stop playing around. If you'd really called the cops they'd have been here by now. You invited me in, and at the moment you're not even aiming your gun at me."

A quick gasp escaped her, and she quickly leveled the weapon back up.

"So tell me. Exactly why did you let me in just now?"

She tried to stare him down, but it didn't work. Ron had the innate advantage of having practically nothing left to lose. He considered telling her that it had gotten to the point where the cops, at least Lipscomb and Hollis, had pretty much discounted him as a suspect, but decided to keep that particular hole card concealed for the moment.

Shrugging, the lady placed the gun on a nearby end table, stood up and went over to a small, teak liquor cabinet up against one wall.

Without offering Ron anything, she poured herself several fingers of straight whiskey, then stood there and downed nearly half of it in one swallow.

Ron doubted if he knew many men who could do such a feat.

With a finger or two left in the glass, she put it down and turned back to him.

"Can't stand that stuff," she said in a hoarse tone.

"So why drink it?"

"Need something to make the aches go away. And

damn have there been a lot of aches lately."

Walking back into the main part of the living room, she spurned the small recliner and stretched herself out on a teal-colored sofa, her slippered feet at one end, and leaned her back against the other end.

"Howerton," she said.

"Excuse me?"

"Mike Howerton. You're responsible for your part of this mess. Mike Howerton's responsible for mine."

"And who is Mike Howerton?"

"He was the project director for the Rawlings campaign. The man who liaised with their people and oversaw our end of things."

"In other words?"

"In other words," she said as she rolled her eyes upwards, as if seeking something from on high, "he's the man who put together the focus group."

Ron stood up a bit straighter and took a deep breath, setting himself in the hope that the last few pieces of the puzzle were about to fall into place.

"So why are you mentioning him now?"

She sighed again, then swung her feet to the floor, got up from the couch and walked back over to the counter where she'd left her unfinished drink. Her back to Ron, she finished the rest of the whiskey, slowly placed the glass down and turned back to Ron.

"AK's been in trouble for some time now, much longer than John wants to admit. He and the money people have done a fairly decent job of shifting funds around, nothing illegal or anything, just moving amounts from one department to another, to keep up the appearances of a solvent firm."

"Okay."

"And all the time, they've been quietly letting people go. One or two a month, usually on some pretext, so that it doesn't look like a mass dumping. But they haven't replaced any of the positions, making the rest of us work that much harder, and they've been pulling more than the usual number of interns from the local universities to take up the slack."

Ron thought for a moment of Andrew, his former student, talking about how lucky he'd been to get a foot in the door at such a well-established, stable firm. A sour taste formed in his mouth as he realized the disappointment coming the kid's way.

"So what does that have to do with this Howerton fellow? Did any of us ever meet him?"

"Probably not. He would have spent most of his time behind the privacy glass, helping to monitor your reactions, but the actual person who interviewed you, remember that tall red-headed guy with the glasses, was one of Mike's assistants."

She glanced over at the whiskey decanter, as if contemplating another glass. Then she kind of shook herself and turned back to Ron.

"So when your group came back with such negative results on Mike's program, it gave Kettering a decent excuse to get rid of a fairly high level person."

Remembering what Lipscomb had told him about the cops' suspicions of the Rawlings aide (at the moment he couldn't remember the man's name) Ron thought he saw where this was going.

"So this Howerton fellow got canned?" he asked.

"Right."

"Because of us?"

"Well, that was the pretext used. If it hadn't been

that, it would sooner or later have been some other reason. At the rate it's going, another six months or so, and the whole place will be shut down."

"But as far as Howerton knew—"

She lifted her head and for the first time since he'd arrived looked Ron straight in the eye.

"As far as he knows, and Kettering took pains to be very specific about it, he was fired because of the focus group's reactions to his work on the Rawlings account."

For a moment, Ron felt as if the entire world had gone out of synch. It couldn't be that callous of a proposition. Nobody would kill, how many people was it now, simply because he'd been fired from a job. Would they?

"So you think Howerton may be the one behind all these deaths?" he asked, almost hoping the woman would say no.

"I didn't at first. It never even entered my mind. After all, I didn't have any direct involvement with the work, never even set eyes on any of you people. But when you showed up at AK, with that dumb stunt of yours, and I realized that all the records of that program were gone, I thought of Mike."

"When did he leave the firm?"

"The middle of October. After we scrubbed the initial project, we started up a second round in hopes of saving the account. That one didn't even get off the ground before the Rawlings people dumped us."

"But that would have been–what–sometime in the summer. And he didn't leave until October?"

"You've got to understand, Mr. Green. John Kettering is doing–more like was doing–everything possible to keep his situation under wraps. He inherited the company, you know. At least his share of it. And from the time his dad brought him in and began grooming him to take over, he's been considered something of a lightweight, both in the company and in the larger business community. So with each executive he's let go, he's given several months notice and allowed them the use of company facilities. So Mike physically left in mid October, but he was basically just shambling around there the last few months."

For a moment, Ron felt a deep empathy for the man. He himself had done his share of "just shambling around" the university in those last painful weeks before the end of the spring semester. So he knew all too well what it felt like to be suddenly thrust aside by an employer.

But still that didn't seem enough to account for....

"Did he manage to find another job?" he asked.

"Not last I heard. Talk through the grapevine says that he's had his share of interviews, but I don't think anything's come out of it. Last I heard, he was trying to land a job out of state, but I don't think that one panned out either."

"Still doesn't seem like much," Ron said. "Lots of people lose their jobs. What made you think of this guy?"

"When all the information on your group disappeared. Without expending a whole lot of effort, he was the only one on staff who had access to all the records."

"My God." Ron stood up and took out his cell phone. He only hoped that either Lipscomb or Hollis were answering, because he didn't dare try to explain this to anyone not completely familiar with the case.

"Do you have an address for this guy?" he asked, the

phone to his ear.

"I did. But I heard a while back that his wife finally gave up and left him. Last I'd heard he'd taken an apartment somewhere."

Not that big a deal, Ron thought. Surely the cops could track the guy down, as long as they knew who they were looking for.

He got Lipscomb's voice mail. Hurriedly, he gave her the basic info and asked her to call him back.

Hanging up, he turned back to the Baxter woman.

"Did you tell this to the cops this afternoon?"

"Are you kidding? With my boss breathing down my neck the whole time?"

"So you didn't point them in his direction?"

She shrugged.

"I was still holding out hope that I could save my job, for however long it would be worth anything. But I don't think you need to worry about that. The way they were tearing through our place, I'm sure they dug all this up."

Ron paused and thought for a moment, his head practically aching with everything rushing through it.

"You said he and his wife split, right?"

"That's right."

More and more, Ron felt a strong empathy for this guy.

"Would you know if his wife's still at their old address?"

"I've no idea, and believe me when I say that I really don't care. But if you hold on a minute, I'll see if I can find it."

As she headed off into an inner room, Ron began dialing again, hoping this time to reach Hollis.

CHAPTER FIFTY

Two bodies lay at either end of the shadowy hallway. As Ron came up the staircase, he first noticed a slumped form at the far end of the hall seconds before seeing the other shape lying prone in front of the door to apartment 5B.

He stopped for a moment at the top of the stairs, but could hear no sound from inside the apartment. As silently as possible, he made his way to the far end of the hall and examined the larger of the two forms.

Detective Hollis. Ron felt for a pulse and fortunately found one. A little weak and thready, but more or less regular. A bloody gash ran up one side of the cop's forehead.

Ron didn't know much first aid, and even if he did, didn't feel as if he could spare the time. The man was alive, and seemingly in no immediate danger, which would have to do for right now.

Running on tiptoe, keeping as silent as possible, Ron made his way to the apartment. The form prone in front of the door was that of a young man, barely out of his teens, wearing a patrolman's uniform. This one wasn't in as good of shape as Hollis, and the young man's twisted, drawn expression reflected the pain he must have felt at the moment of his death. Ron shifted his gaze downward and could in no way miss the large, bloody gaping wound in the kid's midsection.

"Goddammit," Ron muttered, feeling suddenly sicker than he had in a very long time.

Hollis would probably be okay, and Ron could do nothing for the young kid on the floor in front of him. He had no idea whether there were other officers on the way, or even if anyone else knew about this. But he couldn't deal in hypotheticals. Time to stop wasting and waffling, and deal with the problem at hand.

Standing up, he placed his hand on the doorknob. Going through that door would probably be the dumbest thing he could do, yet at the moment he couldn't imagine any other options. A safer bet would have been to grab his cell phone and call the cops out here. They'd no doubt come running in an instant, but what assurance could he possibly have they'd get here in time?

And there were at least two more people unaccounted for.

Squaring his shoulders and taking a deep breath, he twisted the knob and opened the door.

"Come on in," a man's voice said from somewhere inside the apartment, "come on in and join the party."

****

"All the way in," the voice said as Ron crossed the threshold. "All the way in and shut the door behind you."

Ron did so, blinking furiously to try to get his eyes accustomed to the shadowy interior. It didn't take long for him to make out vague shapes, and a few seconds after that, actual forms.

The apartment didn't hold all that much, a few isolated sticks of furniture and lots of bare flooring. The main items of interest were the two people over against the far wall.

Naturally, he recognized Helen Lipscomb. Slumped

in a corner, she looked pale and frightened but, as far as Ron could tell, more or less in one piece. She didn't look as if she'd lost her composure yet, but it was sure frayed and unraveling.

Ron shifted his gaze then to get a good look at the man who'd invited him in.

What he saw kind of disappointed him.

After all this time of being haunted by the spectre of some sort of bloody killer, after the increasing and unrelenting savagery of the various killings, each one seemingly more brutal than the last, Ron had really expected to see someone fearsome as all get out.

Instead, he saw an ordinary man, of average height, but not average weight. His clothes, a plain tee-shirt and blue jeans, seemed to hang off him, as if he'd bought them just before going on a crash weight loss program.

His hair was all tangled, even while thinning in places, making him look like an aging heavy metal rocker. Ron found it hard to equate him with the same person who had, among other things, bludgeoned a man to death, strangled someone with his bare hands and managed with a knife to stab a person nearly thirty times.

No, this guy didn't look like he could do any of those things, just as he didn't look as if he could knock out a policeman and gut shoot a kid barely in his twenties.

Except that, looking at him, Ron knew that the man had done all of those things, and possibly more. He had for sure killed at least eight people, seven from the group and the poor patrolman lying out in the hallway.

And it stood a better than even chance that he intended to add a few more to his tally before the night was out.

The only thing in the tableau that made the guy seem

like a dangerous killer, and it was a doozy, was the automatic he held canted at Helen's head.

"It was nice of you to come along, Green," the stranger said. "Saved me the trouble of hunting you down."

Ron mentally flipped a coin on the question of taking the chance of antagonizing the guy even further, and decided to give it a shot.

Either way, at the moment, he was standing there practically dead, he and Helen both.

"I'm sorry," Ron said, deciding to play it ignorant. "But I don't know who you are."

A twitch jumped in the stranger's eye, and for a moment his hand, the one holding the gun on Helen, trembled.

"Don't know me, huh? That pretty much bites. All you did was ruin my life, you and all your buddies."

The next few seconds would tell the tale on the man's mental state. Would he buy Ron's plea of ignorance, or would he realize Ron had to know his identity to have tracked him down here?

"Howerton, damnit!" His voice nearly cracking as he screamed. "Mike goddamned Howerton. Ring a bell now?"

The gun trained on Helen trembled even more, and Ron had to force himself to breathe.

"I'm sorry, no. I don't know you."

As if a switch had been thrown, the man started to chuckle, then laugh, eventually tipping his head back in near hysteria. Ron took a step towards him, then noticed that, despite his hilarity, his gun hand hadn't wavered.

After several seconds of the mirth, he calmed down.

"Don't feel too bad," he finally said. "No reason you

should know me. You see, we never met. I was the man behind the shadows. The account manager who developed the whole Rawlings campaign for AK. I wasn't one of the minions you met actually doing the work; I was the brain guy."

"Look, Howerton, I'm sorry, but…"

"My big moment. You get that, Green? It was supposed to be my big moment. I get called into Kettering's office one day and he tells me that I'm in charge of AK's end of the Rawlings account. Fourteen years in the business, the last six right there at AK, and finally I've got a chance to show them what I'm made of."

"You were the one who put together the ad campaign?" Ron asked, still pretending ignorance.

"That's right, I…"

Helen stirred, shifted a bit to the side, and in the same instant Howerton half turned, the gun now pointed straight at her. Ron was a civilian, and he didn't know one type of pistol from another, but he knew that if the detective wasn't careful, she was on the verge of becoming another casualty.

"Helen," he said, "don't."

She glared at him, no doubt still considering him an unwanted intrusion in her investigation. But from her position, she couldn't see the man's eyes, couldn't know how close to the edge he was. Further, she could possibly be suffering from mild shock and not thinking clearly, so Ron had to keep her out of action for as long as possible.

"You were saying?" he said, trying to draw the gunman's attention back to him.

It worked, barely. Howerton shifted about half a pace, his focus now evenly divided between Ron and the lady cop.

"I was saying that I worked like a son of a bitch on that campaign. Sixty hour weeks, like a lot of PR people do? Forget it. My team and I were putting in damned near seventy-five hours a week. And every single frame of film, every splice of video, every freakin' comma on all the copy, getting my personal approval."

Ron, knowing from direct experience how all the man's work had turned out, felt his stomach drop even more.

"And then you compiled the group," he said.

"That's right." His attention shifted slightly more away from Helen and towards Ron. As Ron sharpened his focus, trying to gauge if there was any possible way for him to pull some sort of miracle, he noticed a slight bulge on one side of Helen's lower right leg. It was hard to tell with the blue jeans she wore, but he was pretty sure he saw a protuberance on her leg.

"That's right." Howerton repeated. "We compiled the group, ready to test out all that hard work. That's the way the business goes. You work your asses off for weeks, or even months, straight through, and then bring in a bunch of numb nuts to evaluate your work."

If anything, Ron's mouth felt even drier than a moment before. His brain had shifted into overdrive, assorted stray bits and pieces of the last several months clicking into place.

"And when we were done…"

"When you were done, after all of a day and a half, I got called into Kettering's office again. Pathetic me, I strutted in like some kind of a champion, ready to receive my laurels. And you know what I got instead?"

"I can guess," Ron said.

"Damned right you can guess. Big K dressed me down worse than I ever had in my life. Cussed me out like a first-day intern. Called me every possible synonym you can think of for worthless and incompetent."

Slumped against the wall, Helen sat up a little straighter and her eyes began to clear.

"I still don't see—"

"You pricks trashed my entire campaign. Totally fucking trashed it. The best comments were middling at best, and most of them were downright derogatory. What did you guys think you were doing?"

"We were told to give our honest—"

"Bullshit! You were there to validate my campaign, all my work. I wouldn't expect all the comments and observations to be totally glowing, but you weren't supposed to throw the whole damned thing down the sewer. And you know what happened next?"

Ron's head began to hurt even more, struggling to figure a way out of this and wondering why he'd come in here in the first place. The only thing he could think to do was to keep the man talking.

At least until he could think of a way out of this mess.

Or until Helen, still looking somewhat groggy, snapped out of it.

Or Hollis, out there in the hallway came back to consciousness.

Or dammit, until *something* happened.

"Yeah," Ron said, "I kind of think I know what happened next."

"Damned right you know. They canned me. That was the upshot of the meeting in Kettering's office the day after you all left. Took exactly that long to throw me out on my ass."

Ron, who had recently gone through something similar, felt another sympathetic pang for the guy.

"Is that what this is about?" he asked. "You decided to get back at us for losing you your job?"

Howerton laughed, actually more of a bark, and shook his head.

"Seriously? You think I'd actually go on some kind of rampage just because I lost my job? What kind of person do you think I am? I've lost jobs before, who the hell hasn't, and haven't gone off my rocker. Why would you think I would this time?"

Ron frowned, figuring he, or maybe Amy Baxter, must have misread the situation somehow. At the same time he wasn't sure, but it seemed as if Helen, still slumped against the wall had raised her right knee a little higher in the air, bringing her ankle closer within reach.

Dammit, he had to keep the man talking.

"So if that wasn't what this was about, losing your job, what was it? You've killed a whole lot of people, Mr. Howerton, and I don't see what—"

"Because," the man said through gritted teeth, "I couldn't find another one."

"What?"

"You heard me. Come on, Green, weren't you a business teacher? At least before you got bounced out on your ass. How's it feel by the way?"

"Like hell, but what you said—"

"You know what it's like finding a white collar job in this economy? If you don't yet, you soon will. I'm telling you, it's murder."

A soft bump came from out in the hall, and Howerton turned slightly away from Helen and in Ron's direction. Hoping he knew what the bump was, Ron did his best to stare Howerton down. He didn't want to make it too obvious, but he wanted Howerton to focus on him so much that he wouldn't notice anything going on out in the hall. Meanwhile, Helen's ankle was now just inches from her hand.

"After a while," Howerton continued, "it wears you down. Sending resumes, networking, calling in old favors from 'friends' who don't want to be seen with you. It comes close to breaking you."

It seemed to Ron that the process actually had broken Howerton, but he naturally didn't say so.

"Did you have any luck at all? Any interviews or anything?"

That short, barking laugh again.

"Of course I had interviews. If you want to call them that. First, several right here in town. Then I had to go farther afield, eventually having a couple outside of the state. But with most of them, it was obvious within about five minutes they had someone else picked for the job and were just going through the paces, filling a quota, as it were."

Ron, who had had a similar experience when trying to land his first academic job, and feared something similar in his own future, felt another twinge of empathy.

Another thumping sound from the hall, softer than the first one, and Ron saw Helen's eyes brighten even more.

"I had seven or eight interviews all told, none of them amounting to squat."

"Seven or—"

And then Ron had it, even more so than before, he had the whole thing. Like a road map unfurled in front of him, he saw the complete truth.

"Oh man," he said.

"I had the first one just about a month after I got canned." Howerton's voice had taken on a dreamy quality, as if he'd somehow moved beyond the confines of the apartment and was in some other place and time. "It actually seemed almost too good to be true. A bigger firm than AK, and the job was senior account manager. We still had plenty of money in the bank, weren't even close to having to touch our retirement accounts, so my wife and I both figured that I'd hit a slight speed bump but had gotten over it."

Glancing at Lipscomb, Ron noticed her eyes had entirely cleared, and he read a tension in her face that hadn't been there before.

Even more, her right hand now rested solidly on her ankle.

"But I didn't get it," Howerton continued. "They took me in, introduced me to a lot of people, gave me the complete soft glove treatment. Hell, I thought I had it locked up."

"But?" Ron was playing for time. A second ago, he'd thought he heard, but couldn't be sure, a mild slithering from the hallway, and Helen was definitely doing something with that ankle, but from his position he couldn't tell what.

Howerton didn't notice any of this, his mind clearly occupied with events from months in the past.

"But then, while I was meeting with the firm's president, the subject of my time at AK came up, and also the Rawlings campaign."

As the man kept talking, it turned out just as Ron had it figured. A series of close calls, but no jobs offered.

The reason each time, his work on the busted campaign, his clear failure on such a major account. Eventually, a few financial turns and having to dip into retirement savings, cash out pension funds, and finally the wife having had enough and booting him out of their house.

But what Ron focused on most was all those job interviews, and as the tale continued he could see that his earlier assumption had been spot on.

"Every time," Howerton said, now staring directly at Ron, as if he'd forgotten Helen was even in the room, "it kept coming back to you, you and the other eleven. When it came right down to it, it was all your fault."

"But I don't see how—".

"You were the ones, dammit!" The gun began to shake and wobble in his grip. "The ones who queered it all with AK. If you all hadn't panned my work, it would have sailed through, Rawlings would have been reelected, and I would have gotten a lion's share of the credit. Instead, you ruined the whole thing with your lousy responses and got me tossed out on my ear."

Ron could see Helen's muscles, at least on her left side, tensing and, terrified as he was, he knew he had to keep the man's attention focused exclusively on him.

To ratchet up his fright a few more notches, for the last several seconds he hadn't heard anything from the hallway, and he didn't even want to think what that meant.

"And the interviews?" Ron prodded, not knowing what else to do but keep the guy talking.

"Yeah, the interviews. Each time, I'd get all psyched up, go out and do the dog and pony show, then lose it all. So tell me, mister big-shot business professor, who else would I have to blame but the twelve of you?"

Just as Ron had thought. He would have bet money that when they went back and checked, provided any of them lived past the next few minutes, they'd find that each of the killings, beginning with Randall Cummings the furniture store manager, had taken place right after, or at the least shortly after, one of Howerton's failed interviews.

Each time, that would have been the catalyst that set him off, making him increasingly angrier and more frustrated.

And, even though Ron wasn't even close to being a professional psychoanalyst, it probably also explained the attacks becoming more and more brutal, culminating in that absolutely savage attack on the Latham kid.

For several seconds now, almost total silence from the hallway. Ron felt his nerves as close to snapping as he could imagine possible. Then, from the corner of his eye, he saw Helen nod. What did she mean by that?

"So," Howerton was still talking, "there's only a couple left after you. And I may not be better off then, but I'll feel a whole hell of a lot better. There was actually someone else ahead of you on the list, but what the hell. You're here now so I might as well tie it up."

"Look, Howerton…" Then he saw Helen nod again, more vigorously this time, and in another of those instant flashes of insight realized what she wanted.

When he was a kid, Ron had a package of those trick playing cards. The kind with a series of pictures drawn on them, each almost immeasurably different from the last. And when you placed your thumb along a corner and ruffled them really fast, the pictures flashed past, telling a complete story.

Ron hadn't thought about that pack of cards in years,

but it came to his mind now as real life seemed to play out in just such a manner.

After Helen's second, frustrated nod, Ron collapsed. He didn't drop to the floor; he simply fell, as if all his bones had dissolved at once.

Howerton took a step backwards, no doubt confused by his victim's sudden action.

Helen snapped herself up, her hand whipping upwards to reveal the small pistol she'd had strapped to an ankle holster.

She fired off a shot, catching Howerton in the shoulder.

He whirled around, leveling his pistol towards her, only to catch two more bullets, one from Helen entering his chest and the other from the hallway, passing over Ron and plowing into Howerton's spine.

The man collapsed.

All of this, to Ron's fevered brain, had seemed like nothing more than a sequence of fast moving, individual frames, even though all of those actions, including his dropping, had occurred nearly simultaneously.

Pressing his palms flat on the floor, Ron levered himself up, deliberately not looking at the shot-up body right in front of him. He turned towards the open doorway and saw Hollis, hand held up to his still-bleeding head, then looked back at Helen, who had once again slumped against the wall.

He understood how she felt.

Finally, he looked down at the recumbent form on the floor, a pool of blood widening out from it.

This was the man, the one who had killed his lover, murdered over half a dozen people all told, and turned Ron's life into a complete and utter hell. Now he lay dead, and Ron knew he should have felt, if not elated, at least relieved. With Howerton dead, and the truth finally out, he could start picking up the pieces of his life.

Except he couldn't.

No matter what the end result here, his life remained a shambles.

And he seriously doubted he could ever put it back together again.

CHAPTER FIFTY-ONE

June 15

As he sealed the lid on the final box, Ron heard footsteps coming up the stairs. He glanced out the window but couldn't see the moving company truck. He discounted the steps as belonging to one of his neighbors and pulled out a marker to label the contents of the box.

"Hello?"

He looked up to see Helen standing in the doorway, her left arm still in a sling.

"Door was open," she said.

"Yeah. I've been placing stuff out in the hallway all morning. Figured I'd save time when the movers show up."

He finished labeling the box of clothes and stood up, capping the marker.

"What'd you need?" he asked.

"Nothing much. Just figured I'd come by to see how you were doing."

She looked around the apartment, and Ron wondered if she was detective enough to figure it out. Although for the most part still furnished, a few places seemed somehow empty, with half the cabinets open and empty and the other half closed.

It didn't take her long to look as if she wished she could swallow her words.

"Sorry. That was kind of thoughtless."

"It's okay," he said, "considering how things could have turned out, I should really feel rather lucky."

She nodded, but still avoided eye contact with him.

"So your wife and kids…"

"Will be moving back as soon as I'm out."

"Rough," she said.

Ron shrugged.

"You want a beer?" he asked. "I still have a few things in the fridge."

"It's only eleven."

"True. But lately I'm not worried a whole lot about social convention."

She nodded, and he stepped into the kitchen.

"How's your partner?" he called out.

"Healing. They figure he'll be back on duty next month."

Ron stepped out from the kitchen and handed her an opened bottle. He briefly raised the one he held, then began guzzling.

Helen, despite her initial reluctance, drank nearly a third of the bottle at once.

"He's really grateful to you," she said when she came up for air.

"The feeling's not exactly mutual," Ron said as he placed his bottle on the countertop. "You guys really put me through some kind of hell."

Helen frowned for a second.

"I guess you're entitled to feel that way, but we really did act the way we thought best."

"And almost railroaded me into a murder trial, let alone almost getting me killed."

Helen shrugged, as if knowing anything she said

would be pointless.

Sighing, Ron walked over to the window and stared down into the street, watching for the movers.

"So where are you headed?" Helen asked from behind him.

"Ohio. There's a school there that just sent me a contract."

"College?"

"No,"—he stared down at the street—"high school. They were fully staffed, then at the last minute someone in their business department got called up to Afghanistan. But hey, it' a salary."

"I'm sorry."

Ron turned away from the window, shoulders slumped in resignation, and perched on the sill.

"Not your fault. Guess I'm really just pissed at myself. I had a decent life once, and I still haven't quite come to grips with how it all fell apart."

"I know it sounds cheap coming from me," Helen said, "but like you said a minute ago, there are some positives to look at. You are alive, and your name's been cleared. Plus…"

"Yeah?"

"Well, I'll deny I ever mentioned this, but if you found the right lawyer you may have a decent shot at a lawsuit against the city."

Ron, for what seemed like the first time in months, smiled.

"Maybe," he said, "but the cost of going back and forth between here and Ohio would get a little prohibitive, especially since my new salary is almost exactly half what I was making at the university."

"It's another possibility. I don't claim to know how

it all works, but since you've been cleared, wouldn't you have a shot at getting your job back, if not your tenure?"

"Maybe. But it would take a long time, be a bloody fight, and in the end what would I really get? The chance to work at a place that doesn't want or trust me? Naw, it's better to just go somewhere and start fresh."

Helen shifted her arm, wincing a bit as she did so.

"How long is it going to take to heal?"

"Not sure. They said no more than a month, but only if I take it as easy as possible."

Ron grinned.

"At least someone got more physically damaged out of this than I did."

She smiled back, if somewhat wistfully.

"Take care of yourself, okay? Drop me a line when you get where you're going."

"Will do," he said.

She reached over to pat him on the arm, then turned on her heel and left the apartment. Ron walked over to the window, and a minute later saw her come out the front of the building and head off down the street.

He looked around at all the packed boxes, the detritus of a life in ruins, before thinking, what the hell, and headed to the refrigerator for another beer.

He had nothing to do now but wait.

A word about the author…

A high-school teacher, former college instructor and fiction writer, Kevin R. Doyle is the author of numerous short stories, mainly in the horror field. He's also written three crime thrillers, *The Group*, *When You Have to Go There*, and *And the Devil Walks Away* and one horror novel, *The Litter*. Recently, he's begun working on the Sam Quinton private eye series. The first Quinton book, *Squatter's Rights*, was nominated for the 2021 Shamus award as Best First PI Novel. The second book, *Heel Turn*, was released in March of 2021. More information can be found at kevindoylefiction.com.

Thank you for purchasing
this publication of The Wild Rose Press, Inc.

For questions or more information
contact us at
info@thewildrosepress.com.

The Wild Rose Press, Inc.
www.thewildrosepress.com